CH

Venturess

BETSY CORNWELL

CLARION BOOKS
Houghton Mifflin Harcourt
Boston ✳ New York

Clarion Books
3 Park Avenue
New York, New York 10016

Clarion Books is an imprint of Houghton Mifflin Harcourt Publishing Company.

www.hmhco.com

The text was set in Monotype Spectrum.
Hand-lettering by Leah Palmer Preiss

Library of Congress Cataloging-in-Publication Data
Names: Cornwell, Betsy, author.
Title: Venturess / Betsy Cornwell.
Description: Boston ; New York : Clarion Books/Houghton Mifflin Harcourt, [2017]
| Sequel to: Mechanica. | Summary: An indomitable inventor and her loyal (and
royal) friends cross the ocean to the lush world of Faerie, where they join a rising
rebellion.
Identifiers: LCCN 2016032623 | ISBN 9780544319271 (hardcover)
Subjects: | CYAC: Fairy tales. | Magic—Fiction. | Inventors—Fiction.
Classification: LCC PZ8.C8155 Ve 2017 | DDC [Fic]—dc23
LC record available at https://lccn.loc.gov/2016032623

Manufactured in the United States of America
DOC 10 9 8 7 6 5 4 3 2 1
4500659347

For the teachers at Moharimet Elementary, Berwick Academy, the Johns Hopkins Center for Talented Youth, Smith College, and the University of Notre Dame for helping me become a writer; Sara Crowe and Lynne Polvino for their care of and faith in my work; the Mechanica street team for their boundless creativity; Anna, Alex, and Trish for being comrades in arms; and Richie, for every day, and for "a kind of love called maintenance": thank you

⁕

The famine queen stood tall and proud.
On either bank the people bowed.
From Passage West came a Fenian yell:
"Rule Britannia, rule in Hell!"

The grass grows green on the other side
And mighty ships sail out the tide
To far-flung harbors across the sea,
Far away from Passage, my love, and me.

Oh love, will you go, will you go, will you go?
Or love, will you stay, will you stay, will you stay?

—John Spillane, "Passage West"

PART I

THE furnace rumbling in my horse's belly warmed my feet, and puffs of smoke from his nostrils drifted over me as we cantered toward the palace. Snowflakes melted and hissed on his flanks.

My patron, Lord Alming, had teased me the first time he saw the saddle I'd designed for Jules. He couldn't understand why on earth I would want to ride in the open air when I could stay warm and dry inside the glass carriage I'd already built.

But I missed Jules when I was inside the carriage, and there was something weirdly impersonal about pulling levers to direct him, as if the levers were reins and Jules no more than a normal horse. After all, I needed only to tell him where I wanted to go, and he would take us there.

I didn't need reins when I was riding Jules either. I had fitted retractable handles into a slot between his steel shoulder blades just in case, for my own comfort until I got used to riding again.

But I knew he would never try to throw me. Whose best friend would do that?

Riding had been Jules's suggestion, not long after last year's ball; it was the day I left the Steps to start my own workshop, in fact.

I had walked out of the house that used to belong to my parents with my head held high, the little mechanical insects Mother and I had made buzzing around me in a protective swarm. Mother's books and journals, which she'd left in her workshop after she died, were boxed and stacked inside my carriage. Even with my sewing machine and dress form wedged on top of them, the small compartment was barely half full; it had been years since the Steps had let me keep anything of my own — at least anything they knew about. I carried the ball gown Jules and the insects had made for me over my arm.

Lord Alming had been waiting for me in his own elegant barouche; I was to ride with him to my new workshop and apartments in Esting City, and Jules, pulling my carriage, would follow.

Stepmother had been there at the door when we first arrived at the house. I'd steeled myself for her icy cruelty as Lord Alming helped me out of my glass carriage, but she'd held her arms out to me and smiled, wide and beatific.

"Nicolette!" she'd cooed, grasping the hand Lord Alming

wasn't holding. She'd pressed my palm to her own cheek. Her large gray eyes fluttered closed for a moment, and her face took on the glowing expression of a painted saint. "I am so happy for you," she'd said, with never a glance toward Lord Alming, even though this act of hers was for his benefit.

I couldn't move, couldn't look away from her; I'd felt a bone-deep revulsion that rooted me where I stood. My throat felt too thick and full to speak. I sensed Lord Alming watching me.

I'd torn my gaze away and glanced back at Jules, where he stood in the drive with steam rising around him in the cold morning air. His immense metal strength reassured me, and I could do what I'd intended: ignore Stepmother completely. I squeezed Lord Alming's hand and led him forward, sweeping past her and into my parents' house. The huge manservant who had accompanied us followed silently.

Stepmother had stayed with us, hovering like a malevolent bird as I made my way up the main staircase and down the winding corridor that led to the servants' quarters. My bedroom there was spare and small, and it had already been ransacked, the threadbare quilt tossed in a corner, the thin mattress overturned.

But I'd always known Stepmother went through my things, and the journal I'd come for was still safely hidden in the spring-loaded slot I'd installed under the bed. I relished the small hiss she made as I took the book out.

"I wish you could have trusted me, Nicolette," she'd said

in a sweet but weakened voice. I watched not her but Lord Alming, to see if her virtuous charade was having any effect on him.

He'd given me a look of such disbelief through his monocle that I couldn't help laughing. And when Stepmother would have followed me into the cellar, down to my mother's secret workshop, he'd waved his hand, and his manservant had stepped forward to block Stepmother's path.

"I won't be gainsaid in my own house!" she'd said, more weakly still; but she didn't struggle. She couldn't unleash any real venom in front of Lord Alming.

When everything had finally been packed into my carriage, when I was walking at last out of that house and toward the happily-ever-after I'd built, Stepmother caught me by the wrist. She brought her other hand up to my cheek and turned my face firmly toward her, so that I had to look.

"My darling girl," she'd said, as if intoning a prayer, "I wish you a joyful life, today and evermore." Her words were just loud enough for Lord Alming to hear.

I'd pulled away, and my legs started to shake as I walked toward the carriages. It wasn't her obvious attempt to play mother in front of Lord Alming that had disturbed me; it was that I'd suddenly known that she meant what she said. That even after everything she'd done to me, and everything she'd stood back and let my stepsisters, Piety and Chastity, do, she somehow believed that she wished me well now. I'd known that, when she said her real prayers that evening, she would tell the Lord that she'd tried her best to do right by me—and that at least part of her would believe it.

I'd started to feel dizzy. I'd nearly stumbled as I kept walking away.

But Jules had stepped forward, pulling the weight of my laden carriage behind him. His bright glass eyes looked into mine and he pricked his ears and tilted his head to the side, beckoning me to come toward him. As soon as I got close enough I put my hand on his neck and leaned against him; I'd felt so sick by then that I didn't think I could have made it even one more step on my own.

"Ride," Jules had huffed, blowing steam against my cheek.

I'd pulled back a little to look at him. "Are you sure?"

He'd flicked one ear in annoyance. Jules meant everything he said; using his voice box caused him pain, and he never spoke unless he had to. No one else even knew he could speak.

I was too shaken to do anything but agree. I'd called to Lord Alming that we'd follow behind him, and I hoisted myself up onto Jules. My arms wrapped around his neck, I felt strength flowing into me with every step that he took. I turned for one last look at Lampton Manor and glimpsed my stepsisters' beautiful faces framed in a first-floor window. As soon as they saw me looking, they ducked out of sight. The edges of my skirts were smoking and singed by the time we got to Esting City, but I haven't ridden in the carriage since.

A few days later, after we'd settled into my new workshop, I'd brought back a tooled leather saddle from Market.

When Jules balked at it, I'd sighed. "Well, what would you have me do? Ruin all the beautiful clothes you and the buzzers make for me every time I ride?"

He had snorted like laughter and picked up a piece of fabric left over from another gown. It was a lovely claret color, a rich brocade.

I'd had to laugh too. "I should have expected nothing less from a horse who designs gowns," I'd said. Jules had the final say on all the dresses we created, even my own wardrobe. He led my mechanical insects through all the sewing and tailoring, just as he'd done when he was no bigger than my hand, though now he was as huge and solid as any draft horse. He loved the work, and I'd long since admitted that my horse somehow had better taste than I did.

In fact, the dress I'd be wearing to the palace that night was another of Jules's creations. It was a lovely, ethereal periwinkle silk, embroidered with small white starflowers that drifted down from the bodice and all around the bustled skirt. I had asked for a pale gown, since the one I'd worn to last year's ball had started such a popular trend of dark purple dresses among the ladies of the court. They all absolutely had to have the adjustable glass slippers I'd designed too, but I didn't mind that. The huge success of the slippers had allowed me to pay off the mortgage on my very own workshop, and I had nearly enough money saved to make a reasonable offer on Lampton Manor.

I didn't want to make a reasonable offer, though. I wanted to make an offer Stepmother could never refuse.

But while the slippers' sales had held strong, ever since King Corsin had officially declared war on Faerie again, I'd had a hard time selling my other inventions. Before the declaration, the Fey rebellion had grown stronger and more organized until they were close to winning back their independence. Our armies had since put Faerie under martial law and regained control of much of the continent, but waging a war was expensive, and Esting's once-decadent courtiers had far less money to spend on my beautiful clockwork trinkets now that their funds were needed to help quell the rebellion.

My workshop was near the heart of Esting City, and Jules and I reached the palace in only a few minutes. Its blackstone walls loomed like huge shadows, lit at intervals by the bright glow of gaslights in the evening gloom.

I suddenly remembered how I had looked and felt exactly one year ago, riding up to the palace doors in my glass carriage. I saw myself as if in a vision: I had been shivering inside my old, patched, oversize work coat and thinking of Fin, the boy I daydreamed about, waiting for me in the ballroom. I didn't even know he was the Heir then. There were so many things I didn't know.

Watching that ghostly girl, I wished for a moment that

she—that I—could stay in the glass bubble of Jules's carriage, heart beating fast, hoping to dance with a boy I'd met more times in my imagination than I ever had in waking life.

By the time I'd walked out of that ballroom last year, I'd left those fantasies behind. I didn't live there anymore, in that place where I dreamed of a hazy, perfect future. I lived in my happy ending now, but it was nothing like those simple dreams.

For one thing, I couldn't approach the palace anonymously this time. As soon as Jules stepped into the halos of gaslight, guards emerged and bowed to us, and a groom I didn't recognize hurried toward Jules.

"The guards will send word to announce you within, my lady," the groom said. "I shall see to your mount."

He reached mechanically for Jules's reins and his hand closed on nothing but air.

I smiled at his baffled expression; he must be new. "It's all right," I said. "I'll bring Jules to the stables myself. Please don't announce me."

"But my lady—"

Jules and I were already off.

We knew the way to the stables blindfolded. Jules crunched nimbly through the three or four inches of snow on the ground, and I pulled down the hood of my fine cloak and took a deep breath. My vision of the girl in the carriage had faded away, and my nostalgia for her had gone with it. I always had thick cloaks and fine dresses now, and my back and feet were never cold nor my stomach empty, as hers had so often been.

Whatever complications I faced here in my happily-ever-after, I had saved myself from real hardship. I must always remember that.

As we reached our destination, a tiny, lithe figure came jogging out to meet us. The stable hand's red hair was almost bigger than she was.

"Hello, you beauty!" Bex cried.

I grinned. I knew she wasn't talking to me.

"So Nick's brought you back at last, hey? Oh, I missed you so much!" She approached Jules and held her hands under his nose for him to sniff, a huge smile painted across her freckled face.

"Honestly, Bex, it's only been a few days," I said, dismounting. I had to fairly leap down; I'd built Jules bigger than even a quarry horse. He rose like a shining glass-and-steel mountain next to diminutive Bex, steam crowning his head like clouds.

"So long?" With considerable effort, Bex arranged her face into an expression of dramatic woe.

Jules huffed smoke at her and nosed through her pockets.

"Only apples in that one," she said, "but I have what you're looking for right here." Bex slipped her hand inside her coat and came out with two big, dusty nuggets of black coal. She opened the hatch in Jules's side and dropped them into his belly.

Jules whinnied his thanks, a screeching-springs noise that always made me wince and smile at the same time.

"You two will be all right till I come back, then?" I asked.

Bex and Jules both nodded. Jules had never spoken in her presence, or in anyone's presence but mine, but she'd figured out long ago that he could respond to human speech in a way that no other horse could.

Most of the kingdom thought Jules was just a fine simulacrum, with no life of his own at all. But he *was* alive, and all I knew about the Ashes that gave him life was that they had to do with illegal Fey magic. I guarded Jules's secrets closely.

But I trusted Bex with him, at first because my friend Caro did, and later on her own merits. Bex was sharper, harder-edged, and more mischievous than Caro, but they shared the same golden optimism and the easy honesty that comes with it.

"Are you sure you don't mind missing the party?" I called as Bex and Jules walked into the stables.

Bex's laugh cracked through the darkness. "And lose the chance to ride this lad? Don't worry, Nick, he'll be right here when you're done waltzing." She looked back at me, her eyes reflecting just enough of the reddish glow from Jules's furnace that I could see her wink. "Just kiss my girl for me, will you?"

I took the back way in, through the huge, labyrinthine underground servants' quarters that supported the palace in every sense of the word. I had no desire to walk down those wide marble steps at the front entrance, where the aristocrats would get to inspect me at their leisure, the way I'd done at last year's ball. I still felt a little embarrassed by my own naiveté back then. Waiting to be kissed by my prince, when I didn't even know he was a prince yet.

I knew the palace now, and I knew which of the servants' hidden doors would let me out just behind the orchestra pit in the ballroom. From there, I could peer around the curtains and assess the lay of the land while remaining well concealed.

It was easy to spot Fin: He lounged on a throne opposite the main staircase, chatting with a young man who clearly wasn't holding his interest. He looked like the picture of a bored Prince Charming from any story book, except for the snap of good humor in his eyes that even his mask couldn't quite conceal. King Corsin sat at a small distance in an even bigger throne. A tall platinum crown rested heavily on his brow, and he was dressed in grand military regalia, yet despite his finery, he seemed faded and worn, almost beneath notice. The somber, black-robed Brethren advisors that flanked him had more presence than their monarch did.

I wanted to say hello to Fin, but any public interaction between us was highly scrutinized these days. In fact, I had to be careful when I showed myself in public at all, which was why I was so relieved that Fin had agreed to make this second annual Exposition Ball a masquerade. My mask gave me at least some sense of anonymity, of armor for the broken heart I'd had at last year's ball.

But I had worked hard since then to mend my heart and remake my understanding of love and family from the simple, binary ideas I'd had before. Fin and I weren't the starry-eyed couple I'd dreamed of last winter, true; we were simply a unit, together with our Caro. We were three people who loved and needed one another, and it was as easy and as hard as that.

Just then I was attacked from behind. A pair of strong, soft arms locked around my waist, I felt the pressure on my back of an enveloping hug, and I heard the rustle of another gown's worth of fine fabric colliding with my own.

"Caro!" I squeaked. I managed to wriggle around in her arms, and I bent down to plant a happy kiss on her forehead. "Bex sent you that."

"What," Caro said, "am I not to have a kiss from you, then?" She fluttered her eyelashes coquettishly.

We both laughed. I kissed Caro again, for myself this time.

Caro was wearing a gorgeous marigold-orange gown that I hoped would cause back orders at my shop tomorrow. Any Jules creation became the latest craze; I just wished he could take the credit for them.

And I hoped at least a few courtiers would have enough money to buy them. Given the War Contributions urns placed strategically around the ballroom, though, and the propaganda announcements that periodically interrupted the music, I suspected very few people would have money to spare.

Caro looped her arm through mine, and together we stepped out onto the ballroom floor. "Now, what's our charming prince up to?" she asked.

"Dying of boredom, I believe," I said, but when I glanced up at Fin, I found that wasn't true at all.

He was talking animatedly with a slim young man in a mask of pristine white lace, angled at the edges to emphasize the sharp lines of his cheekbones and mouth. Thick, shining auburn hair rose above his pale forehead. Even masked, his face was handsome.

I knew at once who it was and what he and Fin were discussing. And then I knew that another public interaction with the Heir was quite unavoidable, whatever rumors it might restart.

Caro knew, too, that there was only one type of conversation that could get Fin so excited these days.

"Ugh, politics," she tutted under her breath.

I'm sure she would have left him to it, but I clamped her arm against my side and fairly dragged her up to the dais. Fin could use our help, I was certain, and he was my friend (and I would have to radiate friendship and no other emotion for every instant that we were together in public, I reminded myself) and therefore I was going to help him.

The handsome courtier's barrage of talk didn't cease

when we reached them, but Fin glanced over and sent us the flicker of a wink, all the while keeping his face arranged in an expression of intense interest.

"But Your Highness," the young man was saying in his voice like treacle, "we must think of your *safety*." Coming from anyone other than Fitzwilliam Covington, that tone would have sounded condescending, even wheedling. But Fitz was never anything but slick and smooth.

Fin's dark eyes flashed behind his crimson silk mask. "There are others whose safety I value far more," he said. "There are lives far more endangered than mine ever was."

If Fitz's voice was treacle, then Fin's was blackstrap molasses, the sweetness still there but made dark and rough. He'd talked more in the past year than he had in probably the whole rest of his life taken together, what with the speeches he was making all over the country now, trying to persuade the public to feel sympathy for Faerie, trying to pull back the tide of war that already threatened to drown us. Our army and Faerie's were both decimated already, and reports of more battles, more deaths, came back every day.

Dark clothes were still fashionable, to be sure, but many of this year's gowns were worn in mourning.

Fitzwilliam Covington himself wore a black satin band on his arm. He had recently inherited a minor lordhood after his father died in a Fey ambush. Fitz was among the most vocal advocates of the war. He was ambitious, already using his new position any way he could, and he was rising through the ranks in the military too. Yet he had his eyes on a much higher title.

"Duchess Cerese-Jessine Listro of Soleil Domine," the announcer called from the staircase, his dignified voice amplified through a series of copper tubes leading to blossom-shaped horns installed along the ceiling of the vast ballroom.

Fitz's gaze darted to the tall, stately form of a beautiful young woman descending the main staircase, her hair woven in hundreds of intricate braids on top of her head, a leaf-green gown of Jules's and a golden mask of my own design setting off the warmth of her brown skin. I liked Cerese, and I'd had great fun dressing her and her sisters for the ball; foreign nobles had been my best customers for months now, and the Listros had a large domain in the Sudlands. I hoped I'd get to speak with her before the end of the night.

Fitz clearly shared that hope. He kept watching the lovely duchess as he made his excuses to Fin. "Your Highness, you know how I would love to continue reminding you of the duties you hold toward your own precious person," he said drily, "but I'm afraid true love calls." As if he had only just noticed that I was there, he made an overelaborate, nearly mocking flourish of a bow. "Of course, you both know how that feels." The look he shot me made it clear that Cerese wasn't the real reason he was leaving Fin's company; I was. It was the same look he once gave me when I walked in on him with my stepsister Piety — when he was supposed to be courting Chastity. He'd never been one for scruples.

But I'd kept Fitz's secrets, and so far he'd kept mine. I met his eyes, imagining frost creeping over the leaves on my mask.

"Yes, yes, Fitz, go on," Fin said. Fitz turned away just a hair earlier than was really polite for leaving the presence of royalty, bowing before him just a hair less fully than one ought to bow to the Heir of all Esting.

"Thank the Lord," Fin said with a fierce clap of his hands, turning toward Caro and me. "That idiot might have gone on forever if you hadn't shown up. He's the only soul in the kingdom who dislikes *you,* Nick, and although I can't possibly fathom why, I am glad of it. At least he's gone now."

I knew perfectly well why Fitz didn't like me: it was because I hadn't married Fin. I'd refused to play the game Fitz played, the favor-for-favor court intrigue that he was sure I could win as the Heir's fiancée, the Heiress Apparent to our powerful kingdom and all its empire. As Heiress, I could have done Fitz any favor he wanted; I could have given him his own dukedom outright so that he was not forced to court beautiful women in order to earn the rank.

But to Fitz's outrage, I hadn't taken the bait, hadn't taken the offer, but had remained only Nicolette Lampton — not that that wasn't enough to give me some power these days. The glass slippers I'd danced in a year ago had turned me into the most famous inventor in the country overnight. I was wearing them again today, of course, like almost all the court ladies. I'd never been able to find other shoes quite as comfortable for dancing.

I'd not been able to resist creating my own mask, either. My handiwork was well-known enough that its style might have revealed my identity, but a few other nobles had ordered masks from me, so this one didn't stand out. It was fine-hammered silver, inlaid with delicate leaves that fluttered when I moved, controlled by minuscule hidden gears. I wasn't willing to deprive myself of the gift of pride in my work.

"Was Fitz talking about the automaton again?" I asked, looking warily at the Brethren beside Corsin's throne. They both watched Fin, and they didn't look away even when I glared at them. The king moved his thin fingers slowly back and forth over the sash on his jacket, his eyes half-closed and unfocused. He coughed, and the Brethren turned to him at once, fawning.

Fin glowered. "What else? But I won't be made a puppet, Nick. If I won't let my father secret me away anymore, I certainly won't let a snake like Fitz make a simulacrum for me to hide behind."

It had been nearly six months since Fitz had proposed creating a decoy version of the Heir to make his speeches for him, but clearly Fin remained unmoved.

"I'm surprised to see you here, Caro," Fin said suddenly, shifting in his seat. "Shouldn't you be following Bex around the stables?"

Though his voice was teasing, not bitter, I couldn't help but remember the way I'd seen him look at Caro at the previous year's ball, the moment I realized he was in love with her and therefore couldn't possibly be in love with me.

How little I had known back then.

Caro shot Fin a sardonic look. "Not glad to see me, then?"

"I'm always glad to see you," Fin said carefully. Pointedly.

We all knew Caro was spending more of her free time in the stables with Bex than she was at either the palace or my workshop. I was so occupied with my business that I didn't mind much. But Fin . . . Fin was tired, lonely, and desperate for conversation with someone who wasn't trying to change his mind about the war. He'd taken so many verbal beatings, public and private, for advocating for Faerie in the past year. Even his father, King Corsin, couldn't speak to him without shouting anymore.

We three dear friends, my beloved family, stood there silent. Caro and Fin glared at each other. As for myself, I did not know what to say.

So I was disproportionately grateful to the shy young man who tapped my shoulder just then and requested a waltz. I whirled away in his arms, wishing I could take my heart with me.

I danced with four partners in quick succession, and when I finally stopped to catch my breath I had to refuse several more requests.

"You're the belle of the ball again, my dear," said a familiar deep voice.

I turned to see my patron, who was wearing a typically flamboyant outfit: gold-and-green pinstriped coat and tails, with a carved pearl pin stuck into his sky-blue tie. He winked at me through his thick monocle.

"Hardly, Lord Alming," I said with a quick curtsy. "They saw me with the Heir, and they still believe they might be dancing with their future queen. It's only about power."

He chuckled. "I don't go in for romance myself," he said, "but I know it when I see it. Not all of your partners were thinking of their ambitions — not their political ambitions, at least." He raised his eyebrows and slipped a hand into his pocket. "But I didn't seek you out to talk of your beaux, Miss Lampton. I have something for you." He pulled out an envelope stamped with an elaborate blue wax seal. I didn't recognize the design.

"I have last quarter's royalties for you as well," he said. "Come by the factory this week and pick them up. I'm afraid sales have sunk a fraction again, but I'm holding out hope for the spring. Glass shoes are so impractical in winter."

I was clutching the envelope, trying to think if I *did* know the seal. There was something familiar about the handwriting on the front, although I couldn't quite place it.

N— L—
Care of Gerald, Lord Alming
Alming Abbey, Woodshire
ESTING

And under the seal on the back: *Contents Secret.*

"If I've earned enough to save a bit more toward buying Lampton, I'll be happy," I said distractedly, turning the envelope over in my hands. "Are you sure I'm the N.L. for whom this is intended?"

"Oh, yes," Lord Alming confirmed with utter confidence. But then he cleared his throat. "Ah," he said. "My dear, I'm afraid I have some news on that score. On Lampton, I mean."

I looked up. "News?"

He frowned, lowering his voice and stepping closer to me. "You know I try to keep abreast of the Brethren's doings," he murmured.

I nodded, remembering the hawklike men who hovered around Corsin. The Brethren were the increasingly extremist religious group that held far too much sway over the king, or so Lord Alming and I and a very few other Estingers thought. The Brethren were unwaveringly anti-magic, and their priests had been the first to advocate banishing all the Fey from Esting and imposing a quarantine on their country. Lord Alming, who kept his own part-Fey lineage a closely guarded secret, suspected them of even more evil than they openly displayed. He'd spent much of his fortune on bribes and espionage, trying to learn their secrets.

"They've been gathering monies to support the war" — he clicked his tongue — "which really supports them, of course. There's more room for religion without magic coming in and making miracles so *practical*. They've just received a sizable donation in the form of a manor and estate grounds from one Lady Coronetta Halving and daughters."

I winced. Stepmother had always been pious, even naming her daughters after Brethren-approved virtues: Piety and Chastity. She hated magic and the Fey nearly as much as she hated me. It would be just like her to donate Lampton Manor to the Brethren to keep it out of my hands. I often wondered if she feared I'd try to claim that it was legally mine, an avenue I unfortunately couldn't pursue. Since she had married my father, the estate had passed to her on his death. My only hope had been to buy it back.

I remembered her last wish for me, *a joyful life,* how it had sounded at once sincere and menacing, and my skin crawled.

My home, the house where I'd been born. My mother's secret basement workshop, the place where I had found hope, where I had found Jules and the fleet of mechanical insects I loved so much, where I had become the inventor I was today. I'd been working to buy back the house since before I'd even left.

And now it was gone. The Brethren were too self-righteous to sell to a nonbeliever like me at any price — and even if they would, I didn't think I could bear to give them money that they'd use to help fund the war.

The envelope started to crumple in my fists. I forced my hands to relax.

Lord Alming touched my shoulder. "I am so sorry, my

dear, but I thought you'd want to hear it from . . . well. Not from them." He surveyed the ballroom, and I caught a glimpse of my stepsister Chastity in a far corner, flirting half-heartedly with an elderly baron and wearing, I was surprised to see, one of the last dresses I'd made her.

When I caught her eye, she flinched and turned away.

"Coward," I whispered.

But I tried not to think about the Steps if I could help it, so I looked back at Lord Alming and nodded resolutely.

"What's done is done, my dear," he said, "and perhaps it's for the best. You can move forward, you know, rather than longing to return to the past. You can use your savings to expand your workshop, or . . ." He waved his hand. "Or anything you like. You've thought about travel, haven't you?"

"Mm." I was looking at the envelope again, trying to drag my thoughts away from my lost home.

Lord Alming made a short bow. "I'll take my leave of you now, Miss Lampton," he said. "I'm planning an early morning at the Exposition tomorrow. A source tells me the priests have some plans of their own I'd like to keep an eye on . . . and I never know when I might come across some young genius in need of an angel investor." He winked, bowed again, and walked away.

I retreated behind one of the hidden servants' doors to read my letter. I took the warning on the back seriously, and the ballroom was too crowded for me to be sure that no one would be looking over my shoulder.

And if I was going to cry about the loss of Lampton Manor, I didn't want to risk the Steps seeing me do it.

I opened the envelope. The wax seal melted against my fingers, sticking unpleasantly, and I felt a brief, tingling heat slither up my arms.

The feeling vanished almost instantly. The wax hardened and fell away from my hands, leaving them clean.

A spell—to check my identity, no doubt. I wondered what spell had told Lord Alming I was the correct recipient—or was I simply the only N.L. he knew? It was so hard to tell with magic sometimes.

I swatted away my tears and began to read.

My dear Nicolette,

I cannot tell you how glad I am to pen this letter. I have longed to write to you for years. Perhaps I should have done so; I did not wish to take the risk. I can only hope you will forgive me.

My friend has described the remarkable young inventor he met at Market last fall in several of his letters, but it was only when he mentioned your horse that I was sure the lady in question was my own one-time charge. I have sent this letter through him because we know him to be sympathetic to the cause.

I have become an officer in the resistance here, and I write to you on behalf of my commander. We have heard the news of your auspicious engagement, and since I have assured my commander that you are _trustworthy_, we agree that a meeting between the Heir of Esting, the Heiress Apparent, and the Fey leader would be most desirable. I hope — and I believe your charming prince hopes too — that the war need not take so very many more lives than it has already done.

Would you, and would the Heir, be amenable to a diplomatic meeting on our own shores? The Estinger forces have rendered us incapable of travel, as you know. I cannot say too much more in a note that may be intercepted in spite of all our precautions. Again, _I beg your forgiveness_.

You are grown now, and free, and perhaps you still harbor your old sympathy for this place and its people. I remember how you always longed to see Faerie.

Yours ever,

A— C—

I pressed Mr. Candery's letter to my heart. For a moment I wasn't standing in the gloomy service corridor at all, but in the green and humid jungles of Faerie.

Alec Candery had practically raised me, at least until Stepmother dismissed him after Father's death. I'd always missed my old half-Fey housekeeper and wondered what had become of him; not long after he left me, he and the other part-Fey had all been banished from Esting.

He had obviously heard the false rumors of Fin's and my engagement. If only I had the power he believed I had, to arrange a peace talk that could end this war . . . Fin would be the perfect person, the only person, to do it. He'd campaigned tirelessly for Faerie's independence this year. He would leap at a chance like this—wouldn't he?

I folded the letter and slid it into one of the hidden pockets in my skirts. I wasn't engaged to Fin, but I did have his love and respect; he would listen to me. Could I convince him that he'd do more good in Faerie than he would making speeches to unfriendly crowds here in Esting?

A meeting that could end the war, a journey to a magical land . . . I shivered, fearful and enraptured all at once.

I brushed my hands over my face one more time, straightened my skirts, and stepped back into the ballroom. I began to walk toward the dais, but I saw that Fin's throne was empty.

Fin and Caro were on the dance floor, twirling through a fast-paced waltz. They smiled at each other, happy and relaxed. I was so relieved to see they'd made up that I knew Mr. Candery's message could wait until tomorrow. We were hardly going to commission a ship for the journey tonight, and I knew Fin would need some persuading—if going to Faerie was even the right course of action.

We would decide together, the three of us, what to do. That was always the way.

I looked at my pocket watch; it was nearly eleven. I

smiled a little, remembering my dramatic midnight exit from last year's ball. Like Lord Alming, I wanted to make the most of tomorrow's Exposition. This year I'd leave the ball even earlier.

THE morning of the second annual Royal Exposition of Arts and Sciences dawned gray and cold, metallic shafts of light ringing the edges of the sky. I didn't need to take Jules through the forest this year, or set up a Market booth. I merely had to open my workshop's doors.

Still, I'd spent the past few weeks preparing an extra-spectacular display. I was wary of using my buzzers, imbued as they were with Fey magic. Instead, I'd made wind-up automated versions. They had no Ashes, no spark of their own life, but with their intricate clockwork parts, the insects crawled and skittered and fluttered more than convincingly. Long lines of them waited on the table in my shop.

I had been up since two hours before dawn, taking time to drink a cup of my favorite clary-bush tea before I started preparing for the day. I wrapped a cleanish muslin apron around one of my work dresses and set about polishing the butterflies' crystal wings and the caterpillars' jointed sections, made of real pearls that the Night Market trader told me a mermaid had sold to him.

I'd laughed at the idea, but pearls were still a daring choice of material, even for me. They came from the sea, which separated Esting and other civilized countries from Faerie. Their otherworldly sheen seemed to suggest, if not magic, at least sin. The Brethren certainly disapproved of pearls, but that only made me — and a few other not-so-pious Estingers — love them more. In fact, I was counting on the pearls' scandalous appeal to fetch an equally scandalous price.

Finally I was done polishing. I went into Jules's stable to get dressed.

"You won't find clothes like these in most stables," I told him with a laugh, admiring the sage-green striped skirt with its gathered bustle, matching jacket with silk braid trim, and elegant white neckcloth, all waiting on an adjustable dress form. A metallic rustle behind me signaled that the buzzers were ready and waiting to help me dress.

I raised my arms above my head and closed my eyes. I felt dozens of little tickling brushes and pressures, the weight of my work skirts and bodice coming away, my long hair rolled loosely at the back of my neck; I hated wearing it pulled up tight. The new dress settled over my fine cotton chemise and drawers, and the buzzers pulled the jacket over my arms.

I opened my eyes to see my two biggest spiders tying the snowy neckcloth expertly into place while a butterfly swooped in below them to straighten my lapels. I was eager to see myself in the mirror I kept in the front of the shop, but I already knew from the proud, pleased expression in Jules's glass eyes that I looked perfect.

I wondered for the millionth time what the Ashes that had brought life to Jules and the buzzers truly were, but not even Jules would tell me. I didn't press for an answer because it was obvious the first time I'd asked that the question hurt him.

All I knew was that I couldn't keep the Ashes in the same room as Jules and my insects. I'd tried to store them in the stable when I first moved to my new workshop, but the buzzers grew restless and anxious and crowded to the opposite side of the room against their leader, who stiffened his legs and stared at the bureau the Ashes were in with his ears flattened back against his head and his eyes wide and white like a frightened colt's.

I'd moved them to my back room after that and never said another word about it.

"Thank you, Jules," I said now, stroking his warm copper nose. "It's perfect, as ever." I looked at the buzzers, hovering expectantly in the air or waiting on the hems of my skirt and jacket. "And thank you, little tailors."

They whirred and clicked out a soothing purr; Jules whickered and nuzzled my shoulder. I put my arms around his neck and allowed myself the luxury of a long hug before I resumed my work.

Light was only just beginning to streak the sky when I

returned to my storefront, so I lit the gas lamps on the walls to admire myself in the mirror.

As usual, Jules had outdone himself. The whole outfit was marvelous; it fit me like a glove, and everything from its colors to its cut said that I was a brilliant young inventor to be taken seriously.

I twirled slowly before the mirror — and saw a pale face in the window, looking in.

I gasped and lunged toward the door. Whoever had been spying on my work, I wasn't about to let them get away.

The face vanished, but as I dashed outside, my shop door's bell clanging in my wake, I saw a pale scrap of, well, *someone* running away into the predawn darkness, dodging a quick right turn at the end of the block.

I took off in pursuit. I didn't have to carry cords of wood or scrub floors for Stepmother anymore, but I was still fairly fit and more than fairly fast.

I caught up with the spy before the next block. Thank goodness for the ragged long-tailed jacket streaming behind her, which I grabbed with both hands, or she would have gotten away from me again.

The girl was no more than a child, but she was stronger than I'd guessed she would be. I stumbled after her and we both tripped and landed in a heap on the dirty sidewalk.

I sat up and looked myself over. I wasn't hurt, but I saw a long rent in the front of my skirt where my knees had hit the ground. I felt terrible for Jules's and the insects' sake.

But I couldn't dwell on my clothes; my new captive was twisting her jacket out of my hands. Her own hands were small and grubby; the much-darned mitts that covered her palms were grubbier still. I looked down at a face framed by a flannel kerchief: a scowling little mouth, a wide chin bleeding with fresh scrapes, and frightened brown eyes.

"Oh, for goodness' sake," I said. "Don't be scared of me." I took a deep breath, wondering what to do next. I had no reason to trust that she'd stick around if I let go of her jacket.

"Here," I said, making my voice as gentle as I could while I used one hand to rummage for my handkerchief, keeping the other clenched tightly around her ragged coat. I didn't know for whom this girl was spying, or why, but I thought kindness was a better way to find out than force — and I had used more than enough of that to chase her down.

The girl looked at the clean handkerchief, then up at me with an expression that was at once worried and skeptical. She pressed the cloth hard to her swelling chin.

"Right," I said. "I am sorry I, um . . . I'm sorry I hurt you. I honestly didn't mean any harm. Would you please tell me your name?"

The girl shook her head quickly. A few wisps of dark hair fell across her forehead. Her scowl tightened.

"Well," I said, "come back to the shop with me, and we'll have a chat. That's what you wanted to see, isn't it?"

She looked down, and I thought we might be at an impasse; I didn't think I had it in me to force a young girl to go anywhere against her will, however dangerous she (or whomever she worked for) might be.

But after a long moment of stillness, she plunged her grubby hand into mine and squeezed. I released her jacket, and she began to lead me back toward my own shop.

The sky was growing lighter as we approached, and a few other windows along the street were starting to glow with gaslight or candles. I smiled at my own storefront; every time I came home to it, the sight warmed my heart.

The sign read simply *Lampton's,* but it was done in an elaborate golden script, inlaid with glass and a few working gears that moved with the wind. It was shaped just like the glass slippers that had made me my fortune.

One of my two window displays featured the shoes front and center, with two clockwork mannequins in ball gowns behind them, waltzing together to a silent beat. Although I sold them as my own, the gowns were Jules's and the buzzers' work, of course. No one could know the extent of their intelligence; even the Fey sympathizers at the contraband Night Market were afraid of the Ashes.

The other window displayed creations that were truly mine, though: my knitting and sewing machines, automatic sweeping brush, stocking-darner, linen folder, chimney-sweeper, spinning mop. All things I'd made from necessity when I slaved for the Steps, inventions that kept house for me so that I could do other work of my own.

But somewhere along the line, those very inventions had

become my work. Now I never had to do a chore I hated, because I could make something to do it for me—and no other woman had to either, so long as she came to me. I was proud of that.

I laid my hand flat on the locked door and it opened of its own accord, ratcheting sounds from its inner gears welcoming us into the shop.

I heard my little captive catch her breath, and too late I berated myself for revealing that small secret to her. I still didn't know who her employer was.

The dragonflies hovered in the air to greet me. They flitted curiously around the child, who laughed when their wire feelers brushed her face and arms.

One landed briefly on my shoulder. "Go to Lord Alming's and bring him here, please," I whispered. The dragonfly zipped out the door before it had time to close again, and the girl was too distracted by the other buzzers even to notice.

I just had to keep her here until Lord Alming arrived. If she was a spy for the Brethren or one of our business rivals, he would surely know.

"Now," I said to the girl, "I am going to have my breakfast. Would you like some too?"

She ducked her head. Her face was too dirty to see a blush, but I suspected one was hiding on her cheeks. She nodded, and there was something desperate and embarrassed in the nod that I recognized. Here was a girl who knew hunger.

We sat down at the table together and the buzzers served

us a lukewarm meal of chocolate toasts and sinnum buns; I've always had a sweet tooth in the morning. The clary-bush tea, at least, was piping hot and perfectly brewed, thanks to the automatic kettle I'd perfected soon after I moved in here.

The girl eyed my kettle. "Why do you always make things like that?" she asked.

I squinted at her. If she was talking, that meant there was a chance of finding out who'd sent her; still, I couldn't give too much away about my work, lest she bring it back to her employer.

Whoever that was could certainly be feeding her a little better, I thought . . . and a plan began to form in my head.

I gestured to the caterpillars, who hooked themselves to wire harnesses on the edge of my serving tray and pulled it forward on tiny wheels. The array of pastries halted before the little girl. "Please, have some more," I said, "you've hardly eaten —"

She popped a whole sinnum bun in her mouth before I could finish my sentence, her brown eyes never wavering from my automatic kettle. In fact, she hadn't glanced once at the food she was eating or at the mug from which she took such long swigs of tea, as if she thought the food and drink would disappear if she admitted it was really there.

I knew that feeling. My guard against this girl slipped away even further in spite of myself.

"Things like what?" I asked her, trying to keep my voice

if not icy at least cool, so as not to betray the amusement and sympathy I felt.

"Little things," she said. "Boot polishers. Kettles." She waved a toast-clutching hand toward my display window, and I saw a strange combination of longing and scorn on her face. "Sewing machines." Then she actually had the nerve to roll her eyes.

"I'm proud of my work, thank you very much!" I said, all worries about concealing my sympathy gone. "What would you suggest I make instead?"

The grubby face lit up.

"Cannons!" she said through a mouthful of chocolate toast, the way some children might have said *toys* or *sweets*. "Armor! Rifles! Spears! Why, with what you can do . . ." She shook her head, still torn between derision and dreamland. "I don't know why you'd spend your time on *girl things*." She wrinkled her nose.

Ah. This was an argument I'd already had plenty of times in the past year . . . only it was always with adults, and mostly men.

"Are you a girl?" I asked.

Scorn won out when she looked at me this time. "Think so."

"Do you think boys are better than girls?"

"No!" she said as stoutly as any soldier, but then I saw her start to buckle. She looked down at her mug. "Only, there's lots of people who do."

My hostility dissipated. "Well," I said gently, "do you think boy things are better than girl things?"

"*I* like them better," she said.

I took a sip of tea. "Ah. If you like them, and you're a girl, then they're girl things too, aren't they?"

"Humph." She looked derisively at my sewing machine again, but I saw the flicker of a grudging smile.

"I don't suppose you've ever spent a whole day mending seams?"

She shrugged. "Maybe not."

"No, because then you'd know how tedious it is, and you'd know the value of a machine that does it for you. And it's a rare girl who doesn't have to do those things, you know—spend her whole day mending and cleaning and boiling water, with not a moment to herself for a thought of her own . . ." I took a deep breath, pushing away the memories of my own forced labor. "It's all right if you *do* like those chores, but so many girls *have* to do them that they never get the chance to discover what they like, all for themselves. So I make helpmeets that give those girls time to find out. To do whatever the things are—the girl things—that *they* like to do."

It was funny; I'd never quite thought about it that way, but I knew as soon as I said the words that they were true.

Meanwhile the girl had gone back to scowling. "I suppose," she mumbled.

I sighed and took a deep drink of my tea, letting the

steam settle my breath and clear my head. "What do you do all day, then?" I asked. "Something that someone else tells you to do?"

Her glance darted to the door. "They call me Runner," she said, "because I'm fast."

"Well, that you are," I said, chagrined. "I barely caught you myself."

"I never thought you'd catch me at all," she said, a grin stealing across her face, "and that's how I let you, I think."

"Hmm. Where do you run to, Runner?"

"From."

I didn't understand, which was clear as day to Runner, who rolled her eyes again as she picked up another bun. "I run away *from,* most times," she said. "The Miss distracts them, and I steal the purse and run away from the mark back to the Big Lad—that's the boss—and maybe he gives me my dinner, or maybe I sleep on the shelf."

"The shelf!"

"The best one of us gets the shelf, Miss Mechanica." She blinked at me as if it were obvious. "Up where there's no rats."

That notion made me cringe, and her use of my nickname did too, the one the Steps had given me, the one Fitz had used when he was parading around the story of Fin's and my supposed love at first sight last year. The story had shifted and grown since then, until it wasn't even Lord Alming who had found my slipper but Fin himself. People said that he'd slid it on my foot like an engagement ring and we'd sailed away to the palace atop my mechanical steed, happily-ever-after-the-end. The whole kingdom had fallen in love with our love story.

An illustrated book titled *Mechanica* even came out a few months later. I'd paged through Caro's copy, trying to crow over it the way she had done—and I admit to smiling when I saw the unkind caricatures of the Steps—but I couldn't quite bring myself to find such untruths amusing.

What the kingdom thought by now, a year later with no royal wedding in sight, I really had no idea. I'd tried to dispel the myth, to make my living as just Nicolette Lampton, the inventor. But if this girl still called me Mechanica, I hadn't done nearly enough.

And right now, at half past seven in the morning on the dawning of the second annual Exposition, I had more pressing matters to deal with than my own image in our nation's folklore, as I was quickly reminded when someone began to knock determinedly on the door.

"Ah, Lord Alming," I said with relief.

But it wasn't my tall, mustachioed patron who waited for me there; it was a short, fat, pretty blonde. Caro bustled past me into the shop. "All right, all right, I'm coming, aren't I?" she told the metal-and-glass dragonfly that plucked at her skirts. "You've done your job, you've done your job!"

Once she was inside, the dragonfly made a loud buzzing

noise, calling all my other flying creatures, more than three dozen now. Together they pushed the door closed.

A butterfly flitted back to my kettle and set it on again. Several steel spiders descended from the ceiling on cotton threads and harnessed themselves to the waiting teapot, ready to wheel it over to us.

"Well, I can't fault the service, Nick," Caro said with a sigh, sitting down at my table as the caterpillars pulled the mostly empty breakfast tray over to her, "even if it is a bit insistent at times." She turned toward Runner, who seemed to be trying to trickle under the table like water. "Now. What on earth are *you* doing here, Miss Harkington?"

Runner's and my noises of disbelief came out in unison, although hers was the louder.

"You know who Runner is?" I asked. "Do you know who she works for?"

Runner was up and making for the exit even as I asked the question, more than fast enough to earn her name.

But this was an inventor's shop; I pushed a lever on the wall just to my side, locking the front door before she got to it. Runner pulled at my elaborate brass door handle with considerable strength in her little arms, but it wouldn't budge.

I hated causing the girl any panic. "Look," I said. "It's only that I don't want any of my, ah, trade secrets getting out to my rivals. So if you could just tell me which one of them sent you to spy on me, I would be most appreciative."

Runner pressed her lips together hard and shook her head. I turned to Caro. "Just tell me who she is."

Caro looked at us both with sympathy. "I don't know her exactly, or the name Runner, but I know she's a Harkington just by looking at her," she said. "One of the minor noble families living at the palace. All of them have those eyes and that chin, you see? And I also happen to know that one of their young girls ran off three months ago. Now," she said in her sweetest voice, turning to the increasingly fidgety Runner, "you wouldn't have any idea who that was, would you?"

Runner's apparently distinctive chin trembled, and it looked as if she was about to burst into tears. At the last minute she swallowed them, took a deep breath, and spilled out more words on its exhale than I would have thought lungs her size could contain: that she'd run away, yes, that she was Purity Harkington, yes, that she had run off in the first place only because her widowed mother had a new beau whom she didn't like at all—he was always bothering her and her mother never believed it—so she figured she could take care of herself, and the Big Lad was mean but at least he was better than her mother's beau, and she wanted to make her own way and someday become an inventor and a princess like Miss Mechanica, except she'd invent useful things like cannons and guns instead of teapots, and she'd come to the shop only because she couldn't help it, couldn't help looking in and dreaming, even though her dream was a better one than Miss Mechanica's was.

At the end of such a fascinating speech I found that my arms were crossed tightly and my lips were pursed. I sympathized with the girl's ambitions, although I certainly didn't appreciate the way she characterized my work, and her story about running away made me so sad, I was afraid to show it on my face.

But Caro was smiling, and she bent down to put a reassuring hand on the girl's arm. "Well, now, Miss Runner," she said, "because I think you like that name better, don't you?"

Runner nodded.

"This beau you mentioned. That would be Lord Whiting, is that right?"

The girl flinched at the sound of the name. She regarded Caro fearfully, then nodded again, more slowly this time.

Caro's voice and her body language stayed as gentle as could be, but she and I shared a look that spoke a whole world of outrage.

"Runner, Lord Whiting's gone," Caro said. "He bothered another girl, and she told my cousin Jamie, who's the head of the palace guards. Lord Whiting's in prison, way up in the north."

Runner's face crumpled, and she buried it in Caro's shoulder. Caro began to stroke her hair, very softly. "If you come back to the palace with me today, and come back to your mama who's been worried sick about you, then I don't doubt Miss Lampton here would be willing to teach you a few tricks of her trade"—Caro gave me a look that wasn't quite a wink—"so long as you stop saying mean things about what she does."

Runner glanced around the workshop, and her eyes widened with longing when she heard Jules's metallic snuffling noises as he moved about in his stable . . . but then something closed up in her face, and she shook her head reluctantly.

"Can't go back," she said. "Mama loves Lord Whiting. She called me a liar." Her voice was quiet now, with none of the bold insouciance she'd had before.

Caro and I exchanged another look.

"Oh, darling," said Caro, with all the force and warmth of someone who's a mother to every lonesome soul she meets, "I'll make well and sure she does believe you, and if she doesn't . . . if she doesn't, you can stay with my family. Nick and I will help you, won't we?"

They both looked up at me.

I nodded, at a loss for words. How did Caro know so exactly how to care for everyone who needed her? It came as naturally to her as the beat of her heart.

"Of course," I said. I had only to look in Runner's eyes to know the truth of her story, to know she wasn't any kind of spy at all, just a girl with tragedy behind her. I had been a girl like that once . . . and Caro had helped me too.

What a blessing my friend was. I felt overwhelmed with how much I loved her.

"I'm in charge of a whole lot of people at the palace, you know," Caro said. "I'm only sorry I didn't know before you ran away. I might have—" She stopped, anger and protectiveness mixing with regret in her eyes.

I found myself walking across the workshop to take the girl's hands in mine. "I'll teach you whatever you'd like to learn, Runner." Then, remembering how I had felt about charity at the times when I'd needed it most, I added, "So long as you help me around here sometimes, of course. Bookkeeping and tidying and things like that."

Runner grinned and raised an eyebrow, a little of her edge returning. "I thought you had machines to do the tidying, miss?"

There were more faces in the window now; my first customers were waiting outside. The Exposition would be long and busy, and I needed every sale I could get. I bustled Caro and her new charge out the back door with a few more sinnum buns in their hands and with the promise that Runner could come back as soon as she liked. Finally, and somewhat reluctantly, I changed into the blue day dress I'd worn for last year's Exposition; with the new outfit Jules had made so badly torn, it was the most suitable option I had.

When I finally opened the door, a flood of customers poured in. The next two hours sped by as I rang up purchases and noted down special orders and helped people try out all the different contraptions.

Brethren priests wandered in and out of the shop once in a while too. Solemn and silent, they moved slowly, but I always had the impression that something deep inside of them was coiled and ready to spring. They never bought anything, and my buzzers hid themselves in the rafters whenever a black-robed man walked through the door.

But nearly everyone else who came to my shop was friendly, cheerful, and eager to spend money, and I could only feel surprised and grateful that they had it to spend. Maybe business was looking up again after all.

I kept so busy that I didn't even notice the trumpets announcing Fin's speech, which he'd lobbied so hard to be allowed to make today.

I missed its beginning, too, as I rang up a customer who had for some unfathomable reason purchased *seven* of my cuckoo clocks.

I asked my next customer to wait a moment, explaining that I was eager to hear the Heir. She looked at me knowingly, but I ignored her.

". . . No one feels the pain of our history with Faerie more than my family does, more than I do," Fin was saying. Copper speakers like the ones in the ballroom amplified his voice all over Esting City, and his words fairly rang in my little shop. "I lost my own mother, my brother—and you lost your queen, and the prince who ought truly to have been Heir, your next king—"

I heard the faintest tremble in his husky voice, the smallest hitch. I closed my eyes in sympathy and wished that I could send him strength from where I stood.

"Both of them, lost to Fey assassins. But I must ask myself, and I must ask each of you: Will we judge an entire nation on the works of a few, no matter how horrible those works may be?"

All of Esting loved Fin, our shining young prince, with the light of conviction always burning in his dark eyes, pouring out in his passionate and eloquent speeches. Many more commoners than nobles agreed with his views on Faerie, much to his father's frustration. And of course they loved Fin even more now that he was the hero of Esting's favorite romance. I was grateful that at least I could stay in my shop during his speech, away from the crowd's demanding eyes, though I received more and more curious glances from customers as the moments wore on.

"Would we have the citizens of Faerie judge us on the way a fraction of our own people have treated them?" Fin demanded now.

That was good, I thought—that was something it would be hard for them to get around. All you have to do to make them see, Fin always said, is hold up a mirror.

The customer asked me for a kettle in the display behind

my register, and I missed Fin's next few statements while I rustled brown paper and twine, took the woman's coins, and thanked her for her business. Perhaps I *should* hire a shop assistant, as Lord Alming had often suggested—

A gunshot stopped my thoughts.

A moment of perfect silence. Silence in my shop, in the streets, in the square, silence blossoming out of the projection horns that had carried Fin's speech to everyone in Esting City, that had amplified the gunshot as his words stopped.

That silence lasted only half a heartbeat, half the tick of one second on my perfectly synchronized clocks, but it lanced through me like a spear.

Then screams.

I was running before I knew what I was about.

"You'll be safe here," I said to the wide-eyed patrons who had flattened themselves to the walls or the floor or whatever other protective barrier was closest to them. "The door locks, and it's strong." And before I'd even finished the sentence I was in the stable. I leaped up onto Jules and we dashed into the street, surging toward the square against the panicked current of people running away.

I had a sense of machinery around me, large and small—all the wonders of this year's Exposition, none of which were important enough even to notice anymore. I felt the giant presence of a military airship lurking in the sky, its black bulk looming above me like the weight of guilt, like the weight of despair.

I already knew who had been shot. Fin would have said something else, some instruction for safety, some word of rallying or comfort or leadership, if he could have.

I was grateful, perhaps for the first time ever, for the nature of my fame in Esting: As soon as the crowds saw me, they parted, and as I dismounted I saw a guard I vaguely recognized take hold of Jules. One huge man even lifted me up onto the stage.

The Heir's lady love, come to mourn her beloved.

Fin lay on the wooden floor behind the podium. I could see his knee-high black boots and military trousers with their pale gray stripe, his legs splayed awkwardly.

It had been perhaps a minute since the shot. I felt a tear through my heart, a certainty that I was too late. I had only enough time to think that there had never been anything I could do to help him, and then I was behind the podium and I saw him moving, struggling in a pool of blood but moving, and I cried out and pressed myself down next to my dear friend, my beloved in all the ways that mattered because I loved him as much as anyone I knew.

Fin gripped my arm with one cold, ashen hand. "Nick," he said, his lips pale, "don't believe it, don't believe it . . ."

Then a doctor was there, a Su chirurgienne with her bag and gloves and steel mask, and there were guards holding a stretcher, and they were going to carry him away from me.

"We will take care of him, my lady," the doctor said tersely, prying Fin's trembling hand from my forearm. "He is not going to die. Let us take him now."

But I couldn't let them go without me. "No," I said. "You have to let me stay with him. I—I am his fiancée."

It was the first time I'd ever said the words, or even hinted that they were true.

I gathered all the authority inside me and pushed it into my voice, willing myself to stop shaking. "I am the Heiress Apparent, and I will remain with the Heir."

TOO late I heard the echo of my words and realized that the mouthpiece on the podium had carried them all through Esting City. Everyone at the Exposition had heard from my own lips what I had always refused to say: that Fin and I were going to marry.

But that didn't matter now, with Fin bleeding out and weak, being carried away by doctors and guards who cared more about his royalty than his humanity. He needed a friend with him. At whatever cost it might come, that friend would be me.

The next few hours were harrowing in a way I'd never known before. I stayed with Fin through all of it, the sweeping rush to the palace via a hidden trapdoor beneath the Exposition stage, through the honeycomb of servants' passages, up into a small chamber of white marble, lit with bright gaslights that were magnified in a hundred precise and garish mirrors, each one of them reflecting the gory hole in his shoulder, his drained, sunken-looking face.

I watched, stunned, as a clearly Fey painkiller was poured into Fin's wound and dribbled into his slack mouth, something silvery blue that seemed to be made of liquid and smoke at the same time, something that made me cripplingly dizzy with one breath of its strange fumes. Fey potions, here? Used on the prince himself, whose mother and brother had both died from such concoctions?

But I, of all people, had nothing against Fey magic. I was grateful for the obvious relief the stuff gave Fin. His grip relaxed when it had been tight with pain only moments before. I kept holding his hand as the chirurgienne dug into his flesh and pulled out shard after shard of a bullet that, she explained, had been designed to shatter into pieces inside him.

When finally the bloody work was done, I remained at his side. A steaming compress of familiar Esting herbs was applied to the wound, a white linen bandage wrapped all around his shoulder and upper torso. He was carried — still magically, blessedly asleep — to his own suite and placed on his wide canopy bed, limp as a doll.

The attendants who laid him down looked at me cautiously. I was sitting next to him, still holding his hand. I'd released it only long enough for them to remove his shirt before the chirurgie, and I was not about to let go again any time soon.

"Would you, ah, like me to call for a chaperone, miss?" one maid asked.

I stared at her. "What?"

"Well, to . . . to preserve my lady's reputation," she stammered. "Not that I mean it's in question, of course, my lady, begging your pardon," she added very quickly, bobbing a deferent little curtsy on just about every word.

"My reputation?" I felt a surge of anger, almost overwhelming, and it was only the realization that I was gripping Fin's hand much too hard that forced me to calm myself down.

"I have no family who could suffer from such a blow," I said in as courtly a tone as I could manage, "and I hardly fear for my honor with my *fiancé*"—I flung the word at her, I couldn't help it—"in such a condition as he is."

The maid blushed. "Of course, my lady," she said quickly. She backed out of the room, curtsying with every other step. The other attendants fled after her.

I turned back to Fin, who was starting to stir, his brow furrowing slightly, his lips moving just a little. They were dry and cracked. There was a crystal jug on a small table near the bed, but I couldn't reach it without letting go of his hand, and that wasn't something I was willing to do yet. Not before he woke up.

"All right," I said, leaning back in my velvet seat. "You can come out now if you like."

I felt a fluttering pressure in my breast pocket, and as I

looked down, my copperwork butterfly emerged, stretching its thin wings. Two dragonflies crawled from my pockets a moment later, and three glow bugs quickly joined them.

"Would you get some water for Fin, please?" I asked, nodding toward the table.

Together four of the insects alighted on the jug, two on the handle and two on the base, and counterbalancing each other, they tipped it forward so that iced water poured smoothly into a waiting goblet. After they set down the jug, they gripped the edges of the cup's lip and lifted it slowly, laboriously, into the air, then brought it to me.

They'd known to the last drop how much weight they could carry together. They used tools. They made calculations. They looked like simple clockwork bugs from the outside—well, not simple, but at least straightforward in concept and purpose—but inside of each of them there was a tiny soldered-shut box, barely larger than the head of a pin, containing an even tinier pinch of Ashes, taken from one of the hundreds of samples my mother had kept in carefully labeled drawers, one for each species.

I shivered. As grateful as I was for the insects, their lives were always tied to my mother's death. They weren't a gift from her, but an inheritance; I had them because I *didn't* have her. The way she'd left them for me, left her whole workshop hidden away with magic that only I could see through, was her last challenge: Could I continue her legacy?

Well, I had. I was a more famous inventor than she'd ever

been. I often thought of her strict lessons, her standards that had always seemed impossibly high, and I wished I could show her what I'd done with her buzzers now. Either my mother or I had placed the Ashes inside each insect's lifeless clockwork belly, pressed a hand over it, and made a wish for it to live.

And now they were thinking, planning, working together, and bringing me a perfectly calculated glass of cool water so I could moisten the lips of my unconscious friend.

They were alive. I couldn't think of them as anything else, no matter what my mother had written in her journals, no matter how many times Lord Alming told me evasively that Ashes were just a Fey illusion and not to concern myself with their origins.

They were alive, and the mother I shared with them was dead.

I shook myself out of my reverie and turned to Fin. Here was someone I loved, still living.

I dipped the edge of my handkerchief in the water and dripped one drop at a time onto Fin's chapped lips, and then even more slowly, more carefully, into his mouth. The room was warm and dry, thanks to the spiral chimney that wound around the walls and up into the ceiling; the fires in the vast kitchens heated most of the palace that way. But Fin's lips were cracking and I hated to see him—to see anyone— in discomfort, especially when they could not remedy it themselves.

"I told everyone we're getting married, you know," I said. "The least you could do is wake up." I squeezed his hand.

Fin actually squeezed back, so faintly but, oh, it was there. I brought the now weeping goblet to his mouth.

"Fin!" came a loud cry behind us as the heavy wood-and-iron doors burst open.

It was Caro, sweeping in when she was most needed, as she always did.

"Is he all right?" she asked frantically, kneeling beside the bed. Her hands shook, and I saw the huge restraint it took for her not to fling her arms around him, not to do him more injury by accident. Instead, she placed her hands, so carefully, on his arm. "I heard the shot, even from the palace, it's those damned projectors we made, everyone in Esting City heard that horrible noise, but they wouldn't let me come into the operating room, and I didn't know when—when he would—" She took one great shuddering breath, and then she started to cry.

"He'll be all right." I handed the goblet to my hovering insects and began to stroke Caro's hair.

We stayed like that for I don't know how long, Caro weeping over Fin's and my clasped hands, my fingers wandering in her curls. It was strange to me how much comfort I took from being the strong one, from being there for both my friends when they could not stand on their own.

After Caro's tears were spent, the buzzers offered her a

fresh cup of water. She swallowed it quickly, then rose and walked to the table to refill it from the jug.

"You should have some," she said. "When did you last eat?"

It was comforting to be cared for too. As I drank, I felt the cold water wash away a headache I hadn't let myself notice. "At breakfast, I think," I said. "With you and that girl, that Runner. Is she all right?"

"I think so," Caro said weakly, but clearly grateful to have something else to talk about. "I talked to Lady Harkington and told her, well, what had really happened, and that craven woman wouldn't believe a word. She says she'll be loyal to Lord Whiting no matter what, says he's her *true love*." Caro flung the last words out as if they were poison. We shared another look, and I wondered how any mother could be so heartless. I tried to imagine what my mother might have done to someone who hurt me when I was young . . . but then her devastating absence from my life just reared its head again, all that grief I tamped down to get through each day. I took a breath and forced it to retreat once more.

Caro waved her hand as if to say Lady Harkington wasn't worth another thought. "I brought Runner to my own mother and explained everything, and I doubt Mum will leave the girl's side for the next year. It's a good thing too, because if she didn't have that tired, hungry child to mind, I imagine she'd be off to the north to have Lord Whiting's head . . . or off upstairs to have Lady Harkington's, at least." Caro grimaced. "Not that I'm particularly concerned about their well-being. But you know how my mother gets with anyone who needs to be cared for."

I knew very well; she was exactly like Caro.

"I do want to tutor her, you know," I said, "just as soon as she's ready. Maybe we can convince one of the science academies to admit a girl."

Caro smiled. "If a recommendation from the most famous inventor in the country doesn't convince them, I can't imagine what will."

Fin stirred again, his long-lashed eyes fluttering open. We both snapped our attention to him.

"Oh," he muttered. "Oh, I'm awake." He thought for a long moment, then added, "Good."

I laughed weakly, and so did Caro. "It's more than good," I said, smoothing back one of his sweaty curls.

Fin moved his head slightly, then winced. "I wouldn't have wanted . . ." He cleared his throat, a dry, cracking sound. "You don't believe them, do you?" His bloodshot eyes flickered from one to the other of us.

"Believe what, dear heart?" Caro asked, taking his other hand in hers.

"You don't believe them about who did this to me . . ."

"No one knows who shot you," Caro said. "It's only been a few hours." She looked at me.

"I was there almost as soon as it happened," I agreed,

trying to comfort him. "I was there in the chirurgie with you . . . Don't worry, Fin. No one's said anything yet." I didn't know that for sure, of course, but he was starting to look so agitated that I would have said anything to keep him from aggravating his injuries.

Fin frowned. "That doesn't make sense." He tried to look down at himself but couldn't manage to lift his head more than an inch off the pillow. "In the shoulder," he said. "Anywhere else? I can't feel my arm . . ."

"Just the one shot," I told him. "Just the shoulder. The chirurgienne said the bullet broke up inside of you, but she's from that women's medical academy in Soleil, she's very good, she got it all out . . . They used some Fey painkiller on you, that must be why you can't feel your arm."

Fin nodded, as if everything we'd told him was just what he'd expected. "They didn't mean to kill me, then."

Caro tutted. "Kill you," she said, trying to sound as if she found the very notion ridiculous. She could barely get the words out.

"If they'd wanted to kill me, they'd have done it." Fin was growing more alert by the moment, and now he tried to pull himself up in the bed, but he still didn't have the strength. "It was a warning." He licked his dry lips. "Lord, it's hot in here. Nick, would you mind opening a window?"

I stood up. Fin's rooms were spacious, and it took me more than a few long strides to reach the nearest tall window. I fiddled with the multiple latches, then put my weight into pulling the heavy sash upward. Once I got it going, it rolled up smoothly, with the satisfying sound of hidden, well-oiled wheels. Fresh winter air swept into the room, and we all breathed deep.

Noise came in too. It took me a moment to realize what I was hearing, and another to understand just why I found it so disconcerting.

There was another speech being made in the square, amplified through the network of tubes and horns that Caro had helped design. "My fellow Estingers, forgive me," the speaker was saying. "I have been punished for my blindness."

I realized suddenly why I found the voice frightening. It was Fin's.

I looked at Fin and Caro, wide-eyed. Caro stared back at me with equal bafflement, but Fin was trembling on the bed, trying even harder to prop himself up. His face was set with rage.

"We must take back the safety of our lands from those who have betrayed us," Fin's sweet and husky voice was saying from the square. "We must show Faerie once and for all who rules this world that I once claimed we shared."

Then I heard it, that tiny difference in the tone that only someone who'd spent a lot of time with both young men would know. This voice was sweet and husky, yes, but it was lighter and smoother than Fin's. As smooth as treacle.

Fitz.

"I'll go, Fin," I said. "I'll find out what's happening. Don't worry, don't strain yourself—" I had to physically push him back down onto the bed. He looked as though he could have killed Fitz if given the chance, grave injury or no. "You'll only hurt yourself worse, can't you see? Stay here with Caro, and I'll go down to the square and find out . . . all that I can. They'll have to let me, you know. I told them I'm your fiancée, and the whole city heard it."

That last bit of information, at least, distracted Fin enough that he stopped struggling against me. "Did you?" he said, with a trace of his old good humor coming back into his eyes. "I thought I must've hallucinated that."

"Seems more likely," I replied, catching Caro's eye. She smiled at me fondly, then down at Fin. "Just don't go getting any notions that it's true, my charming prince."

"Right," Fin muttered. "Why would I want to marry anybody I love?"

But none of us wanted to dredge up that particular debate, and all of us *did* want to find out exactly what Fitz was attempting with his superlative Fin imitation down in the square—although I already had an idea.

"I'll come back as soon as I can," I said, and I fled.

I took the hidden servants' door just outside Fin's suite. After a frantic dash down seven flights of stairs and through the basement kitchens, I was back in the stables, where I knew Jules would be waiting for me.

"What in the Lord's name's happening, Nick?" Bex called as I ran past her to the stall reserved especially for Jules.

"Don't know yet," I said, sorry I couldn't tell her more but aware that every second Fitz spoke with Fin's voice presented a grave danger. I had to put a stop to it as soon as I could.

Jules had me out through the palace gates in a flash, but the streets had grown so crowded that even with people recognizing and making way for us, we had to push through the throng to get close enough to the stage to see anything.

What I saw stopped my breath.

It was Fin.

Not a voice emanating from behind a curtain to hide the Heir's injuries or protect his safety, not Fitz acting as spokesperson on the Heir's behalf, not even the metal automaton I'd half expected . . . not anything but Fin himself, looking perhaps more beautiful than ever, even with a large white sling wrapped artfully around his right arm and shoulder. This perfect, radiant Fin was demanding a genocide, an extermination of the people he'd campaigned for so long to keep alive and even independent.

"Oh, Fin," I murmured in despair, not knowing whether I spoke to the haggard youth who lay in his bed or the gorgeous false prince who now pounded his fist on the podium in the passion of his speech.

I was conspicuous in the crowd, I knew, in my famous

blue dress from last year's Exposition, riding my legendary steel-and-glass horse. Everyone who'd heard my quiet exclamation turned to me to see my reaction to my fiancé's speech. I arranged my face into a carefully neutral expression, and I kept it determinedly set as I edged closer to the stage.

The impostor's gaze darted to me. "My beloved!" he said, right into the lip of the tube that projected his speech all over the city. "See her, countrymen? This is a woman who knows what Esting should be: self-made, independent, elegant, ambitious. And, of course, exquisitely beautiful." The slightly derisive note in his voice when he called me beautiful made me even more certain that it was Fitz who spoke.

What was happening? I couldn't understand it.

"Come up here, my darling," the prince was saying now. He leaned away from the podium and extended one gloved hand toward me in a stiff, formal gesture that held none of the real Fin's fluid grace.

The people that remained between me and the stage backed away. I urged Jules forward. He balked and flattened his long, jointed ears.

"It's all right," I whispered. "I know it's not really him."

Jules whuffled smoke and took a few slow steps. I was relieved to see that the guard who stood at this side of the stage was one we both knew, at least: Ben Walworth, one of my favorites of Caro's many cousins. "Thank you, Ben,"

I murmured, dismounting as the tall man came to us and took Jules's handles. Jules nudged Ben affectionately but kept both wary glass eyes on me.

I climbed the steps at the side of the stage and took the false Fin's proffered hand, which felt almost feverishly hot, even through the kidskin glove. Up close, he was lovelier still. His eyes were so clear, their whites so bright, his dark skin so perfectly smooth . . .

He pulled me to him and embraced me with his one good arm, there at the podium, before the crowd. I struggled against his grip, but it was incredibly hard and strong — far more so than the real Fin's, who was strong enough.

"What's going on?" I hissed to whoever this was, this too-perfect Fin with Fitz's treacle voice.

I took a breath and caught the scent of warm, deep spice, like whiskey and sinnum . . .

Ombrossus oil.

And then I knew.

It was the strangest sensation. I pulled back from the impostor as he changed before my eyes — no longer one whole human being, but a conglomeration of moving parts. Porcelain eyes rolled in a molded face, and dark curls made from silk tumbled across his painted forehead. His body was hard and strong and uncomfortably warm because it wasn't a human body but an automaton after all, unimaginably life-like, running on coal and clothed in military garb. I could see wisps of smoke, fine and faint, rising above his head like halos—or horns.

Where was the furnace? My admiration for such impressive work distracted me for a moment, which was more than enough time for the thing that wasn't Fin to wrap its arm more tightly around my waist.

I struggled to get free from its grasp again, but I could not. I felt the framework of its hands under the gloves, just a steel skeleton, not flesh and bone at all. I could have sworn I'd felt the pads of his fingers and his palm before, when I'd thought he was a real person, some clever impersonator Fitz had hired, wearing some brilliant disguise! How could I not have known?

It was the ombrossus oil, of course; the Fey disguising potion that Mr. Candery had left me a tiny precious vial of. I'd used it only a few times, but I'd know its alluring deep, spicy scent anywhere. It had been prohibitively expensive even when it was legal, and since it had been banned with all other magic, very few Estingers would remember it—and none of them would be close enough to catch its scent. Only recognizing ombrossus could break its spell.

"What on earth!" I whispered, louder now, speaking not to the automaton but to Fitz, who I was certain could hear me. "Fitz, what do you—"

"My fiancée is clearly distraught by the recent attempt on my life," the automaton said. "Who could blame her? If a Fey assassin had threatened my darling Mechanica's life, why . . ." The automaton trailed off, shaking its perfect head. "No punishment can be too harsh for these savages," it went on. "I will speak with my father this evening, and we will announce our course of action as soon as possible. In the meantime, I beg of you, continue with the Exposition festivities. Let us show these monsters what civilization truly means."

The automaton made a respectful nod as the crowd burst into wild, adoring applause. Gray curtains swirled around the stage, cutting us off from public view.

I had to act quickly and choose my move well. I grabbed both sides of the automaton's head and pulled with all my strength. My hands started to blister where they touched its scalding-hot ears. Then, finally, with a horrid metallic whine, Fin's face broke free from the mechanical prince's smoking head. I stumbled backward with my prize.

Once I recovered my balance and tucked the face inside my jacket, I began to look around for Fitz.

He rushed forward from a shadowed corner, dropping a small metal mouthpiece as he did. He fretted over the faceless automaton, which was slumped against the podium like a corpse.

"For the Lord's sake, Miss Nick, there was no possible reason for you to do that," Fitz snapped, speaking in his own voice now and cold as ice. "If you had any idea how long it has taken to craft this — this — why, I'd think an inventor such as yourself would respect another's masterpiece! I mean, honestly—"

"Masterpiece." I had regained enough composure to match the ice in his voice. "That's an apt description for this puppet, isn't it? You're its master, aren't you?"

Fitz shot me a look that would have soured wine. "You always did lack imagination, Miss Nick. You who might have been Heiress." He eyed me up and down slowly. "Of course, it may not be too late. You may keep the face if it pleases you—and if you'll have supper with me tonight. Clearly your involvement is inevitable now."

I narrowed my eyes. "I have to return to the real Heir. The one who's lying abed with a bullet wound that could well have been fatal." A horrible idea began to blossom and twist across my mind. "Lord, that's what this thing is for, isn't it? So that you can use Fin even if he's dead?"

"Certainly not," Fitz hissed, quickly stepping closer to me. "It's entirely for his safety, as I explained to him just last night. And one paltry shoulder shot wouldn't kill Fin, Nick, for the Lord's sake."

The idea had grown into a whole sickening garden. "You know, Fitz, I wouldn't put it past you to shoot him yourself to get the opportunity to use this little toy." I was shaking all over with rage.

Fitz pursed his lips, completely composed. It was obvious I hadn't struck the nerve I'd aimed for. "Come to supper in my quarters tonight, Miss Nick, and I shall reveal all. Then you can decide if I am in fact the pantomime villain you've made me out to be."

I stormed away without replying. The automaton would need repairs before it could do any more damage, and I needed to get back to Fin.

"Well, are you going?" Caro asked.

Fin frowned. "Don't be absurd. Of course she is."

I glared at him. "I am doing no such thing," I said. "To go into that . . . that villain's lair—"

"Oh, for goodness' sake!" said Caro. "People aren't heroes or villains, all bad or all good, you know. I have to agree with Fin. You should go, Nick."

"You two are," I said quietly.

"We are what?"

"All good." I had felt as rigid as an automaton myself ever since the false Fin had pulled me up onto that stage. But now the iron rod through my spine started to soften, to turn into something as fragile and mutable as human bone, after all.

I sank down onto the edge of Fin's bed. I didn't feel as if I could support myself upright anymore.

Caro put her hand on my knee. "We aren't all good, darling, and you know it," she said.

I wanted to rebuke her, but my throat closed and I couldn't find words.

"I certainly wouldn't have led you on the way I did last year if there were nothing wrong with me," Fin added, a bit harshly.

I couldn't argue with that. I laughed a little, with a hiccup in it. "The Steps are all bad," I said. "I know that much."

But even as I spoke, I remembered the last night I'd spent at Lampton, when I'd snuck into Stepmother's room to return my ball gown to her closet. I'd heard her calling out in her sleep for my father, for the man we'd both lost, and I had felt a sympathy for her in that moment that had never quite gone away.

Now, my father—he was a complicated man, that was certain. And my mother . . .

"My mother was good," I said. "Infinitely good. I wouldn't be here, wouldn't be anywhere, without her."

"Well, no one will deny it," said Fin, all briskness. "But you have to admit, it's much easier for someone to be good once they're dead."

I felt a flash of startled anger and glared at him, my spine iron again, but when I saw the understanding in his face, my retort died before I could speak. We silently shared a whole conversation about parents, dying, grief, and loss, just looking in each other's eyes.

Finally I said, "I don't want to meet Fitz alone. I don't trust him."

"That's easily solved," Fin said. He was propped up on the

bed now, leaning against several stacked down pillows. His color was better, but his every movement was still painted with pain. "We'll go with you."

"You will not!" I cried. "He might be the one who shot you; I wouldn't put it past him."

Fin tried to roll his eyes, then winced and closed them. "Fitz is a climber, Nick, not a murderer. He could hardly use me to his advantage if he killed me."

I wasn't convinced, but I didn't want to aggravate Fin anymore, so I stayed silent.

"Even so," Caro said thoughtfully, "you can't be left here alone. If someone does try to attack you again, you're in no condition to do anything about it. You have to admit, Fin, *someone* shot you today."

Fin settled back on his pillows, grimacing in discomfort. "I know."

I had always felt that the three of us were so strong together, unassailable. But just then it seemed that if even one of us was in danger, the rest became incapacitated.

"You can't go alone either, though, Nick . . . Ah," Caro said, snapping her fingers. "I know what to do. Fitz will hate it, too, so of course you'll both be pleased."

BEX chattered about horses and reeked of them, too, all through Fitz's formal supper. The look on our host's handsome face when he realized his politely phrased barbs didn't do anything to silence her and that in order to preserve his own sense of etiquette he would in fact have to listen to her talk all night, would have to *smell* her . . . that alone was worth spending the evening with him.

I stayed quiet throughout the meal, and just as Bex and I had planned, her constant stream of talk gave me ample opportunity for silent observation.

Fitz seemed the same as he'd always been: charming at first, witty, but with an edge of cruelty that he enjoyed brandishing at those he deemed less intelligent or sophisticated than himself. He especially liked landing insults that he believed his victim didn't even notice; several times he complimented Bex on her horsemanship in ways that were meant to emphasize just how coarse and common she really was.

Bex, of course, noticed every one of those supposedly hidden insults—they just glanced right off her. If anything, her generosity and knack for storytelling shone out the brighter in contrast with Fitz's mean-spirited witticisms. I was genuinely enjoying myself, thanks to Bex. I could certainly understand what Caro saw in her.

The delicious, clearly expensive food did its part to help me enjoy the evening too, from the first appetizer of light, citrus-scented soup to the delicately crisp sugared pears for dessert, as, of course, did the sparkling wine that accompanied each course. Fitz would never stoop to being a less than impeccable host, however little regard he might have for his guests. The meal also made it obvious that he wasn't giving so much of his family's money to the war effort that he couldn't afford a few luxuries for himself. Perhaps he wasn't as vehemently imperialist as I'd thought.

"Won't you join me for tea in my library, Miss Nick?" Fitz said when his manservant, a sullen youth whom Caro had told me she'd never liked, was clearing our dessert cups away. Fitz pointedly looked only at me, but Bex rubbed her hands together and smacked her lips.

"Ooh, lovely! Hope you've got honey for it. I've a terrible sweet tooth." She winked at me and waggled her eyebrows suggestively at the word *sweet,* and I had to work hard to keep from laughing.

Fitz pursed his lips and turned away. He had no choice

but to serve the tea to both of us in his small, dark, and admittedly beautiful library.

After we'd finished our first cup, though, even his rigorous sense of correct behavior reached its limits.

"You know perfectly well why I invited you here, Miss Nick," he snapped suddenly, putting down his cup and saucer with an ungentlemanly clatter. "Now, will I have the chance to defend myself or not?" He glared sideways at my companion, then at the door behind her.

I took a slow sip of my tea and looked at him levelly. "You mean the automaton? Why, of course. Let's talk about it now." I smiled. "Why *did* you decide to build a replica of our prince without his knowledge or consent, Fitz?"

"My goodness," Bex said, "a real automaton! That's a fancy notion for a simple stable hand like me, sirrah, but I'll try to keep up." She fluttered her lashes in exaggerated innocence, adjusting her seat on Fitz's white satin chaise longue. Essence of silage and horsehair came off her in waves.

I couldn't help it; I laughed and laughed. I remembered every time Fitz had been condescending or cruel in the past — and all the times, when I'd first known him, that I'd fallen under the spell of his shallow charms — and I was overwhelmed with mirth.

"Right," Fitz said. "I can see this is useless. Go back to the prince, Nick, and tell him whatever you like. Tell him I was the shooter, even, since you're so obviously determined to vilify me." He walked to the library door and held it open. "I assume you know your way back," he said through clenched teeth.

"Fitz," I said, catching my breath, "if you have anything to prove to me, now is the time."

We stared each other down.

"I can assure you," Bex said, switching to a perfect imitation of Fitz's aristocratic accent, "the Heiress Apparent doesn't extend her favor indefinitely." And in her own voice, low and menacing: "I'd take this chance if I were you."

Finally, his jaw and fists still clenched, Fitz nodded.

"Come with me," he said.

"How many?" Fin asked. He was still sitting up in bed and he looked remarkably well, or at least he had until I'd brought back the news.

I shook my head. "A thousand, at least. They weren't finished yet, Fitz said—but if he has the manpower, it won't be long. A few months."

Enough automaton soldiers to kill every last person in Faerie. Their metal bodies were stacked like building blocks, filling up the huge storeroom.

"Does the king know?" Fin muttered as if to himself. He never called him Father anymore.

"Fitz said he had Corsin's approval." I hadn't wanted to believe it, but I did. Fin's father's health had been failing for years, and as his body weakened, he became more pious, more worshipful of new Estinger technology, and more embittered by his rebellious colony. Fey assassins had killed his wife and then Fin's older brother; the king's heart had never recovered.

"Lord, it never stops!" Fin punched the bed. He used his good arm, but his shoulders lurched with the movement and his face grew drawn. He hissed in pain. "I can never stop it."

"Don't," said Caro. "You'll hurt yourself."

Fin twisted the edge of a blanket in his fist. "Why should it matter?"

Caro stood, her face full of rage, ready to rebuke him, but Fin kept talking. "I've tried so hard this past year, so hard, to make some kind of difference, to do something to be worthy of all these opportunities I've been given. This title, this power. And just when I thought I was maybe getting somewhere, changing people's minds, I'm pushed back into the shadows." His knuckles were pale; he looked down at the blanket and slowly relaxed his hand. "I don't think Fitz was the one who shot me," he murmured. "I don't think he was behind it at all."

I had to admit that I agreed with him; I hadn't seen a murderer in Fitz that night, not someone who could aim a pistol at his future king and pull the trigger. All he could talk of when he showed me the stacks of automatons was how pleased King Corsin was with them, with him; he'd even mentioned the relief Fin would feel when the war was over. By ending the war — by whatever means — Fitz hoped only to gain more favor with those in power. If nothing else, killing Fin would pose too big a risk to his career.

Lord, I despised him. If I still thought he'd shot Fin, I'd have someone easy to blame. He couldn't even give me that.

"Who did shoot you, then?" Caro asked, her voice still tight with anger. "A Fey assassin? After everything you've done for them?"

Fin's laugh quickly turned into a wince when his shoulder moved. "I've done nothing for the Fey," he said, "nothing. In the single year since I've even been allowed to speak in public, what's happened? We're at war now, full-blown war. Once Fitz and the king get that army moving, we'll kill them all. I've done worse than nothing." He was staring at a tapestry on the far side of the room, a depiction of an old hero-and-dragon story, and there was longing, almost hatred, in his face. He yearned to see himself in the hero, I knew that, but whether the dragon he battled was the war, or the Brethren advisors who breathed down the king's neck, or even his father himself, I wasn't sure.

"You're right, Fin," I said, standing up. "You can't make any difference here and now. But I know a place where you can."

I'd kept Mr. Candery's letter close to my heart ever since I received it, for the warmth that thinking of my old housekeeper brought me as much as for fear that it might somehow be stolen. I had tried hard to make my workshop secure, but as today had proven, none of us could be fully sure of our safety anymore.

I took the letter out and handed it to Fin. As he read it through, the warmth started to come back into his cheeks, and his face began to look a little less haggard. Caro leaned over his shoulder and read along, one hand touching his hair; as always, her anger had quickly vanished inside compassion.

"It's brilliant," he said, looking up at me. "It's perfect. It's the chance I've been hoping for."

Caro bit her lip. "How do you know you can trust fer?" she said.

The Fey pronoun threw me for a moment. "Mr. Candery? I trust him the same way I trust you. He raised me. He loves me." Seeing the look she gave me, I added, "He's always used *him*. He's only half Fey." Full-blooded Fey had no gender, and only people who reviled them most—like the Brethren—insisted on calling them *he* and *she*.

"No, I have faith in your Mr. Candery," Caro said. "I meant the Fey leader."

Fin sighed, then nodded reluctantly. "Look at this," he said, "the words he's underlined. *I cannot tell you*, first of all. And at the end of the letter: *I beg your forgiveness*. What if he's trying to tell you not to come? What if the leader had him write this to set a trap for us?"

I sat next to Fin and took the letter back, scanning through it for possibly the hundredth time. I was supposed to be the analytical one with the inventor's mind; how hadn't I noticed?

"But see," I said, "there's another word underlined, there." I stroked my finger over Mr. Candery's writing, as if I could read his intent in the shape of the words. *"Trustworthy."*

They both looked at me. "What do you think it means?" Fin asked.

I took a breath; I knew he would believe me, whatever I said. I felt the weight of all our futures hanging in the balance.

I cannot tell you. Trustworthy. I beg your forgiveness.

I remembered the quiet, gentle way Mr. Candery had moved through the house, had moved through my life; how he'd cared for my mother, and for me, far beyond the duties required by his position. I remembered how he had never hurt me, even with a word; how when Stepmother dismissed him, he'd risked leaving behind illegal magic to help me through the life he knew she'd make hard for me.

Fin was right; Mr. Candery was attempting to tell me something he couldn't put in the letter. But I couldn't believe he would set a trap for me, even if someone was forcing him to do it.

I looked at Fin on the bed, at the bandage wrapped around his shoulder, the badge of all he'd tried and, he thought, failed to do in Esting.

I squared my shoulders. "It means we should go to Faerie," I said.

King Corsin slumped in his throne like a man whose bones had dissolved. His long white braid snaked around his shoulder and down one arm, and he stroked it listlessly. Brethren clerics stood rigidly on either side of him; as always, it was obvious that the real power in the room lay with them.

Fin leaned on my arm more than we let his father or the Brethren see. He had to look strong for this, had to look capable; we both did.

Corsin gazed at us with mournful, watery eyes. "You want to leave me?" he asked, his voice a quaver.

I felt Fin tense next to me, and then I felt the hidden shiver when even that small movement hurt his shoulder.

"We want to help you, sire," I said. I held out Mr. Candery's letter, forcing my hand not to tremble. "We can help the whole country, if you'll let us. So many Estinger soldiers have died already, and the Fey have still pushed us out to the very edges of the continent—"

The cleric standing on Corsin's left side scoffed. "You're a military expert now, are you? Or a political one?" he asked slowly. "You gave up your right to speak for Esting when you refused to become Heiress."

The king looked up at his advisor, then back to me. "Yes," he said slowly. "You refused to marry my son, my son who loves you. Everyone loved your story." He sighed weakly. "It was perfect."

"Father," Fin said through gritted teeth, "you know I don't want—"

"Yet you called yourself Heiress yesterday," murmured another cleric, stepping smoothly forward, closer to the throne. "Just as the Heir was nearly killed. And now you produce this letter." He smiled serenely. "How convenient."

Corsin nodded, his eyes narrowing as he took in the cleric's words.

"No!" Fin pulled us both toward his father, and he couldn't hide the shudder of pain the movement gave him. The Brethren watched him impassively. Up close I could see many broken capillaries around the king's eyes and nose. His skin seemed translucent, sagging, as if it no longer had the strength to hold in his vitals. How old was Corsin—fifty? Sixty? I couldn't remember, but he wasn't old enough to look like this.

"Please, Father," Fin whispered. "Listen to me for once, and not to them." He glared at the closest cleric so fiercely that the man backed up a few steps. "Nicolette is the last person in the world who means me harm. I do love her, and she loves me." Our eyes met briefly, and I nodded at him, giving permission one last time for him to say what we'd agreed must be said in order for the king to let us go.

Fin continued, in a louder voice: "If you allow us to take this voyage, you may confirm the news of our engagement."

The Brethren murmured to each other in rippling whispers. This story was a powerful one, one they could use to charm the divided people of Esting, to give them a common dream again, a common loyalty to the royal family — which would really be loyalty to the Brethren. We knew they would twist our story to suit their own ends, but all the while we'd be in Faerie, enacting real change. They might have this frail, broken old man in their grasp, but Fin was stronger, braver than his father. They would not get him in their clutches too.

Corsin straightened and held a thin, veiny hand out to his son. "The Fey have killed enough of my family," he whispered. "My firstborn, your brother. Nerali . . ." But his wife's name proved too much for him to bear. A tear slipped down Corsin's cheek, and he slumped back in the throne.

"Which is why the war must continue, sire," said one of the clerics, slipping closer. "History has proven that the Fey cannot be reformed, cannot be educated or converted. So they must be eradicated."

Fin tensed again; if he'd had his strength, I thought he might have hit the man. "Please, Father," he repeated. "You're right; there's been enough death for us. Let me try to make peace instead. Please."

The cleric opened his mouth to speak. Corsin kept him silent with a raised hand, and when the king looked at his son, I saw the ghost of the leader he must once have been before grief and dogmatism eroded him.

"You may go," he said finally. "Put an end to this . . . loss, if you can."

My heart began to thud with relief, even as I felt the cold

glares of the Brethren all around us, their anger filling the air like poison.

Late that night I crept back to Fitz's storeroom. Breaking in was easy when I had so many friends among the palace servants and especially when my target was someone they disliked so much.

I'd calculated that there were at least a thousand half-finished automatons in his storeroom. I wasn't sure how many he planned to create; how many would it take? Did he want only to defeat the Fey or to obliterate them? From the predatory gleam in his eye, and from the way the Brethren advisors had spoken to Corsin, I was sure it was the latter.

Even in the pale light of my small gas lantern, I could see what marvels of engineering they were. I hated their purpose, but I had to admire their design. Runner, with her rapturous dreams of cannons and battle machines, would adore these.

I'd seen her earlier in the evening, tucked snugly into Caro's own childhood bed while Mrs. Hart sat at its foot, turning the crank on one of my knitting machines ferociously and glaring at anyone who threatened to wake the child up. I almost wished I could stay, that I could make good right away on my promise to start teaching her engineering, but there would be time. I'd lend her some of my books before we left, and I'd see to it that Lord Alming looked after her; he'd be glad of another brilliant young protégée to encourage.

The thought of the voyage made me realize how tired I was. There was so much to do, to organize, before we departed. I'd learned all I could here, and it was time to go home.

As I turned to leave, I saw something familiar: the broken remnants of the Fin automaton I had attacked the previous morning. I smiled and moved closer, the better to inspect the damage I'd done. The scent of ombrossus grew stronger as I approached.

The light from my lantern caught another human shape next to the false Fin. I jumped back, thinking it was Fitz lying in wait for me, but it didn't move.

I realized it was another automaton. I stepped forward again to examine it. I held my light up to its face, and then I let go of the lantern to cover my mouth with both hands and muffle my scream.

The lantern clattered to the ground; the flame guttered and went out.

The face I had seen was my own.

PART II

THE month before our embarkation sped by in a haze of hard work. Any time I didn't spend on the special orders I'd received at the Exposition, I was working with Lord Alming, hammering out the finer points of his stewardship over my business while I was away. I had total faith in his intentions; he was so proud of me and my successes that he would never do me wrong. His ambitions still centered not on increasing his already-massive fortune, but on using his own money to spy on the Brethren. I'd constructed a few cunning little devices to aid in that goal, but I drew the line at leaving any of the buzzers with him.

The buzzers and Jules were coming with me, as much because of how lonesome I'd be for them as to make sure they didn't fall into the wrong hands while I was away. They slept peacefully now, tucked opposite the Ashes that they always avoided when awake. I'd had to take those with me too, packed carefully into slender glass tubes and stored in a padded and reinforced briefcase I designed myself. While I still didn't know what the Ashes really were, I was certain that they would spell more trouble than I could get out of if the Brethren found them. And if I was ever going to discover the origin of this particular magic, which even the part-Fey smugglers I'd met seemed to fear . . . well, Faerie had to be the place to do it. Mr. Candery used to buy them for my mother; surely he would know.

I could imagine our reunion already. My arms ached to hug him again.

Before I knew it, Fin, Caro, and I were in Port's End, stepping onto the gangway that led up to the *Imperator*.

It was a glorious creation, a sleek ebony vessel inlaid with brass portholes, big enough to hold a crew of six as well as twelve passengers—although for this voyage there would be only Fin, Caro, and me.

The great black balloon rising above the ship bore the triple stars of the Esting flag, just like the first airship I'd ever seen, at last year's Exposition. It was strange to think how quickly they'd gone from being newfangled wonders to everyday sights; military airships patrolled the sky above Esting City every day now, airborne defenses that somehow felt more intrusive than reassuring.

This one seemed designed more for luxury travel than warfare, but even so, the cannons lining its hull were hardly decorative. The *Imperator* was prepared to defend itself.

The thought should have filled me with fear, but at that

moment, walking up a gangplank into the sky, all I could feel was excitement and the thrill of freedom. I was getting out of Esting City, out of Esting entire, out of all the things that haunted and constricted me there. I was going on an adventure to visit the land I'd dreamed of ever since I was a small child falling asleep in my bed to the sound of Mother's stories. I was going to Faerie, and I would see Mr. Candery there.

Jules trotted ahead of me, and the buzzers sprang one by one from my pockets and hand luggage and followed him. I smiled at their eagerness, but I stayed with Fin and Caro.

"Do you suppose they feel they're going home?" Caro asked. She'd worn a sensible brown traveling outfit for the day, having specifically requested that Jules make her something without frills. She wanted to seem as inconspicuous as possible when Fin and I waved our goodbyes to the Port's End crowd that had gathered to watch us leave on our engagement voyage.

"Surely they do," said Fin. "The Ashes come from Faerie, don't they, Nick?" He looked perhaps more princely than ever in his official military regalia, turning to wave at the throng.

"That's the only thing I know for sure," I said as people cheered. I was a little afraid to learn the Ashes' secrets, but . . . they had brought life to Jules and the buzzers, and I loved them so much. I could only long to know more.

A Brethren priest waved incense across the prow of the

airship, chanting prayers in such low, sonorous tones that I couldn't understand his words. I shivered. I didn't know how so many of my countrypeople could fear magic so much and yet implicitly trust the Brethren's dour, menacing brand of mysticism. I didn't believe the priest's prayers and incense would have any effect on our voyage one way or the other, but somehow I still wanted him to stop. I knew the Brethren wished nothing good for me, or Fin, or this venture. They wanted only to use us like puppets, the way they did Corsin.

I thought of the likeness of myself that I'd found in Fitz's storeroom. I'd gone back there just last night with a wrench and a torch and a bottle of oil, and I'd destroyed my simulacrum utterly. I'd burned a few of those frightening soldiers in the process, and I could only hope I'd bought us a little more time before Fitz's army would be finished and ready for travel.

I looked at the crowd that had gathered to see us off, and I suddenly wished it were larger. The more people who saw Fin and me leaving the country, the better; it would take Fitz months to rebuild those automatons, but still, the idea of his using my likeness to promote his own agenda, let alone of his using another false Fin, made me feel ill.

The walk up the gangplank was longer than it had seemed from the safety of the ground. It took several minutes before we reached the ship itself. I made the mistake of looking back down as we boarded, and all the empty sky between that spindly gangplank we'd climbed and the earth made my stomach clench.

The feeling didn't abate once we were on deck. But at least there was plenty to distract me from the idea that we all stood on nothing but air.

First, the *Imperator*'s six crew members greeted us with formal salutes. I'd never felt comfortable with the servants in the palace, at least not the way Fin was, and the crew's deferential body language made me self-conscious too. I'd had plenty of fun at the palace's "downstairs" parties with Caro, carousing with her mother and her scores of cousins. But I could never get used to servants *serving* me. Fin knew nothing different, but he was always respectful to them, friendly and conversational without demanding that they like him — and exactly because of that, they tended to like him very much.

Only two people didn't seem so pleased to greet us. The first, dressed in white robes and headscarf, was clearly the ship's doctor, a Su chirurgienne like the one who had fixed Fin's bullet wound. She nodded coolly, keeping her hands clasped behind her back; still, she didn't seem unfriendly, only reserved.

But the Brother that King Corsin had insisted accompany us on the voyage didn't even join the welcoming line. He stood at the prow of the ship, swinging an incense burner at the end of a long chain — what about the fire risk, I wondered? — and chanting words I couldn't hear.

I felt my skin prickle, and I was glad everyone else on board seemed to be ignoring the Brother. I turned away from him, deciding to do the same.

Fin met the crew first, and their regard for him was obvious from the real warmth in their smiles when he shook their hands. Caro and I received polite bows from the men and a bobbing curtsy from the one female sailor, who introduced herself with a shy smile as Sneha. We smiled shyly back; it was obvious that Caro felt as awkward as I did.

"I wish I could have come as your lady's maid," she muttered.

"Lord, no!" I whispered back. "This is disorienting enough!"

The word *disorienting* reminded me that I was standing in midair, and my stomach lurched. When Caro grinned at me, all I could manage in return was a queasy smile.

The ship's captain, a surprisingly young man named Wheelock who greeted us with an impeccable formal bow, said that our heavy luggage had been sent on ahead and was already waiting in our rooms. "There will be refreshments in the galley in one hour's time," he said gravely, as if tea and cakes were the most serious matter in the world. "Perhaps you wish to inspect your quarters before launch, to ensure that you have everything you need."

"Thank you, Wheelock," Fin said with a genuine smile. "We're grateful for your forethought." Ever since we'd decided on a course of action, he had seemed much more relaxed and healthier, and while he still wore a sling, his wound was nearly healed. The chirurgienne had told us that his shoulder would likely always be stiff, but you'd never guess it from his straight and vigorous stance.

The three of us followed Wheelock through an ebony door into the belly of the airship, and the idea that we really would be spending a month on board began to sink in. It was a long time — and at the end of it we would come ashore on a magical and exceedingly dangerous foreign continent.

But I was my father's daughter as well as my mother's, and William Lampton had loved nothing more than travel to foreign lands. I was glad I hadn't inherited his prejudice against Faerie, but I liked to think I had something of his sense of adventure. I called on it now. My father had been a traveling trader, a venturer; perhaps I could be a venturess.

We neared the end of a long, tall, narrow corridor lined with long, tall, narrow doors and lit with small glimmering lanterns that hung from the ceiling by ropes — to keep them steady in case of storm or wind, I remembered from a book about shipbuilding that I'd read some years ago. It seemed many things from those old ocean-sailing ships translated directly to the air, including words like *galley* and *berth*.

"Miss Caroline Hart," Wheelock said with another flourishing bow as he stopped before a copper-inlaid door, "your quarters are here."

He opened the door, and Caro gasped with delight.

Inside the intensely neat little room I could see built-in bunk beds and shelves, and Caro's steamer trunk was strapped to the opposite wall with thick leather belts. There was a copper basin secured there too, and a small round mirror above it. A brass porthole let light in at the far wall, and a fresh-smelling posy hung by the mirror. The severe economy of space might have made the room seem cramped, but instead it had a cheerful simplicity that made its size perfect.

"The shared water closet is at the end of the hall, miss," said Wheelock, "and if you require anything you may ring the pull here." He indicated a silk rope hanging by the door that disappeared into a discreet space in the ceiling.

"Thank you," Caro said, "but I do like to take care of myself. I'm used to it, you see."

"So I've heard, miss," said Wheelock, and the two shared a conspiratorial little smile that suddenly made the captain seem like a young person after all.

Caro tossed her hat onto the lower bunk. "Right," she said briskly to Fin and me. "See you in an hour? I want to write Bex a note before I freshen up. We won't want to miss those refreshments!"

We nodded and Caro disappeared into her cozy room, closing the door behind her.

"The royal suite is just here," Wheelock said with a bow, indicating the grand door at the end of the hallway. "I can only hope everything is to your satisfaction."

He kept looking at me as he spoke, and I couldn't

understand why I should have any say in the appointment of Fin's rooms.

Then he opened the door and I saw the big double bed, decked out in silver and gray.

"We're to share a room!" I exclaimed, not quite able to control my surprise. What about the palace maid who'd been so worried about my reputation that she didn't want to leave me alone with Fin even when he was wounded and unconscious?

Wheelock's eyes widened with horror. "A suite, my lady! I thought it would be best, since there's room for the, ah, supplies you brought here . . . I do apologize . . . Anything you'd like changed, anything at all . . . I'm truly sorry, I meant no insult, with the engagement announced—"

Fin smiled his beam-of-light smile. "It's quite all right, Wheelock," he said. "Nicolette would prefer a separate room, that's all. Please don't worry."

The color was still drained from Wheelock's face, but he composed his expression quickly. "Thank you, Your Highness," he said. "I am very grateful for your understanding." He bowed low before me. "And for yours, my lady."

"Not at all," I said, embarrassed. Had I given the game away by my surprise at sharing a bed with Fin? The public belief in our engagement was key to our whole mission.

"Ah, Wheelock?" I said, trying to sound natural when I'd never in my life called someone by a surname alone. "It's perfectly all right. I will stay in these, ah, quarters after all;

they are far too lovely to change in the least." In addition to keeping up the pretense of our engagement, I realized I couldn't possibly let Fin sleep alone and unguarded . . . at least not before we'd gotten to know the crew much, much better.

I took Wheelock's gloved hand, then quickly pulled back for fear it wasn't proper; it was clear that the oddly stiff young captain set great store by such things. "It's fine, truly," I said.

His dark gray eyes met mine just long enough to startle me with their sharp perception. Then he looked away, formal and reticent again.

"Not at all, my lady." He bowed and turned to leave.

Fin gave me a roguish grin over Wheelock's shoulder.

As soon as the captain left, I rolled my eyes. "I'm staying here simply for your own safety, Your Highness," I said pointedly.

"Of course, of course!" Fin agreed, imbuing his husky voice with the innocence of an angel. "Why would I ever think otherwise?" His smile broke out again, although he tried to hide it as he added: "And will you be thinking of our captain's safety next?"

Since neither question was worthy of reply, I turned away with great dignity and went to my steamer trunk, wanting to change so I could get to the galley. I hoped a little food and something hot to drink would settle my mind. The wobble in my legs and belly had subsided, and inside this room I could almost convince myself I stood on solid ground. The small round portholes instead of windows, the slight concavity of the walls, and the way everything was either bolted or strapped down to the floor were the only elements that gave any indication that this was not the case.

I was so intently busy with my clothes that I didn't notice Fin walking up behind me until he put a hand on my arm. "Truly, Nick, don't worry," he said. "I hope I didn't make you uncomfortable just there."

I touched his hand with mine, then turned to face him. "You didn't," I said. "It's just . . . it's always there, isn't it? You're such a dear friend to me now, but sometimes I just . . . I remember. The way I used to feel about you."

Fin smiled again, but gently and seriously this time. "I know. It's not always easy, what you and I and Caro have. But we don't need to let the past keep us apart."

I hugged him close. "A good thing, too," I said. "Someone's got to keep you from getting assassinated on this voyage."

Fin laughed. "I'm safe as kittens with you and Caro, and don't I know it," he said, but he wouldn't quite meet my eyes.

He left me in the bedroom and went to the suite's tiny sitting room so we could both change; I bustled my dusty traveling clothes into a fascinating suction laundry shoot. Then we each had our turn in the suite's private water closet. It had brass plumbing and an amusingly tiny chairlike bathtub; it seemed space in an airship was at a premium even in the royal suite.

Once we'd freshened up, Fin and I sat side by side at an ornate little desk that folded out of the wall, following Caro's example and writing our own last letters home. Airships flew so fast that we had only a short time until the *Imperator* would pass its mail limit; after that point, carrier pigeons released from the ship wouldn't be able to reach the shore of Esting. I wrote a final thank-you and a few instructions for Lord Alming, plus an encouraging note to Runner; Fin wrote to his father. His face was so full of quiet longing that I didn't feel I could ask what he'd written.

We finished our letters just in time for refreshments in the galley, which was located on the opposite end of the ship from the sleeping quarters. As we walked down the hallway and ascended the stairs to the deck, I had the uncomfortable feeling that my body was rising at a faster rate than it would have from just my feet taking it up the steps.

That feeling was horridly confirmed when I came out into the open air and a huge white shape rushed down upon me.

"Fin, look out!" I cried, pushing him farther behind me and shielding my face with my arm.

I felt a cool, gentle sprinkle of water on my hands and hair, and then it was past.

Fin burst out laughing, as did the nearby members of the crew . . . and Caro, who was already waiting for us on deck.

I quickly lowered my arm. I knew, of course, that clouds were nothing more than high-altitude mist. But that one had seemed so solid, and so *swift,* moving toward us like that.

I decided it wouldn't do to feel ashamed that my protective instinct toward Fin was working so well, so I joined in the laughter around me, exaggeratedly miming my own frightened reaction to, of all things, a cloud. I fixed my gaze firmly on the wooden floor of the deck and very firmly *not* on the ropes and chains that attached our ship to the great balloon that kept us floating through the (don't look at it) sky.

With my eyes on the ground, even if that wasn't the right word, I was able to walk confidently in the direction of the galley hatch, fairly dragging Fin along behind me.

But before I could return to the security of indoors, Caro ran—ran!—across the deck and grabbed my arm.

"Come on, Nick," she said. "You have to see!"

"Oh no," I said, still looking toward the galley. "The only thing I'd like to see at the moment is a strong cup of tea."

Caro looked at me sympathetically, but she shook her head. "Soon enough we'll only be able to see ocean, and for a whole month," she said. "When else will you get to see Esting from above?"

"On a map?" I suggested, but I had to acknowledge that such a sight might be worthwhile.

Fin grabbed one of my hands, Caro took the other, and I followed them slowly to the high railings at the edge of the top deck.

I grasped my friends' hands tightly and gratefully. Even my shaky ankles and wobbly stomach couldn't completely distract me from the wonder of the landscape below us.

How could I not have realized before how lovely Esting was? Had I been too close, too familiar, to see it?

Gentle hills, deep green woodlands so dark they looked almost black, the spiraling roads of little valley-cradled villages . . . and, already far away in the distance, the forbidding blackstone turrets of the royal palace, rising out of Esting City's geometric grid of streets. Why, that meant the trees in front of the city were the beginning of Woodshire Forest, and hidden somewhere at their edge was Lampton Manor. I couldn't see it from here, but the thought of my childhood home in the Brethren's hands twisted in my heart.

Woodshire Forest was far vaster than I'd realized; the path from the manor to Esting City, though it had seemed so long to me before, cut through only one sliver of the forest's huge expanse.

I thought of the Forest Queen, Caro's five-times-great-grandmother, who had lived in those woods with her merry band and had so many adventures. Thinking of Silviana gave me courage, and I found that my feet stood a little steadier on the rising deck.

"The Forest Queen had a vast demesne," Fin said quietly at my side, echoing my thoughts.

I nodded, staring dreamily at the undulating treetops, wondering if that's what the ocean would look like once we crossed over the shoreline. I'd never seen the ocean before, even though it was only a day's hard ride from Lampton.

I heard a loud rushing sound far above us. The airship

swept upward, lifting us who knew how much farther into the air. The movement was too smooth to call a lurch, but my legs certainly didn't like it, and I felt the warmth drain from my face.

The higher we went up into the sky, the colder the atmosphere around us grew, and I had to take deeper breaths to get the same amount of air. We'd been warned of this before our trip, and I began to think longingly of the lovely boiled-wool cloak in my steamer trunk. I hadn't liked the idea of being wrapped up tight while I felt motion sick, but cold was quickly becoming the more pressing concern.

Yet I couldn't bear to tear my gaze away from the receding land below us. Everything looked small and perfect and ordered, like the clockwork I had loved and studied all my life. I started to wonder how I'd ever thought any problem I had, down there in that tiny clock country, had ever seemed insurmountable.

Woodshire Forest rolled on and on, even when the palace became nothing more than a black speck on the horizon. Then suddenly it cut off into a jagged face of gray cliffs, so small from up here, and . . .

Below the cliffs, the crashing sea.

"Oh," Fin and I gasped together, and I could tell from the way his tone matched mine that he had never seen the ocean before either. The thought startled me until I remembered that he'd spent most of his royal childhood behind the closed doors of the palace, except for when he went riding or when

Caro snuck him out to the Market. When his mother was still alive, surely the journeys they made were to the desert Sudlands where her family ruled, connected to Esting by a thin strip of barren land. I knew from the time Fin, Caro, Bex, and I spent in the paddock's pond last summer that Fin was a strong swimmer, but there would have been no need for him ever to visit the sea.

The ocean was its own continent, dark as the forest above it, churning and roiling white froth so that it seemed as if at any moment it might swallow the cliffs. Yet it was seductive, too, in the way it rolled and beckoned and sang, waves stroking the edge of the land like lovers. Infinitely fierce and infinitely gentle, like every love I'd ever known.

"It's something, isn't it?" Caro asked. When I looked over at her, she was radiant, her cheeks red and sweet as apples in the cold wind. "I told you both you'd want to see it."

I shivered. "It's fantastic," I said. "I couldn't have even imagined it."

Caro put her arm around me from my right, and Fin did the same from my left. Bending our heads together for warmth, we watched our home country slip into the hazy distance.

The refreshments laid out in the galley far exceeded my idea of an airship's food stores. I was surprised at how hungry I felt when I looked at the laden table, given how wobbly my stomach had been a few minutes ago, but something about the cold ocean air made me feel both refreshed and somehow famished.

To begin with there was fresh fruit, at least a dozen different kinds: the apples and dark grapes that grew so well near Esting City, of course, as well as large, translucent golden plums from southern Esting, syrupy green succulents from the Sudlands, and tapered bunches of the tiny, sour orange frostberries that grew year-round in Nordsk, where so few other fruits could weather the cold.

Fat rolls of the fine wheat bread that the palace kitchens always served were stacked in pyramids at one end of the table, still warm enough to let out little puffs of yeast-scented steam when you ripped into them, which all three of us did with abandon. We hadn't eaten since a very early and hurried breakfast back in Esting City, and it seemed the cold, thin air on deck had woken Fin's and Caro's appetites too.

Gooey triple-crème cheese, shards of aged cheddar, fresh goat's-milk butter, and smoked wild pheasant from Woodshire Forest were all arranged amid dripping chunks of honeycomb on a platter near the bread. The pheasant, a smear of cheese, and a few grapes on one of the warm rolls made just about the nicest sandwich I'd ever had.

My favorite clary-bush tea wasn't there, of course, nor was there any other Fey food or drink on this royal journey (although I remembered the strange liquid painkiller the chirurgienne had used on Fin, and once again I wondered how stringent the quarantine really was), but the black tea and coffee were strong and delicious.

After we'd eaten, Wheelock appeared again, as silently and suddenly as if he'd arrived, I whispered to Caro, "by magic."

"Treacherous thought!" she murmured, barely suppressing a giggle. I had to hide an unladylike snort.

"Would Your Highness and my ladies wish for some entertainment after your meal?" he asked with another bow. "We have an excellent portable phonograph, or I can show you into the ship's library."

An airship's library appealed to me indeed, and I glanced at Fin eagerly.

"Well, if you don't mind," he said with a courteous nod to Caro and me, "I would love to see our balloon up close. Would it be possible for one of the crew to take us up the ropes?"

My eyes widened, and my perfect sandwich began to tumble unpleasantly in my stomach. "Ah, I'm not sure I could manage that yet," I said, a little embarrassed. Was I so poor a venturess as this?

"Nick, I'm so sorry!" Fin said quickly. "I'd quite forgotten about your seasickness. Airsickness?"

"The latter is the correct term, Your Highness," Wheelock said with utter deference and with the same gravity he'd used on our first meeting, which made his voice seem so much older than his face.

"Airsickness, then." Fin looked at me with genuine

sympathy. "I'll certainly wait to see the balloon until we can all manage it," he said stoutly.

"You will do no such thing!" I exclaimed. "You've been talking about seeing that balloon up close for the last month—and I'll expect a full report of its engineering," I added, more to Caro than to Fin. She had a better mind for such things. Fin was always the artist . . . and the idealist, the politician who really believed in what he said.

I just hoped it wouldn't get him hurt again.

Caro nodded squarely, silently conveying that she'd look after Fin's safety so that I needn't worry about leaving him for a while.

"I would love to see the library," I said to Wheelock, who bowed yet again in acknowledgment.

"At your convenience, my lady," he said, then backed out the door and shut it so silently that it was hard to notice even while you were watching him.

"Are you sure, Nick?" Fin asked. "I really don't mind waiting. I'd like for all of us to see it together."

"Not at all," I said sincerely. "I couldn't enjoy it now, not until my legs get a little bit better—and my stomach. A nice, slow look around the library seems like exactly what I need. But I meant it when I said I want to hear all about it."

The library was a small, ovoid room in the very stern of the ship with a huge curved window displaying a little more open sky than I was prepared for when I walked through the door. I felt briefly vertiginous, as if I were about to fall through that reinforced glass and away into the endless air. We were high enough that I could see neither land nor sea, nor even horizon; nothing but blue, scudded through with white cloud.

There were two big, brass-lined bubbles of some kind at the lower corners of the window, but I couldn't look at them quite long enough to get a clear impression of what their function might be. Instead I focused my gaze on the tightly packed bookshelves, the leather club chairs bolted to the floor, and the library's main table, which displayed a gigantic, pinned-down map.

I looked back at Wheelock. He was standing by the library door, as still and rigid as a statue. I wondered if he even felt allowed to blink.

"Could you show me our route, please, Wheelock?" I asked, indicating the table. I wanted to examine the map, and it would have felt peculiar to do so alone while he waited in the corner.

He nodded and silently came to stand before the map with me. From a shallow drawer under the table he produced brass pins and a black thread.

"We began here, at Port's End," he murmured, sticking a pin into the city and deftly looping the thread around it.

I traced my fingers over the outline of Esting's shores. "I know the geography of our country well enough," I said, "and of our neighbors, Nordsk and the Sudlands. I devoured maps of Faerie as a child, too, but this one . . . it makes the place seem much larger than I had imagined." I gestured toward the vaguely teardrop-shaped continent on the opposite side of the map. It was so far away that I couldn't touch the outlines of Esting and Faerie at the same time even if I stretched out both my arms.

"The area of Faerie is thirty-one thousand square miles," Wheelock recited, gently sticking pins into the vast expanse of ocean between the two countries.

I sucked in my breath at the figure, although I supposed I must have heard it before. Esting was barely a third of that size.

"It's not a straight line," I said. "Our route."

He gestured over the smooth arc of the thread. "We follow the trade winds," he said.

"Of course. And then there's the curve of the earth, I suppose; it would be hard to account for that on a flat map."

"Yes."

Somehow the space between Esting and Faerie made the strongest impression on me; all the space we were about to cross, our journey hanging on Wheelock's thread. The paper ocean wasn't blank, either. Here and there the inked forms of huge curling serpents broke the water.

"Here be monsters," I whispered, reading the inscription under one such beast.

Wheelock looked up at me; just for a moment I caught the trace of a secret smile behind his eyes, as if he were a young adventurer too. But he quickly looked down at the map and tacked in the last pin, on a Faerie beach not too far from their capital. "Yes," he said again, in old-man tones, and the secret smile was gone.

I turned away from the paper monsters.

"Thank you, Wheelock," I said. "I think I'd like to go back to the suite now, please. I would like to see to my, ah, work for a while. I might return to the library afterward."

"As you like, my lady," Wheelock said. "Your animal companions have already settled themselves in your suite's storeroom. I took the liberty of installing an extra lock on your storeroom door. I thought an inventor must value privacy in her work." He pulled a brass key from his pocket and offered it to me. I smiled and accepted the key, and when he bowed once more and extended his arm, I took it gladly. I felt brave enough to look out that huge window again when I had someone else to lean on.

For all his funny, elderly-gentleman mannerisms, I decided I liked Wheelock. I appreciated the utterly normal way he spoke of my buzzers, without the awe or cautious judgment I heard so often. I felt quite cheerful, and even a little less airsick, holding on to his arm as we made our way back to the royal suite.

After I helped the buzzers settle into the briefcase I'd made to house them for the month-long voyage, and I'd stroked their heads in the pattern that let them wind down and rest until I needed them again, I turned to Jules.

"You'll be able to rest soon too," I said, "and it's very well deserved."

He shook his head and nudged me toward the largest of the three tool chests I'd brought. Jules took up nearly half the space in this little windowless storeroom, and I knew that he and the supplies that filled up the rest of it had more than doubled the *Imperator*'s weight. But I was so far into my work on Jules's modifications that I couldn't bear to leave the project behind unfinished. Leaving him or the buzzers behind in Esting had been even more unthinkable.

My lightest luggage was the stuff I guarded most carefully, though: the briefcase with my buzzers and the unused Ashes from my mother's cupboards, labeled with their different animal species and carefully sorted into more than a hundred little boxes and cork-topped vials.

It was Jules who'd insisted I bring them, strangely enough, in spite of how he usually couldn't stand even to be in their presence. "Not safe," he'd said in his gravelly, pained voice when I explained that I'd leave them locked in one of Lord Alming's vaults. I'd brushed him off at first. But "Not safe!" he'd said again, stamping the floor of his stall hard enough to raise sparks.

"Would you like to sleep now, Jules?" I asked after I'd been toiling away at his modifications for several hours. He shifted back and forth on his feet, trying out the new weight I'd added to his frame, and then he nodded.

I stroked the three spirals on his shoulders, the way I'd learned from Mother's old journals. Jules's clockwork wound to a stop, and I doused the low burn in his furnace.

I fastened all the bulky padlocks I'd brought to secure the storeroom door, turning Wheelock's key last of all; he was right that I valued my privacy, even from him.

When I emerged onto the deck, snugly wrapped in my wool cloak, night had already fallen. Caro and Fin lounged on deck chairs near the bow, talking quietly and now and then pointing up at a dark sky that overflowed with the brightest stars I'd ever seen. A huge moon glowed above us, smooth and bright as a crystal ball.

I walked confidently toward them, relieved to find that my shaky legs and stomach had returned to normal in the past few hours. They smiled when they saw me, and Caro patted the empty deck chair next to hers.

"That's the Cryptid, those six stars," said Fin, gesturing upward at a cluster that did, perhaps, look a little bit like a vicious beast if one squinted just right. I had often envied Fin the many excellent tutors he'd had as a child and his result-ing knowledge on such a wide array of subjects. I'd always been a voracious reader, but the only real schooling I'd had was in engineering and physics with Mother, and Faerie his-tory and housekeeping with Mr. Candery. Those had come in handy, of course, but I would have given nearly anything to listen in on one of Fin's private lessons in languages or poetry or music. I hoped to begin taking such lessons myself, or even to travel to one of the women's academies in the Sudlands, once my business was established and once I'd bought back Lampton—

But I couldn't buy back Lampton. I kept forgetting that my home was lost to me.

I refocused on the bright river of stars above us and on the low murmur of Fin's voice as he told their stories.

After a while, Wheelock brought us some hot port in little hammered cups. I was surprised he hadn't delegated the task to one of his crew and was pleased to see him.

The captain clicked his heels together and made Fin a little salute. "A toast, if I may," he said, taking a small flask out of his peacoat.

Fin raised his cup with a smile, and Caro and I followed suit.

"To Your Highness's long life, to success in your journey's aim and in your coming marriage," he said, with a salute to me this time. "Long life and love to you all." He saluted Caro last, then touched his flask to each of our cups and took a quick drink.

"Thank you, Wheelock," Fin said. "To a safe and happy voyage, led by your skill and guidance."

Wheelock looked startled at having the toast returned, and after we'd all sipped another time he bowed stiffly and hurried away into the darkness.

I found myself smiling after him with amusement and sympathy.

"How formal he is," Caro whispered, not unkindly. "You'd think him a man of sixty, but he couldn't possibly be older than, oh—"

"Twenty," Fin said. "He's the youngest airship captain who's ever qualified, and one of the most promising; everyone says so. I requested him specifically for this journey." He frowned. "I hoped his youth might make him more sympathetic to my, ah, views of things, but now I'm not so sure."

"I think it's shyness," I offered. "Part of it, at least. If he's the youngest captain ever, he'd hardly be used to the company of people his own age." I remembered how terrifying it had been when I'd started to make friends my age for the first time, not much more than a year ago. But I'd gotten extraordinarily lucky: my first friends had been Fin and Caro, and it was impossible to feel ill at ease with them for long.

Caro nodded. "He'd probably have to act older for the other sailors to take him seriously too."

We nestled back onto the deck chairs with our hot drinks, our conversation gradually turning to the month-long journey ahead of us.

"I think I'll be busy with Jules's mods for most of the days," I said, "but I did notice the library is well stocked, and Wheelock mentioned that phonograph. I don't think either of you will be bored."

Fin straightened in his chair. "Did you see the pods in the library? Lord, I can't wait to try them."

I vaguely remembered the rounded shapes at the edges of that huge window. "I was still a little seasick — airsick, I mean — so I didn't really examine them," I admitted. "Although I think that's passed now."

Fin smiled. "Oh, I'm glad."

"What are they for?" Caro asked.

"They're bathysphere pods," Fin said, and I gasped with sudden delight at the word. He grinned at me and nodded excitedly. "They're for underwater sightseeing," he explained to Caro, whose eyes widened. "They're lowered from the stern of the ship on calm days when we go down close to the water to catch fish. This is the first time a Faerie-bound ship has been equipped with them. Something else I requested specifically," he confessed.

Caro laughed. "You must admit, Fin, there are times when it's good to be a prince."

He raised his cup to her with a wink and we all sat in silence for a moment, imagining voyages underwater.

But Fin's expression soon changed. He looked up at the sky with a grave determination, and I knew that Caro's mentioning his title had turned his thoughts toward the heavy responsibilities he carried with him on our voyage.

"What are those stars there?" I asked, trying to help him return to lighter thoughts, at least for now.

Fin blinked and smiled at me, relieved.

It must have been very late, but the events of the day and the prospect of all the adventures to come had made us too excited to sleep. We stayed up talking until the stars began to fade.

When we finally wandered below deck, still talking quietly through our yawns, we all went to the royal suite without saying a word about it. We lounged on the bed together just as we'd done on the deck above, sharing little jokes and memories, little hopes for our journey. I'm not sure when we fell asleep.

I woke up a few hours later with Caro's and Fin's arms thrown loosely over my waist, our heads sharing a pillow. I stayed still, breathing softly, nestled between them.

Caro woke soon after and slipped silently out of our room to her own berth, placing a soft kiss on Fin's and my foreheads first.

As we looked at one another with sleepy happiness over breakfast later that morning, I knew without asking that we'd spend every night of the voyage together. Somehow, just knowing that made the ship seem more like home.

TEN days into our journey, Wheelock declared the wind conditions safe enough to fly low the next morning. Billowing nets would be cast out from the sides of the boat to catch fresh fish for the galley, and Fin, Caro, and I were cleared to use the bathysphere pods.

It was amazing how quickly we'd adjusted to life on the *Imperator*. My motion sickness was entirely gone. Although I hadn't yet managed to scurry up the ropes with the crew, as Fin and Caro had done several times, I'd helped pull those ropes from the ground when the folding, fin-like sails had to be adjusted to catch the wind. We needed stiff breezes for this voyage, especially if we were to reach Faerie in only a month, but a few slow days were necessary too if we wanted to eat any fresh food at all.

After my years of eating the Steps' scraps, I knew better than to complain about having a plentiful supply of food, but I was still looking forward to a fish fry instead of the salted-meat stew that had become our standard dinner fare. The luxury of the first day's refreshments had turned out to be just a ceremonial anomaly. I yearned for rhodopis berries, which could pop back into freshness at the touch of a finger and would have been perfect on the long voyage. I felt more annoyed than ever about Esting's embargo on Fey goods.

That was one of the many things Fin and I would try to fix once we reached Faerie.

On the morning of our voyage underwater, all three of us woke up early and excited. Caro rose before dawn every day in order to return to her own bunk undetected, but on that particular morning we were all up and dressed with starlight still whispering through the portals in the royal suite.

When we got to the galley, Wheelock was already there, spinning his empty teacup on its saucer like a toy top. His hands hovered over the cup and he watched it intently, as if he could keep it spinning through sheer willpower.

It was the first unserious thing I'd ever seen him do, and I couldn't help the little giggle I let out. But when he heard the noise, Wheelock flinched and clamped his hands down over the cup.

Twin ruddy spots appeared on his cheeks as he quickly stood up. "Good morning, Your Highness, my ladies," he said. He hurried to the side of the galley. "Would you like some tea? Cook isn't up yet, but I'd be honored to serve you my — myself." He turned away from us, hiding his face, but I could see his hands shaking a little as he poured.

I smiled at him gratefully when he handed me my cup, but he wouldn't meet my eyes. After he brought us our drinks he bowed deeply and hurried out the galley door.

"Poor fellow," said Fin. "I wish I could make him feel more at ease."

"I think Caro was right—he's afraid he won't be taken seriously if he acts his age," I murmured. "Did you notice how excited he was when he told us about the sailing conditions last night? He was trying so hard not to show it, but . . ."

I pushed my chair away from the long galley table and stood up. "I'll be right back," I told Fin and Caro, who didn't seem surprised at all by my leaving.

I walked swiftly across the deck. The bridge was raised to provide the best possible view to the navigators, and I climbed the steep spiral half-staircase to reach it. Sure enough, Wheelock was there, twirling a dial on the side of a large compass while he examined it closely. He looked completely absorbed, but those spots of color still burned in his cheeks.

I knocked softly. He flinched again, and when he turned and saw me through the window, he snapped into such rigid formality that I almost believed the cup-spinning had been just a hallucination.

"Hello, my lady," he said, opening the door. "I apologize for my inappropriate comportment earlier. How may I be of service?"

I bit my lip. I wanted to tell him that I was sure I knew just how he felt: young and successful and smart, and, well, terrified that people wouldn't take the latter two seriously because of the first one. Terrified, too, of spending any time around other young people because he'd spent his life working so hard that he'd never learned to make friends. I knew that story all too well.

But saying so might only embarrass him further. "I hoped you might show me the navigation equipment," I told him instead. In fact, that was very true; I'd been waiting for a clear day so that I wouldn't be in the way on the bridge, but I had longed to see the machinations of the ship's steering.

Wheelock nodded, still as formal as an elderly butler, but his face relaxed by degrees as he showed me around the bridge's equipment. By the time Sneha arrived to take over helmsman duties, I was helping Wheelock steer the ship down toward the water, both of us putting our weight into the huge wheel at the front of the bridge. I was smiling even as I breathed heavily with the effort, and I thought I nearly had Wheelock smiling too.

"Now," said Wheelock, nodding at Sneha as she took over the wheel, "I must take you to your companions in the library. Soon we'll be able to release the bathyspheres." He said the word with a little envy, and I was suddenly sure that he'd woken early in excitement about seeing them work, just as we had . . . except, of course, that he'd be confined to the ship.

I opened my mouth to invite him to join us, but he was already halfway down the staircase that led back to the deck. I followed him, chagrined.

In the library, Caro was running her hands over one bathysphere's exterior, examining it thoughtfully, while Fin paced the room with barely suppressed impatience. "Oh, good!" he cried when he saw us, making sure to smile at both Wheelock and me. "Come on, Nick." He rushed to the second bathysphere and opened the door. "I want you to ride with me, if you don't mind."

I smiled at him and nodded. I turned to meet Caro's eyes, then glanced toward Wheelock. She winked at me in understanding.

"Won't you join me, Wheelock?" Caro asked, grinning. "There's plenty of room."

A surprisingly youthful smile swept across Wheelock's face for a moment. When his old-gentleman expression came back, it seemed almost like a mask.

"Thank you very much, Miss Hart," Wheelock said. "However, it's proper for a captain to remain with his ship. I'm afraid I must decline." But he watched a little enviously as Fin and I settled ourselves onto the brass seats inside one triple-sealed pod and as he helped Caro into the other. We pulled on the oilskin life jackets Wheelock handed us and smiled at one another in nervous excitement.

When the porter arrived to man the crank that would lower us into the sea, Wheelock's expression of quiet longing only increased.

The porter, a hardy-looking man named Walsh, let out an amused huff.

Wheelock spun around and fixed him with a lofty glare. "Yes, Sailor?"

Walsh quickly saluted, looking both ashamed and genuinely embarrassed. "Meaning no offense, Captain. It's just, you've talked of hardly nothing else but . . . it's nothing, sir."

This was a surprising development, as was the evident friendship between Walsh and the inscrutable young captain; they both smiled a little even as the porter submitted to his captain's authority.

Wheelock sighed. He looked at the empty seat beside Caro and finally he gave one curt nod, as if convincing himself to go rather than accepting her invitation.

"You won't be leaving the *Imperator,* you know," said Fin, a twinkle in his eye. "The pods stay attached to the hull with those telescoping pipes, and therefore they're part of the ship, don't you think?"

That youthful smile stole across Wheelock's face again. "Indeed, Your Highness," he said. Turning back to Walsh, he added, "Gunning's been wanting to give his first-mate duties a real run, has he not?"

"Aye, sir." Walsh smiled and stepped aside to let Wheelock past. The captain stepped into the bathysphere pod and settled down beside Caro, his posture ramrod-straight, his face severe and formal again. I was sure that spark was still hidden somewhere . . .

But I didn't watch Wheelock's face very long, because the porter started to turn the crank, and we began to move.

I winced and reached for Fin. I'd looked forward to this part of the voyage more than any other ever since I'd learned that it was possible, yet my heart beat wildly as the glass egg in which we sat detached from the stability of the airship.

Fin caught my hand at once and held firm. That gave me the courage to look around. Once I did, I was so very glad.

The ship had descended even more since Wheelock and I had left the bridge, and we were only thirty or so feet above the surface. Our pods were connected to the *Imperator* by a series of reassuringly strong, metal-reinforced ropes and two telescoping pipes. One of these attached to the top of the glass pod and was clearly structural; the other was thinner, jointed, and flexible, and it extended through the three reinforced layers of glass to a perforated brass circle, from which I heard the voice of the porter, tinny and barely comprehensible.

"All well on board?" he asked.

"All well here, sir," Fin and I chorused, as we'd been instructed.

"All clear, so!" the porter shouted, and then the pod touched water.

I stood up involuntarily. For a moment it was like walking on waves, skimming ahead toward the horizon as sea foam frothed at my feet.

"Oh!" I gasped.

"I know," Fin said, laughing, standing up with me.

Then we were going under, smooth and slow. The waves

swallowed us, reaching the brass reinforcement at waist height, and then the level of our eyes, and at last closing over the top of our pod with a small gulp.

The light underwater was green and gold at once, streaming down in changing ribbons that looked sometimes like swords and sometimes like long golden hair. The space around us receded infinitely into a green, green gloom.

"The nets, Nick, look," Fin said joyfully. His voice sounded different now, more enclosed, bouncing off the curved glass walls.

Already a few fish struggled against the nets billowing and stretching in the currents. I couldn't help feeling a little bad for the fish in that moment, even though I knew that I would be more than happy to eat them for dinner that night. I admonished myself for hypocrisy.

I saw Caro and Wheelock in their pod off to our side, and I waved even though my arm shook a little. I loved this so much, yet it scared me so much at the same time, on such a basic, instinctive level.

Caro waved back, looking perfectly delighted. Wheelock patted the oilskin life jacket he wore and nodded at me reassuringly. I remembered what he had said that morning: If anything happened, we'd be pulled back onto the ship in less than a minute.

I took a deep breath and tried to enjoy the sightseeing, the streaming gold-green light, the billowing nets, the schools of little and not-so-little fish that plunged around our pod.

And then I decided to look down.

All the vertigo I'd felt early in our voyage came rushing into reality below me, where the water grew darker and darker until nothing was there at all except black. I could not guess how deep it was; it seemed utterly endless.

I knew there were many places in the ocean where even our longest anchors could not reach. In bad storms far out at sea, it was safer for an airship to go above the clouds than try to anchor below them, Wheelock had told us.

I wanted to tell Fin to look down so that at least I wouldn't be staring into that void all alone. But my mouth was dry; it took me a moment to find my voice.

And in that moment I saw something that I will never in my life forget.

It was just a shape at first, rising up out of the darkness and into the green ribboning light, moving so fast I almost didn't see it.

Just a shape with a tail, that was all.

But it also had arms. And a head.

And I could have sworn, even in that brief moment, that it had a human face.

I found my voice. "Fin!" I rasped. "Fin, a merman!"

"What on earth?" Fin looked down with me, crouching on the glass floor so that he could see better, but it was gone.

He looked up, disappointment and doubt blending together on his face. I shook my head, not knowing what to say. The shape had come out of the darkness and then vanished so quickly. I began to think that it had only been a strange kind of fish.

As we slipped through the water, Fin and I kept watching the changing light around us and the schools of fish collecting in the nets. Every so often we turned to wave at Caro and Wheelock again, as if seeing their safety could reassure us of our own. They usually smiled and waved right back, although sometimes they were too entranced with the view to notice us. Wheelock, especially, looked around at the ocean with a childlike rapture.

I checked my pocket watch. We would go back aboard in only five minutes, even though we had at least an hour's worth of air remaining in the chamber with us. I realized that I would miss my sojourn here when I returned to the ship. Though I would undoubtedly feel more secure up there—and yet more secure back on land, even in Faerie—there would be a part of me that always missed this green light, this infinite liquid space, this little bubble where all the water in the world rushed over and under and around me while I stayed safe and dry.

Then that bubble shattered.

"No!" Fin hit the glass wall so hard with his fist that a crack appeared in its surface.

"Fin, don't!" I cried, frantically reminding myself that there were three layers of glass around us, not just one, and that we were perfectly safe. "What are you doing?"

"Look, Nick, look! They can't, they can't!" He hit the glass again, and a few splinters fell to our feet.

My breath stopped. There was a shape, a shape with a tail and arms and a human face, tangled up in the fishing nets.

The merman tore at the ropes with his translucent webbed hands, thrust his powerful, sickly-white tail through the water, and bit at the lines with astonishingly long and sharp teeth, but the nets only tangled him tighter. The wire-reinforced ropes sawed against red gills in his sides, and dark blood began to cloud the water.

The creature's movements grew slowly weaker as the ropes wore away at his gills. The sea around him turned muddy and he sagged against the nets, his strange, clear eyes fluttering closed.

Fin punched the glass a third time and breached the first pane. He heaved his body against the side, and the second layer of glass cracked open.

"They can't get him," Fin said. "They can't know. I won't let there be another colony."

He took the emergency hatchet out of its place under our seats, then grabbed the brass speaking pipe that led back up to the airship. "Our hull has been breached," Fin said. His voice was low and angry. "Pull us up now." He tore off his life jacket and pulled me in for a quick, rough embrace.

"Less than a minute, Nick," Fin said, pressing a hard kiss

against my cheek, and he turned away and smashed the hatchet as hard as he could against the third layer of glass.

It shattered and Fin plunged out. The pod flooded with icy salt water. I barely had enough time to take in one deep breath before it closed over my head.

Fin swam as fast as he could toward the trapped merman. The pod was already reeling back up to the surface, and Fin shrank below me as I was pulled up and away.

I clutched at his abandoned life jacket, frantic. I had often gone swimming as a child in a little lake in Woodshire, and I'd gone a few times with Fin, Caro, and Bex in a pond behind the royal horses' paddock last summer. That was nothing at all like swimming in the ocean, of course . . . but if I would struggle to swim here, I knew that Fin would too.

My broken pod burst through the surface and up into the air, and the water came pouring out. I gasped for breath as I flew closer to the airship and to safety, and away from Fin.

His life jacket clutched in my arms, I jumped out through the jagged opening he had made and down into the sea.

I hit the water with a juddering smack that disoriented and frightened me for a few seconds that I couldn't spare. I looked up and briefly saw Caro pounding frantically against the wall of her own swiftly rising pod as Wheelock did his best to hold her back.

I made for the nets.

I couldn't see what was happening under the surface, but I knew Fin hadn't come up yet. I kicked my way over and tied

Fin's life jacket and my own to the rope that connected the nets to the ship. I gripped the edge of a net and used it to drag myself hand over hand underwater.

When I opened my eyes, I couldn't see nearly as clearly as I'd been able to through the glass. I could make out only vague shapes. But I followed the line of the net with my hands, and it led me true.

I saw two blurry forms below me, one dark and one white: Fin and the merman, struggling. Fin sawed at a rope with his hatchet, and the merman at least seemed to understand what he was trying to do and wasn't fighting him. Still, he thrashed wildly against the net itself, tearing his gills and threatening to entangle Fin too. He was keening, almost singing, a plaintive noise that reverberated through the water and seemed to sink into my very bones.

I pulled myself the rest of the way down, and I took the frayed rope from Fin's hands. With every ounce of strength I had, I could just barely tear it apart. Fin didn't acknowledge my presence at all, just moved on to the next section of net and began sawing at it with his hatchet.

The merman's gills were so badly torn that they were painful to look at, even through the blurred lens of the water. As my lungs started to burn I reached out carefully to pull the ropes away where they bound him most tightly. His high song grew louder, spread through the water until I was sure it could be heard even on the ship above. He thrashed and fought against the net, and the long talons in his webbed hands scratched at the ropes. One caught Fin under the eye, and his blood flowed out into the water. When it mixed with the merman's, the creature stopped singing, and his mouth opened wider than ever, revealing serrated fangs. He stared at Fin through clouding eyes.

Fin sawed through the final rope, and in an instant the merman was freed, and he flashed away so quickly I couldn't have said which direction he went.

Someone grabbed me from behind, and I felt myself yanked up and backward, the rope tearing out of my hands and drawing a little of my blood to mix with the merman's. I saw someone else in the water: another sailor diving toward Fin, a thick rope and harness around his torso.

The sailor overtook Fin and pinned his hands behind his back. My own rescuer clamped his arms more tightly around my waist as we broke the surface. I felt the shock of gravity returning as the thick rope pulled us away from the water, back up to the waiting ship.

When we collapsed on the deck, gasping and shivering, Caro rushed at us and embraced us both. "I could pummel you!" she kept saying to Fin. "Why would you do that?" And to me: "You were safe and sound; how dare you risk that? I might have lost you both!"

"I had to save Fin," I said. "You would have done the same if you'd had the chance."

"I'd have looked after myself, with a mind to the people

who love me!" Caro retorted hotly, still holding both of us tight.

With every breath, my lungs were calming, and the pressure in my chest was fading away. "I saw you pounding the glass on your pod," I replied. "You'd have broken through and come after us if Wheelock hadn't held you back, and you know it."

"Yes, well——"

"Shut up, both of you," Fin whispered as two crewmen approached us with blankets and robes. "I'm sorry I made you so afraid and that I endangered you. I'm more sorry than I can say. But we *can't* let them know what we saw."

Caro looked at Fin in bafflement, but I remembered what he'd said as he broke out of the pod.

Wheelock had sprung into action as soon as we came back aboard, and the whole crew was gathered on the deck, securing the nets and ropes that had pulled us up and waiting for the captain's orders. Walsh wheeled out a tall panel, and I didn't understand why until Wheelock bustled me behind it and and called Sneha over to strip off my sopping dress. She pulled a flannel robe around me and wrapped me in a big wool blanket so quickly that I hardly had time to notice her doing it, let alone feel embarrassed. And when I realized that both the robe and blanket had been warmed, I couldn't think of anything but the soft, dry comfort that surrounded me. Fin was similarly wrapped up when I came back out, and Wheelock decorously but firmly pushed mugs of hot black tea into our hands and into Caro's too. She was shaking worse than Fin and I were.

"Come inside where it's warmer, Your Highness, my lady," Wheelock said with a respectful bow that almost hid the residue of fear in his eyes.

"They can't know, Wheelock," Fin said fiercely. His lips still quivered, but they were starting to return to their normal color. "Don't tell them anything. Don't tell anyone."

"As you wish," Wheelock said quietly, his steady gaze meeting Fin's angry one. "Now, please, come inside. You'll need to stay warm if you don't want a case of pneumonia before we arrive in Faerie."

Whatever Fin saw in the other young man's eyes made him nod, and he allowed the captain to lead the three of us to the royal suite. When Caro walked inside with us, Wheelock didn't show the least surprise. We'd tried to be discreet; had it been for nothing?

It didn't matter, not now.

Wheelock laid his hand on the doorknob. "If you need anything at all—"

"Stay a moment, Wheelock," Fin said, easing himself down onto the window seat.

"Yes, Your Highness?" He about-faced and put both hands behind his back, as if he were waiting for orders.

"I don't know you very well," Fin began, "and I wish you hadn't seen what happened—I wish you hadn't seen who was in the water today. Truth be told, I wish none of us had. I wish no one from Esting would ever find out if there's really such a thing as a merman." He shifted, wincing, and it was obvious that his shoulder was hurting again. I went to him and started gently pressing his shoulder blade the way the chirurgienne had shown me after his operation.

Fin looked up with gratitude and with a level of humility that astounded me. "Thank you, Nick," he said. Then, his voice a little stronger: "Wheelock, forgive me for saying that I don't know yet if I can trust you. But it doesn't matter, because I have to trust you now. I have to beg you, please, not to tell anyone else on the ship, anyone else *ever,* what you saw in the water. If my father knew there was another race of people in the world, another nation he could conquer or that the Brethren could convert . . ." Fin trailed off and shook his head. "I can't let that happen. Please, Wheelock. I don't know how you feel about Faerie or about what should be done there now, but perhaps you can understand why I hope that we won't get into another war like this one, another bloody struggle for power. Another nation enslaved." The leadership had come back into Fin's voice. Even though he was speaking quietly, I could almost see the podium in front of him, the adoring crowds. This was what he was born for.

"I understand, sir," Wheelock said in his usual stiff tone.

But then I saw him lose his formality again, and not just for a moment this time. He shrugged it off like a heavy cloak.

Wheelock stepped closer to Fin, and even his gait, the way he held himself, was different; suddenly he seemed like the young man he was. When he spoke, the spark I'd glimpsed that morning had returned to his eyes, and with it came a sincerity that had honesty and passion and even sweetness in it.

"And you must understand, Your Highness," he said, "how glad I was when you requested my service on the *Imperator*. There are those of us who are on this voyage because we believe in what you believe, and we wish to help you if we can." He lowered his voice still further. "There are those of us who are loyal to *you*."

"All of the crew?" Fin asked, a little incredulous. I thought of the silent Su doctor, the Brethren cleric who watched us so suspiciously.

Wheelock smiled, but then he shrugged on his formality again, and the smile vanished inside it. "Most of the crew. Gunning, Walsh, Sneha; they feel as I do. And the others can be managed, Your Highness."

He bowed impeccably as he left the room.

Wheelock seemed to grow shy again over the next few days; even when he and I crossed paths in the library, he would hurry away, avoiding my eyes. I was surprised and even a little frustrated, after the way he'd talked to Fin; why should he insist on thinking we couldn't be friends?

One night I climbed up the stairs to the bridge after

everyone else had fallen asleep. Wheelock was hunched over a rapidly spinning, three-dimensional sextant. I gave myself a little encouraging lecture before I knocked. He jumped when he heard the noise, just as he had the last time, but he quickly opened the door for me.

"I didn't mean to bother you," I said. "If you're busy, I can come back later."

The spots of color had taken over his cheeks again. "Not at all, my lady, not at all."

I chewed my lip, unsure of what to say. Caro was so good at making friends; maybe I should have left this up to her, or to the charming Fin, whom Wheelock already liked and admired. But I was sure the captain and I were kindred spirits somewhere under his stiff formality and my awkwardness. I just had to push past them both.

I gestured toward the compass. "Would you tell me about that instrument?" I asked. "I've only seen flat compasses before."

"Certainly, my lady."

I took a breath. "Please—do you think you could call me Nicolette?"

Just for a moment I saw that flash of a secret smile. "Oh, I couldn't do that, my lady," he said.

I pressed my lips together and looked down.

"Perhaps—perhaps I could call you Miss Lampton, if you dislike the other?"

I looked up again and smiled, although his own secret

smile had vanished. There was an earnest look in his gray eyes, and I was relieved he hadn't offered to call me Mechanica. Miss Lampton was still formal, but at least it was my own name. "That would be fine," I said.

I wanted to ask what his first name was, but I thought it might unsettle him too much. I remembered again how shy I'd been when I'd met Fin and Caro, how prone I was to dramatizing our every interaction.

So I just turned toward the compass again. "How does it work?"

Wheelock seemed relieved to talk about something in his own realm of experience. "It shows one's orientation to the cardinal directions, but also to the center of the earth . . ."

He led me around the bridge again, and I was able to ask all the questions I hadn't thought of the last time.

After a while he stopped and turned back to me with a little bow. "It's surely too late now," he said, nodding toward the bridge's clock.

Midnight. I smiled; time to leave the ball.

"Thank you for, um, indulging my curiosity, Wheelock," I said.

He nodded curtly, an old man again.

But as I turned to go: "Miss Lampton?"

I looked back at him.

"Could you —" He stood in the shadows outside the

circle of the bridge, and I couldn't see his expression. I heard him clear his throat.

"Do you think you might show me some of your own work before the voyage is over?" he asked. "I have admired your inventions since the last Exposition. I would love to—to see them." He cleared his throat again, then quickly added: "You needn't talk to me or anything. I wouldn't want to be a bother."

I laughed, then stopped myself, knowing I'd embarrass him. "I'd be glad to," I said.

He stepped forward, opening the door for me. "Thank you very much, Miss Lampton."

"Thank you," I said, "for showing me the bridge again. I don't want to be a bother either."

He shook his head and looked away. "You couldn't be."

As I walked back to the royal suite, I felt my heart beating a little faster.

I spent most of my days in the suite's private storeroom, working on modifications for Jules while he slept the trip away. I brought Wheelock with me several times, and he would sit quietly and watch me work, sometimes with admiration, sometimes almost with awe. I'd thought I liked to work alone, and I would have found Caro's chatter or even Fin's penchant for political discussions distracting, but I welcomed Wheelock's calm, quiet presence, even when he was fully enveloped in his formality. He helped me forget how much I missed Jules, not to mention my buzzers, who were magically asleep inside the padlocked briefcase.

I missed their company the most, but there were also a million little things I'd come to rely on them for, not the least of which was dressing my long hair in the mornings. It seemed foolish to wake them up for such a trivial reason, plus I was plagued by fears that the strong winds would steal them away from the ship and they'd be lost. My looks were hardly as important as that.

Still, I was completely incapable of executing the elaborate styles they'd done for me nearly every morning for the past year. I started wearing my hair down again, simply tucked back from my face with a narrow ribbon so that I could read and eat and do my work unhindered. It was unfashionable, but who on the boat would care? Fin? Caro? Wheelock and the crew?

It surprised me to realize that I'd grown a bit vain. After all, not long ago I had spent all my days covered in soot and dust, clomping around in old boots and patched coats three sizes too big.

Slowly I realized that my new vanity was actually a reaction to how I'd used to live. Now that I *could* look nice, I wanted to. Returning in any way to my former life, even in appearance, was more frightening than I liked to admit.

I reminded myself that I was moving forward, not back; I was literally an ocean away from the girl I used to be.

But I couldn't shake the feeling that some part of my past was haunting me, hunting me, even as we left Esting far behind us.

As the days wore on, the weather grew increasingly worse. We would never have gotten a chance to use the bathysphere pods again, even if one weren't broken and even if Wheelock hadn't forbidden it.

The *Imperator* spent most nights far, far above storm clouds that would have pummeled the ship, high enough that we could watch frost blossom on the porthole window-panes as we ascended to altitudes where the air was too cold and thin for us to go outside at all.

We couldn't stay so far up for very long; every ten hours or so we had to come back down and open the hatches to get fresh air into the ship and to keep the sails from freezing solid. More than one morning we were warned not to eat breakfast and then spent terrifying stretches of time clutch-ing whatever chairs were bolted to the floor or wall, listen-ing to the wind howl through the open vents and trying to clench our jaws hard enough that our teeth wouldn't chat-ter from the cold. My airsickness didn't return, but I almost wished it would, if getting ill would distract me from imag-ining what would happen if the wind or cold doused the fires under our balloon.

We were unbalanced and on edge for days at a time, and Wheelock kept apologizing, saying such storms were highly unusual over open water at this point in the year, as if the bad weather were his own personal fault.

And sometimes, lying awake at night as the ship tossed and jumped, I did start to think that there was something personal about the storms, something menacing. I'd unfold and reread Mr. Candery's letter, pretending I could hear my housekeeper's words in his gentle, urbane voice. *Trustworthy*, I would repeat to myself, trying to pretend the storms didn't feel like a threat even as they grew stronger.

But we didn't see a real tempest until the day we reached Faerie.

I THOUGHT I'd be unable to sleep the night before our arrival. I'd been anticipating it for so long; not so much the end of the voyage, which I had come to love in spite of our near disaster underwater and the vaguely ominous quality of the recent storms. I'd grown fond of the quiet interludes Wheelock and I shared, and even the repetitive galley food had started to seem reassuringly familiar. Most of all, though, sleeping with Fin and Caro had become such a comfort that I hated the idea of giving it up once the voyage ended.

Still, the notion of finally seeing Faerie, the country I'd dreamed of since I was a little girl—the source of real magic in orderly, insular Esting—was tantalizing beyond comprehension.

I was realizing more and more how much I'd missed Mr. Candery all these years too. So I assumed I'd leap out of bed on the day we were to land, eager to meet him, the Fey leader, everyone.

But days upon days of storms had left us all exhausted. I woke that final morning to find us all in a heap, Caro's mouth slack open and Fin snoring like a train engine, their bright and dark curls tangled together on the pillow. I smiled fondly, then realized I could see them so clearly because of the sunlight streaming in through the porthole.

My heartbeat quickened. Wheelock had told us at dinner last night that we'd likely come within sight of Faerie's shores early the next morning. Even now, I might look through that reinforced glass pane and see the blue-sand shores and jungles and craggy mountains of Faerie.

I sprang out of bed and made a mad dash for the nearest porthole before remembering that our suite was toward the rear of the ship, and I'd be able to see only where we'd been, not where we were going.

I looked back at my sleeping friends and debated whether to wake them. For more than a week now we'd had to keep one another from falling asleep during meals, we were so tired, but I knew they wouldn't forgive me if I deprived them of the chance to watch our approach to Faerie.

I laid a hand lightly on each of their shoulders. "Fin, Caro, wake up," I said, trying to keep my voice gentle, but it came out trembly and excited. "It's morning."

Fin woke with a great snort. "Faerie!" he said, blinking, his voice and eyes still full of sleep. He scrambled out of bed and over to his steamer trunk.

Caro slept a little more soundly. I bent down and kissed

her forehead. "Good morning, darling," I said. "You won't want to miss this, I promise."

She yawned and squinched her eyes more tightly shut. "I'm getting up. I'm getting up." She rolled over and pulled the pillow on top of her head.

I took my turn in the water closet and quickly changed into the arrival-day outfit I'd laid in the bottom of my steamer trunk over a month ago. It was a suitably practical shadowy green-gray, like the venturing outfits Lady Candery and her cohorts had worn on the first-ever expedition to Faerie, two hundred and twelve years ago.

But unlike Lady Candery's ensemble, mine had trousers.

I knew perfectly well how useful trousers would be in the jungle, but fashionable ladies never wore them in Esting. The only girl I'd ever seen them on was Bex, and even she wore skirts when she wasn't working. The thought gave me a small rebellious thrill.

They were Jules's design and the buzzers' creation. Later today, after landing, I'd wake them up at last and let them see the delightfully scandalous outfit they'd made me. Of course, I'd seen Jules regularly while I worked on his improvements, which I'd finally finished just a few days ago. But I hadn't been able to truly see *him,* the real Jules who had slept the month-long voyage away. I missed him the same way I'd miss anyone I loved.

And just as Jules would be excited to see me in the outfit he'd designed, I was eager to see his reaction to the improvements for him I'd worked on so long and so hard. He'd approved my designs back in Esting, but I couldn't wait to give him the chance to test them out.

I stood up on the rim of the chair-size tub to get a view of myself in the mirror before I went out into the bedroom again. The trousers were actually less revealing than I'd anticipated; the button-front waist was very high, and the fabric draped loosely over my hips, growing more fitted at the knee. My calves were clearly delineated, but some of the Nordsk ball gowns I'd seen were gathered in the front to show a stockinged shin. Anyway, I had good, thick, knee-high laced leather boots to put on once I went back outside, and then I'd feel nearly the same as I would have in one of my work dresses back home . . . or so I tried to tell myself. Rebellious or no, I started to feel a bit shy.

I resisted the urge to bundle up under my wool cloak or just change into my normal skirts. It was still cold up here in the thin air above the clouds, but Faerie was a jungle, and I wanted to be prepared.

I marched back into the suite's bedroom in my shocking trousers. Both Caro and Fin were up, dressed, and waiting for their turn in the water closet.

"Love the pants, Nick," Caro said with a wink.

When we came out onto the main deck, the crew was preparing to take the *Imperator* down below the clouds.

All around us was clear morning sky. We sailed perhaps

twenty yards above a billowing white sea of clouds. The sun was high by now, and searingly bright, just enough to take a little of the edge off the freezing-cold wind that slapped at the sails and assaulted any bit of uncovered skin. I tried to remind myself that I was dressed appropriately for Faerie's tropical climate.

"Take her down," Wheelock called, walking swiftly across the deck. The first mate nodded to the crew.

"You may wish to stay inside for the descent, Your Highness, ladies," Wheelock said in his most baleful, officious tones. All hints of the coconspiratorial and perhaps even rebellious Wheelock had vanished. Did he feel self-conscious again now that the voyage was over, I wondered, or was it simply that he had so much to do today?

"Oh, let's stay on deck for the descent," Caro said, clutching Fin's and my hands. "When else will we get the chance to see something like this?"

A hissing sound above indicated the lowering of the flames at the base of the balloon. The crew turned the cranks that pulled the airship's sails, and we began to descend. At the prow of the ship, the Brethren priest was intoning prayers and waving his incense. I was grateful that he stood too far away for me to hear his words.

When we'd gone down to fish and ride in the bathyspheres, the sky had been clear. This time we descended through clouds, and I discovered that I didn't like diving down into them any more than I'd liked rushing up into them. It still felt threatening and alien; this intimacy with the sky was not something that seemed natural.

I thought ruefully of all the mechanical wings I'd built, both insect and avian, and how often I'd considered the logistics of flying without ever imagining the feeling of it, the rising, plunging, baffling freedom from the horizontal mode of living that humans had always known. It turned out I liked having a straight, horizontal line to live on. I found that I was grateful to be returning to dry land after all, even a land as unknown to me as Faerie.

As we sank, millions of water droplets kissed my skin and hair and clothes, clinging like so many tiny diamonds. Breathing in cloud felt strange too; uncomfortably wet. The disastrous journey in the bathyspheres, and especially the sight of the merman's frayed gills, his blood muddying the water as he struggled to breathe, came to me vividly. I coughed and gagged on the mist, and beside me I could hear my friends gasping.

The drops clung to my eyelashes even after we'd finally come down through the bizarre, seemingly unending opacity of the cloud cover. So my first sight of Faerie was fractured through water.

I'd imagined it the way the first Estinger explorers had described the island, small and volcanic, wrapped in blue-sand beaches. They'd only begun to realize how vast a continent it truly was when they had hacked their way through the jungles and seen that immense mountain vista before them, the Faerie palace rising between peaks like a jeweled honeycomb. I'd thought I would see Faerie the way they had, even though I was coming from two hundred and twelve years in the future and down from the sky, not across the water.

I wasn't prepared for the heartrending loveliness below me. I could see only ragged facets of color through the dew on my lashes at first. The endless swelling shards of turquoise and pearl — I knew that was the ocean, even though it was a more intense color than I'd ever imagined water could be. And in front of us there was land, I was sure of that much — dark green land that suggested dense growth. Not the blackish green of Esting's forests, but glowing with the verdancy of emeralds.

I blinked the cloud out of my eyes, and Faerie became clearer, brighter, more vibrant, until I thought I must have been colorblind in Esting.

I'd worried that I'd spent too much time imagining Faerie as a child, and the reality could do nothing but fall short of those childish dreams. Now I wished I could tell my younger self, the little girl who lay in her bed dreaming of far-off lands, that it was even better than she hoped. The sight of Faerie was a gift to the part of me that was still that dreaming girl. I drank in the bright colors, devoured every detail.

I was torn between looking at the ocean and looking at the jungle, and in the end I hardly noticed the descent. I even enjoyed watching the tiny speck of the airship's shadow grow slowly larger as we came closer to the water, because the color of the sea in shade contrasted so gorgeously with the sparkling waves all around it.

Neither Fin nor Caro nor I said a word. We were all too entranced to speak.

I realized that I couldn't see our shadow anymore. The whole body of water underneath us had grown dusky, so that it no longer seemed to throw out light but to suck it in, draw it out of the sky and down into its depths. I shivered.

The air grew dark and cold. Since we'd so recently come through the misty water of the clouds I didn't notice it at first, but it was starting to rain. Little needling drops, hardly harsher than the clouds had been, turned with breathtaking quickness into a torrent. After the rain came an aggressive tapping of hailstones.

They skittered across the deck, then slapped, then pounded. One heavy hailstone knocked splinters from a guardrail post.

"All souls below deck!" Wheelock yelled, and then his arm was around my waist and he was pulling me away from the railing where I'd clung instinctively, knowing only that I needed to hold on to something solid, something safe.

Several crew members rushed to Fin, and Caro started moving toward shelter too. As she walked across my field of vision I saw a hailstone the size of my fist bounce off the back of her head, and she collapsed.

"Caro!" I broke free of Wheelock's grip and ran for her. I

brushed my hand quickly over her head, and when I didn't feel blood or any obvious breaks in the bone, I put my arms under hers and dragged her toward the shelter of the galley hatch. Another large hailstone hit me in the upper arm with shattering force. I bit back a scream and watched it roll away as I pulled my friend to safety. There was something strange about this hail, I thought as Caro regained her footing, something about the way it looked . . . Hardly thinking what I was doing, I reached out and stuffed a few of the smaller hailstones from the deck into my trouser pocket.

"Close the door, Nick!" Wheelock called, forgetting honorifics. But before I did, I heard the most terrible sound: a rending hiss, a death rattle, like all the air let out of a lung at once. I looked up toward the source and saw a ragged spot of light shining through one guttering flap of the balloon above us, with hailstones of increasing size sailing through it.

I slammed the door shut as we all felt the ship lurch. The floor creaked, and wind and hail hammered at the walls around us. All the lights had been doused, all the gas shut off. I thought of the sailors still working the ropes, battered by the storm, risking their lives to keep us sailing true. I felt my old airsickness coming back, and I briefly let my eyes close.

Wheelock was looking at the door too, his face haunted; I knew if it weren't for us he'd be out on the deck with his crew. "Not to worry, Your Highness, my ladies, we shall come ashore in less than an hour now," he said, returning to his formality and clinging to it as if it were the last thing he had. But he opened a hidden hatch under the galley table, and he started pulling out bulky, intricately folded packages.

"Your parachutes and life jackets," he said, handing them out to us. "Just a precaution for you, before I return to my crew outside. Not to worry. You'll hardly need them. Not to worry."

But I heard the fear in his voice, and I'd seen the rent in the balloon. I knew exactly what was going to happen.

Caro, Fin, and I each clutched a parachute. Wheelock helped Fin with his while Caro and I strapped in each other. I watched as Caro and Fin buckled life jackets over their chests and I tried to believe that such flimsy things could keep us safe.

The ship lurched again.

I shook my shoulders to settle my parachute straps, then made for the hatch.

"Nick! What are you doing?" Fin called, lunging forward. "We have to stay in here until we land, unless —" He looked down at his life jacket.

All it would take was a direct order from Fin, and Wheelock would strap me to the wall like one of the trunks. And if Fin thought he needed to give that order for my safety, there was no doubt in my mind that he would.

I looked right into his dark eyes. "I won't leave Jules," I said, quiet and steady. Then I opened the door, and I went back out.

The hail coming down was the size of small melons now, and strangely smooth, seeming almost to glow as it crashed past. The sky overhead was a weird, mottled green-gray of roiling clouds, with spider webs of lightning crawling through them.

I stood in the shelter of the stairwell, eyeing the door across the deck that led down to the living quarters and the storeroom where I kept my beloved Jules and the buzzers. Hailstones were blowing holes in the floor itself now, leaving ragged splinters, and the wood was littered with dark scraps of sail. I could see crew members desperately trying to patch holes in the ragged fabric above. With hailstones this big, I knew it was only a matter of time before even the reinforced hide of the balloon's center segment was punctured.

We wouldn't be landing in one piece.

There was no more time. I lunged across the deck, trying not to think about hailstones connecting with my head. Somehow I made it to the other side safely. Then I went down, down, down the steps, through the corridor, into the royal suite, and across it to the locked door of my storeroom.

My hands were shaking so badly that it took me several seconds to get the keys out of my trouser pocket, where I fumbled with the hailstones I'd collected. But once I had the key ring in my hands I felt better, capable. I remembered why I'd come, what was at stake. I plunged the keys into their locks and shouldered the door open.

Thank goodness I hadn't built Jules's storage box back around him, or I would have lost more precious minutes freeing him. Instead I could rush right up to his sleeping form and stroke the three spirals on his shoulders that would wake him up.

He raised his heavy neck slowly, shaking his head to wake up out of his long sleep.

"I'm so sorry, Jules, but we have to leave right now," I said. "The ship's going to crash."

"Get on," he wheezed.

I felt the biggest shudder yet rack the ship. I grabbed the briefcase with the unused Ashes and the buzzers sleeping safely inside. Using the leather belt that had strapped it to the wall, I secured it to Jules's back, behind the saddle. Then I hoisted myself up over him and astride.

"We'll be running trials a little sooner than I thought," I muttered as I hitched my feet into the retractable stirrups. "I'm sorry about that, Jules, but what else can we do?"

"Hold on, Mechanica," he huffed, and coming from him just then, the reviled name was a wondrous comfort.

I fitted my hands into the steel handles at the base of Jules's neck and flattened myself down onto his back as he made for the door. I feared for my scalp as we charged through, out into the suite and then into the corridor. I mourned a little for the unused supplies I'd left behind and all the other belongings in my trunk, but with more rending hissing sounds coming from outside every moment and most of the portholes cracked or shattered from the impact of the hailstones, there was no time to retrieve anything I didn't absolutely need. My clothes and equipment fit that category. Jules and the buzzers did not. I would work no less hard to save them than to save Fin and Caro—harder, because I knew Fin and Caro had parachutes and could look after themselves and that Wheelock was looking after them too.

No one would bother to save Jules but me.

We came charging up onto the deck to see the whole crew there already. Wheelock was screaming last-minute parachute instructions into the roaring wind, and all of them held their hands over their heads for protection. It wasn't hailing anymore, but that blessing had come too late for the tattered sails and two segments of the balloon that had already punctured. The seascape below us reared and tilted, growing ever closer.

I watched, horrified, as Walsh stepped up to the gate in the railing. The ship pitched again as the man jumped overboard—just jumped into open air and driving rain. He had nothing to meet him below but the water, nothing to help him but the parachute on his back and a flimsy life jacket. And nothing to get to but Faerie, if he even survived the fall.

I couldn't see Fin or Caro anywhere.

I urged Jules toward Wheelock. I worried for a moment about how we'd cross the broken, pitching deck with all of Jules's metal weight, but he managed it nimbly, stepping across from one safe plank to the next as delicately as a show pony.

"Wheelock!" I shouted over the driving wind. "Wheelock, where are they?"

Wheelock fairly shuddered with relief when he saw me. "I thought you were gone for sure," he yelled back, the wind stealing away most of his voice. "I made them go over first. They wouldn't go without you, so we had to—we had to—"

He didn't have to finish. I watched as the courage of the next crew member in line failed; the man behind him gave a short push, and he fell screaming into the blue.

"They've gone over," I whispered.

I knew that no matter how much my own courage might want to fail me, I couldn't avoid following them any longer.

"Come with me," I said to Wheelock.

He stared at Jules, then shook his head. "I can't, Miss Lampton," he said. He shot me a brave smile, the young man showing one more time through the formal shell. "A captain goes down with his ship."

I swallowed. I looked at him, trying to take in both the hidden young rebel and the officious, awkward captain. I knew this was the last time I'd see either of them.

Wheelock looked right back as if he were trying to memorize me too.

The ship lurched again.

"It's time," Jules rasped, stamping his front hooves.

I dug the balls of my feet into the stirrups and gripped the handles in his shoulders. The railing couldn't be much higher than the jumps Bex had taken him through . . . and the fact that I hadn't jumped any horse since I was a child, or jumped Jules ever, didn't bear thinking of.

At least I wouldn't have to worry about sticking the landing.

"All right, Jules," I murmured into his long steel ear. "Let's see if these things work."

He nickered back at me. I pressed my forehead against his neck for a brief moment of comfort, and then he started forward. He moved like rushing water, all fluid forward thrust, and we crossed the length of the deck in mere instants. I felt the gathering force behind me as he pushed out his back legs with all the strength he had, and we were airborne. I had the sense of flying before we even cleared the railing, and it transferred so smoothly into *really* flying that it was all just one extended jump. I could almost hear the call of a hunter's horn.

I kept my gaze straight ahead, my knees locked tight to Jules's sides, my hands gripping the handles for dear life. I took in a deep breath as we left the ship behind.

Jules's huge wings unfurled around us with a flurry of sparks, stretching out so far I couldn't see their tips. Thousands of bronze and tin and aluminum feathers clattered in the wind before they locked into place. Raindrops rang against them like dissonant bells.

I felt Jules's strength as he gave one great flap with those huge wings, felt our descent shift gloriously upward, heaving so powerfully that my own body pressed down on top of Jules's. He began to raise his wings again.

Then I heard a horrible screeching, ratcheting sound from his left wing. Our smooth ascent juddered to a stop.

Jules looked back at me with the whites of his glass eyes showing in panic, and we fell.

The lurch as gravity claimed us was like all the fear and seasickness I'd felt at the start of our voyage wound together into one horrible moment. The plunge downward. The moment of knowing death.

The fall stole my breath away and I couldn't scream, couldn't speak.

Jules kept struggling, kept maneuvering his wings, even though it was obvious that something had happened to the left one. I mentally ran over the designs we'd worked on so long together. I'd learned so much since I'd remade Jules from a toy-size horse into the behemoth he was now, I was sure I had accounted for the changes in mass, in weight, in inertia—

I couldn't think. I could only watch the swiftly rising ocean and silently beg my past work to save us.

A hot gust of updraft crossed us. Jules hooked his wings into the air and locked them in place again, and I felt that blessed, compressing lift. I could breathe, and we were flying once more.

My breath came in short, stuttering bursts, and tears streamed from my eyes and mixed with the warm raindrops. We were flying again, really flying. Jules's left wing still shuddered with every upswing, and our flight was neither straight nor steady, but he was doing it. He was flying. My brilliant Jules.

My hands still gripping the handles as tightly as if they'd been fastened there, I began to scan the ocean below for signs of my friends. I could see black-and-silver parachutes dotting the water. We were maybe three hundred feet in the air, and I could just make out the forms of Fin and Caro, parachutes already discarded behind them, slowly swimming toward the far-off beach.

"Thank goodness," I whispered. My voice came out a teary rasp, and I began to shake with relief. I would rather have plunged to my death on the ship than known that my friends hadn't made it.

Then I heard the blast.

"Jules!" I cried into the wind, but he was already banking around.

The storm was returning, and from this distance I could see that it roiled around the *Imperator* far too perfectly, too specifically, to be anything but magic. The sound we'd heard was lightning hitting the remaining segments of balloon. Forked lightning struck again and again, with the precision of cannon fire. The wall of storm clouds behind the ship was purple and green inside its gray coils, the lightning flashes like angry, knowing eyes. I could hear the hail returning between the rolls of thunder, too, bigger than before, smashing through the deck and sails.

With one last crash, the final balloon segment exploded, and there it was, the sight I'd feared ever since I'd watched the first hailstones crash through our sails—the *Imperator,* breaking up in midair. The bow snapped free of the ship's midsection and plunged downward. Ebony splinters from here, surely huge up close, bobbed in the waves. The midsection clung to the flaming balloon, sinking toward the sea. Black sails like ruined bat wings fluttered on the water. And then with a great hiss like the sound of one of the serpents I'd seen on the map, the balloon hit the ocean and collapsed in on itself with a final convulsion, and the home that we'd known for the past four weeks was gone. The ocean roiled under the storm, raising waves big enough to drown even the strongest swimmer.

Now that it had dealt with the ship, the storm began to spread itself out in the sky, sending lightning down against the water like searching fingers, picking off any crew members who hadn't already gone under the waves. Fin and Caro were farther away from the eye of the storm, a little closer to the shore, but nowhere near close enough.

"Go, Jules!" I yelled.

My horse pressed his new wings back against me and we dove toward the water. The descent was over before I had time to feel sick, before I had time to feel anything.

Caro and Fin struggled in the rising waves, and Jules tossed and flapped above them, dodging the slapping water that threatened to pull us down too. "Take my hand," I called, and for the first time since we'd galloped across the *Imperator*'s deck seven hundred feet in the air, I forced my right hand to give up its hold on Jules's handles. My fingers didn't want to uncurl, and they burned like fire when they finally did, but I had enough strength to help hoist Fin and then Caro up onto Jules's back.

A hailstone hit the water just to our left as Caro clambered up behind me. With his human burden suddenly tripled, Jules fought to get fully clear of the sea. His hooves and the tips of his wings hissed against the waves, raising steam.

And yet somehow, straggling, struggling, we rose. Salt spray stung my eyes and my cheeks, and I could feel Fin's grip around my waist like a vise.

Behind us both, Caro gasped as Jules finally caught the wind again. I assumed she had gasped in fear, but in another moment I heard her awed, grateful laughter.

"The most wonderful thing!" I could just barely hear her say as waves and hail crashed around us.

I saw the joy of it then too: flying astride Jules with the two people I loved most in the world at my back. Caro could find the beauty in any moment, no matter the danger, no matter the fear, and she could make me find it too. How could I do anything but love her?

Jules still dipped and jerked, carrying more weight than I'd ever calculated he could take, his left wing clattering horribly. But he took us away from the eye of the storm above and at last, at last, down onto the blue-sand shores of Faerie.

PART III

As soon as Jules saw beach below us instead of water, his wings gave out and he collapsed, and we all tumbled from his back.

I swallowed a mouthful of sand and coughed and sputtered to bring it back up. Then I tried my hardest to stand, knowing that we had to take cover as soon as possible to avoid the hailstones and lightning, the searching, intelligent force of that storm. My calves, thighs, hands, and shoulders all felt as if they'd been dipped in molten steel, and it was all I could do not to collapse entirely.

While I struggled to raise myself onto my knees, I felt two pairs of hands under my arms, supporting me, pulling me up.

"You saved us, Nick," Fin said.

Caro added: "You were magnificent."

I finally got enough sand out of my mouth to say, "Jules was magnificent."

My wonderful horse was struggling to stand too. Steam and smoke poured from his nostrils, his ears, and a few disturbing fissures in the glass panels along his face and his flanks. His left wing had completely detached from his shoulders in the fall, and it lay splayed and half buried some thirty feet away from us, shining like treasure in the sand.

I limped slowly over to Jules, the muscles in my legs still screaming. I stroked his nose, but he was burning hot and I jerked back. My fingertips blistered instantly.

I started to become aware of another kind of pain along my arms; not just the shaking, strained muscles but something else. I looked down and saw that the fabric of my jacket had burned away, and under its charred edges my skin was burned too, marked all over with swollen pink lines in strangely angular patterns . . . feathers. Jules's metal feathers, which he'd pressed against my arms when we dove down to the water to rescue Fin and Caro.

"Let's get to the forest," Fin said, looking out at the ocean, where the storm still roiled. Lightning struck the water in a disturbingly even rhythm so that the clouds seemed to crawl toward us on glowing legs.

I followed Fin and Caro to the tall, lush trees a few feet ahead, carefully holding my burned arms away from the rest of my body.

"You'll bear those scars forever if you don't cool them off soon," Caro said. "Here." She tore a wide strip off her sopping-wet, sandy skirt and began to walk toward the beach. Lightning hit the sand three feet away from her, and she rushed back under the tree cover.

"I'm sorry, Nick," she said.

I shook my head, trying not to wince at every little movement. "It's all right," I said. "As long as I can move, I'm fine." I looked ahead of us, into the dense, dark jungle. "I think I remember something about the medicinal plants Lady Candery found on her voyage, you know. Mother always loved to tell me about her."

As I said those words, I could almost hear my mother's voice, and feel the soft, light blankets in my big childhood bed, the warmth of her callused hand stroking my forehead, back when I was so young that one bedtime story could fill up the whole scope of my mind, could become my whole reality. Mother would quiz me on the stories' details as she went, and I was always a little too eager to please her, to prove to her my intelligence. But sometimes, when the story was really good, we'd both get swept up and lost inside of it. And she loved to tell the story of Lady Candery, the only woman on the first Estinger voyage to Faerie, the only venturess among venturers. I'd loved Lady Candery too, not least because I liked to imagine that she was an ancestor of our half-Fey housekeeper.

All the neatly tucked-away love and loss that I felt for both my mother and Mr. Candery swept through my exhausted mind like a tidal wave. I missed them both as horribly in that moment as if I had only just learned of my mother's death, Mr. Candery's departure. They had both been parents to me.

"Cap-o'-rushes," I whispered. My throat felt too raw for me to speak clearly. "It grows on the north-facing sides of trees here. Deeper in the jungle. It cools burns." I felt the pain in my muscles with greater intensity now, as if the heartache of losing Mother and Mr. Candery had transferred to a physical ache all over me.

Fin nodded. He straightened his stance, and I could see the hero he wanted to be in the determined expression on his face. "Right," he said. "It's into the jungle, then. I'll go, and you two can stay here until you've rested a bit, until you've got back your strength."

"No!" Caro and I said together.

"We can't let you go off on your own into Fey wilderness," Caro added. "You're the Heir of Esting, Fin. Don't be absurd."

Fin's eyes snapped with anger. "Right now I'm just a body lucky to be in one piece, and I'll help someone if they need helping," he said. "Next you'll build an automaton like Fitz's to keep me safe. I'll go. After we put the cap-o'-rushes on Nick's burns, we'll be able to start moving toward the capital together."

"That took the first explorers more than a week," I said. "And Caro's right. For the sake of all our safety, Fin, and not just yours. Besides, you won't be able to do Faerie much good if you're killed on your first day here."

Fin huffed, but his anger was starting to melt. "All right," he finally agreed. "We'll stay here a while until you feel a bit better, and then we'll all go looking for the rushes."

"We should wait here for other . . . survivors," Caro said.

We looked back at the ocean and the hissing storm slowly growing closer. No broken planks or scraps of parachute floated on the water; no one swam toward us, and no voices called for aid.

We stared silently. All the crew . . .

If it hadn't been for Jules, the storm would have drowned us, too. There were no other survivors.

Near the beach, hailstones smacked into the shallow water, and lightning hit the sand again, leaving a glassy crater.

"We have to leave now!" I said, pulling my friends farther into the safety of the jungle.

Even as we walked away from it, I wondered if there was some way to take Jules's wing with me; flight was an asset we might need to survive on this strange continent, and I hated to see so many months of hard work left behind after so little use.

The rest of Jules was miraculously unharmed, at least in any lasting way. Most of his glass hide and face had shattered, so he looked in places like the metal skeleton of a horse, but even without his skin, he could move and walk unimpeded.

I couldn't feel any pride in my engineering then, only gratitude that he had survived.

As we moved deeper into the jungle, the sound of thunder began to recede behind us. The clatter of hailstones grew quieter too, until finally it was gone. I didn't dare to hope at first, but eventually I had to believe that the storm wasn't following us inland. If it had been a guard, perhaps it guarded only the shore?

But the Fey knew to expect us. Why would a Fey storm attack a ship they were supposed to have invited?

"So, exactly what do those captain's rushes look like, again?" Fin asked. The jungle had grown quiet around us when we first entered, but now sounds of birdcalls were growing loud enough that they threatened to drown out his words.

"Cap-o'-rushes." I took a shallow breath; deep ones stretched the burned skin on my shoulders. "Flat brown fungus. A pattern on top like a woven basket."

"That man at the Night Market had some, didn't he?" Caro asked, circling the base of a tree that was at least twelve feet around.

I looked upward, and the tree was lost in shadowy mists before I could see its top.

We weren't even that far into the jungle yet, and we were already dwarfed. I shivered.

We had come to a place where we would never be able to survive on our own. We were arrogant fools, all of us.

Jules nosed my hair gently, as if he could push the despair from my mind. He stepped more confidently across the slippery fallen leaves and huge protruding roots than any of the rest of us did. Soon he was leading our group.

He had come from this place, after all, or his Ashes had. Watching him walk calmly ahead, I found I was a little less afraid.

"You know," Caro went on. "The night we got the lovesbane for my mother."

"He did," I said. I would always remember that night, because it was the first time I told Caro she was part of my family and that I wanted to be part of hers. I'd been afraid to say it, but thank goodness I had, because then Caro had let me help her buy the lovesbane that saved her mother's life. "He knew what the Ashes were, too, but he wouldn't tell me."

Jules shook his head and I quickly returned to the subject at hand. "Those cap-o'-rushes were dried, though, so they probably looked different."

We kept walking, scanning the trees for fungi. My skin throbbed. Once in a while, the creak or moan of a branch interrupted the strange bird songs around us. There were rustles and scuttlings in the trees too, and once a low, faraway howl that made us freeze in our tracks like prey.

There was something about the light here that reminded me of our underwater sojourn that now seemed so long ago. It was heavy, changing, mysterious light that somehow clung to the skin like liquid and then scattered like shaken dewdrops when you moved into shadow.

We made slow progress through the jungle. I knew I was keeping us back with my stiff, limping walk, and I hated it.

"Could the buzzers help us look, Nick?" Fin asked then. "I mean, if they . . ." He looked stricken and cleared his throat. "I'm sorry, Nick. It's just that I'm so used to them hovering around you all the time. Of course they were still in the ship." He reached out to touch me before he remembered my burns and pulled back.

I started to smile, but even that small movement hurt my skin. I wondered what my face looked like. Had the heat from Jules's wings scarred me there, too?

"No, they're here," I said.

Jules stopped walking, and I reached for the briefcase on his back, then stopped when I heard the skin on my arms crackle.

"Let me," Fin said quickly, pulling the briefcase down and then settling himself on the ground to open it. He fiddled with the clasp for a while, and I watched him blankly for a few moments before remembering that the lock needed my hands, and no one else's. How badly had the fall, the flight, shaken me, that my mind was now working so slowly?

Carefully, I bent down far enough to reach the clasp. I pressed my finger against it. Nothing happened.

I turned my hand over. The palm was red and puffy. My

fingers had swollen with blisters, and I couldn't see their prints.

I stared, willing the burns to disappear, willing the pain to stop.

"We'll have to pick the lock," I whispered. I'd never had to break one of my own locks before, but I knew that if it wasn't done in just the right delicate way, it would shatter and stab the lockpick's hands—and, worse, some of the shards would fly into the briefcase and might damage the sleeping buzzers in ways I couldn't repair outside of my workshop. "We'll have to be very careful, though, and very clever." I looked down at my useless hands in dismay.

"I'll do it," Caro said. "All those years of making music boxes had to come in handy." Fin moved over, and Caro knelt beside him on the ground. She waited patiently for each of my instructions and followed them with remarkable dexterity.

Finally I heard five quick snaps, and the briefcase creaked open.

The first tray contained the copperwork butterfly and five sleeping dragonflies. "Maybe they'd be safer in there," I said, reconsidering. "We'll find the cap-o'-rushes eventually, and I can . . . manage the burns till then."

Jules, who had been watching quietly, shook his head.

"Maybe they'll be safest if they can think for themselves," Fin said.

I hated to risk them in any way at all, but I knew he was right. Caro and Fin woke the buzzers, since even that would have hurt my hands. They crowded affectionately around me for a moment, buzzing anxiously over my burns.

Jules nickered and they flocked to him. He rumbled something quiet, and they took off in small fleets, soaring without hesitation into the shadows.

If Jules knew this place, I supposed the buzzers did too.

I kept thinking about all those people back on the sea, the ones we might have rescued if we'd tried just a little harder, if Jules still had his other wing . . . if I'd built it better and stronger.

I was grateful that Fin had made it to Faerie alive, because I understood that he had important work to do here. And I was grateful for Caro's survival because I couldn't think about a world without her. More than my own life, I needed both of them to live.

But why should I have survived instead of, say, Wheelock? I remembered the stark, stubborn determination on his face when he told me that he would go down with his ship. I had liked Wheelock, really liked him, even more than I'd realized back on the *Imperator*. I thought of his stiff old-man formality and the surprising flashes underneath it and compared him to the young men I'd met at court in the past year, who tended to be variations on the theme of Fitzwilliam Covington: grasping, manipulative, slick.

Wheelock had endeared himself to me in a way that

none of them had, and I mourned the lost possibility that he might have become part of the intimacy that I shared with Caro and Fin. Perhaps we could have had something like Bex and Caro had . . .

But Wheelock was dead, and Walsh and Gunning and Sneha and probably the whole rest of the crew were dead, and they were all lost behind us on that brilliant green sea, and all I could do now was plunge into the darkness of the jungle with the friends I still had with me.

I had to leave Wheelock behind, I had to leave them all, to move forward. So I forced myself to do it.

After less than an hour of picking our way over the huge tree roots and torso-thick vines at our feet, we had to stop for a rest. My mouth was so dry that my blistered lips stuck to each other as I opened them. We had no supplies with us, of course, but I saw some cupped leaves the size of buckets sprouting from a thick stalk ahead.

In the recesses of each leaf's curve was a perfectly clear bowl of rainwater.

I walked up to the closest one, my hands shaking as I raised them to its sides. I wanted to pour the cool water over the burns on my arms almost more than I wanted to drink it . . . My skin felt tightly stretched and uncomfortably hot, a condition that the close, humid air of the jungle only exacerbated.

"Wait!" Fin said as I started to tip the water toward my parched, waiting mouth. "Nick, do you know that plant?"

In that second I almost hated him.

Finally I released my hold on the leaf. "No." I could feel a waxy residue on my hands, and I wiped them against my singed trousers. "You're right, it's too risky."

We rested for a few more precious minutes and walked on.

The buzzers had been gone for nearly an hour now, and I was starting to worry. Every bright flicker in the shadowy jungle around us I hoped was a metallic wing—and not a pair of predatory eyes. Mother hadn't told me as much about the Fey fauna as she had the flora . . . I started to wonder if she'd avoided describing it in order to spare me nightmares.

That wouldn't have been like her, though. She would never spare me or shelter me when she could teach me something instead. I remembered her sharp, demanding intellect and tried to take comfort in it.

Something rustled in the darkness behind us. Without a word we crowded closer together, Caro and I flanking Fin and walking sideways while Jules took the lead, so that we could keep watch in all directions. At least the fear of lurking, hungry monsters meant I paid a little less attention to my still-swelling burns, my screaming muscles, my parched throat.

A series of glassy flickers at the corner of my eye made me flinch, but then I recognized the buzzers as they fluttered out of the shadows. They flew slowly, because they were heavily laden.

The copper butterfly flew directly to Jules's mouth and he began tearing the cap-o'-rushes into narrow strips.

Then Jules ground the fungus in his strong metal jaws. A wonderful astringent smell, clean and earthy at the same time, filled the humid air. The butterfly smeared its wings in the paste and flew to my right arm, where it gently stroked itself along my raw skin.

A sweet, icy tingling spread everywhere the butterfly touched me. The relief was so immediate that tears came to my eyes.

Fin and Caro took the rest of the cap-o'-rushes from Jules's mouth and joined the butterfly's ministrations, carefully spreading the gray-brown paste over my arms, shoulders, neck, and face.

I had never felt anything so wonderful. I had to tighten my jaw to keep myself from crying out with the joy of it, with the gratitude for being suddenly free of such terrible pain.

The dragonflies laid their burden at the ground before us, and it was nearly as welcome as the butterfly's: rhodopis berries, a whole branch of them, larger and plumper and shinier than any I'd seen in Esting. It took all five dragonflies to carry the heavy branch, and they stayed on the ground once they'd laid it at our feet, seemingly too tired to move.

"Thank you so much," I said. I picked the dragonflies up, carried them gently to Jules, and placed them on his back for safety and company. Then I returned to Fin and Caro, and we began to pluck the berries one by one.

I forced myself to eat slowly. I didn't even notice the flavor, just the fresh liquid in my dry mouth. Beside me, Caro and Fin were equally careful, equally shaky. I knew we were all thinking the same thing: If it weren't for the buzzers, we might have collapsed before we found sustenance we could trust, might have resorted to eating plants we didn't know. Might have died before nightfall.

The darkness was coming on impossibly quickly. Many small, layered shadows seemed to tumble down through the thick canopy above us, darkening the spongy, leaf-laden ground with each step we took.

"Wasn't it morning when —" Fin began.

"Yes," Caro and I chorused.

And then it began to rain.

We flinched and huddled closer together. I listened for the hail that was sure to follow, for the malevolent, searching thunder that had seemed to chase us from the beach.

Birds stopped their song, and the movements of unseen animals vanished inside the encompassing noise of soft rainfall. The whole jungle grew quiet except for that gentle sound. The rain fell soft and sweet, washing my hair of its sticky residue of sea spray.

This was no storm; this was ordinary rain. I turned the palms of my hands toward it, and raindrops touched them like blessings.

Fin's hair had been crusted over with sea salt, making it

look as if he had gone gray from the trials of the morning, but now the water sluiced over him and turned his curls black again, draping them down his neck like hanks of dark silk. Beside him, Caro opened her mouth to the sky, and tears fell from her eyes and mixed with the rain. It was the first time I'd seen her cry.

I drank too, my shaking muscles and cramped stomach thanking me for every meager swallow.

I started to feel a strange tightening on my face. I ignored it at first, but soon I couldn't pretend not to notice it; my burns were swelling again. The cap-o'-rushes were washing away.

I watched the feather-shaped blisters on my arms rise again as the paste slipped off them. I hobbled toward the shelter of a huge, heart-shaped leaf, and when Fin and Caro saw what was happening to me, they quickly followed.

I tried to brush the thinned-out paste that remained back over my skin, but it was no use.

"We can go get more," Fin said over the din of the rain, which was slowly growing to a torrent. "Now that we know what it looks like."

"No," I said. "We can't risk getting separated in the storm."

"Maybe the buzzers can . . ." But as he spoke, we watched one dragonfly try to lift off from Jules's back, only to have the raindrops knock it straight to the ground. The rain was coming down hard now. It still didn't feel like magic, and I knew it rained several times a day in Faerie's jungles—but how could I really tell?

Caro started breaking the woody stems of the gigantic leaves around us and weaving them through some low-hanging vines that looped downward from one of the impossibly tall trees. Jules saw what she was doing, bit off another stem, and dragged it over. Fin quickly got the idea and began to help. With my burns shooting pain all over my body, I could only huddle under their makeshift tent, miserable for being unable to help them.

We had a relatively watertight shelter within half an hour. I urged Jules to get behind me, worrying about rust before I remembered that I'd already tested all his materials for both hot- and cold-water resistance, for every environmental variable I could think of. One must always account for the vagaries of truth, Mother used to say.

That phrase echoed unsettlingly in my mind now, as I looked around at a gloomy Fey landscape that seemed at once more and less *true* than the magical world, ripe for exploring, that I'd imagined as a child.

This wasn't a world for exploring . . . it wasn't *for* anything. It just was.

I suddenly wanted to weep with anger for all the wrongs Esting had done to this place, for how even I had thought of it as a place-for-purpose, not a place-that-is. It wasn't a place to explore or conquer or convert, or even to free. It wasn't a place for us at all.

We shouldn't be here, I wanted to tell Fin and Caro, but I hurt too much, and I was too tired, to form words. And what good would it do any of us, grieving and exhausted as we were, to dwell on the mistakes that led us here?

I huddled close to them in our shelter, and I wrapped my aching arms around Jules where he rested against the deep, springy moss of the tree trunk behind us. I was happy to endure the pain of his engine's warmth on my burns for the comfort of having him close.

But Jules, I realized, wasn't nearly as warm as he should be. The whirring ticks and deep rumbles of his mechanisms were slowing down, and when I looked into his furnace I saw the cause: his fuel was running out. Only a few small embers of coal glowed in his belly.

He raised his head slowly and looked at me, his eyes unfocused. I thought frantically of gathering wood to burn, but I knew anything in this jungle would be too fresh and wet to light.

"It's all right, Jules," I murmured, using the last of my strength to speak a few words to soothe him. "I'll find you something soon. I'll keep you safe till then. I promise, I promise."

He nodded, and his head came to rest on my lap as the last sparks in his furnace went out.

I took a deep, shuddering breath that made my arms and shoulders ache. The buzzers tucked themselves into my ragged pockets, sheltering from the rain.

I was overwhelmed with pain and exhaustion. Next to me, Fin and Caro looked haggard and worn.

"We have a shelter," Fin said, looking around at the gloomy jungle. "We need to rest before we do anything else. This is probably the best place to do it. Here." He stood and walked a few steps away, gathered ferns as tall as he was, and then laid them carefully across Jules, Caro, and me to hide us. Finally he sat down again and pulled a last fern over himself.

It was as if the camouflage gave my overtaxed survival instincts permission to relax, and within moments I was asleep.

The pain from my burns and aching muscles bled into my dreams, and I shook with fever and half-imagined fears. I dreamed of my mother's workshop. The damp, organic jungle around me seemed to contract into clockwork and steel; the rain turned to molten glass, the mist to smoke. I heard what I thought were the rhythmic taps of tiny hammers, and I felt my mother's hand on my neck.

Then the hand tightened and wrenched my head upward. I blinked away my visions and stared into an impassive, blue-freckled face.

I CHOKED and struggled to look for Fin and Caro, but the Fey's grip was too strong to let me turn my head.

"Who are you?" fe asked in perfect, harsh Estinger. I looked down and saw a blue kerchief, an emblem of the Fey rebellion, tucked into the collar of fer shirt.

I hesitated. Even if Mr. Candery's letter had been honest, and I held desperately to the belief that it was, I didn't know if this soldier could be trusted.

When fer grip tightened even more, I gasped, then pressed my cracking lips together. I steeled myself for further pain, knowing only that I needed to keep my friends safe.

"I am Prince Christopher Dougray Fadhiri Anton Abdul-Rafi' Finnian, Heir of Esting," I heard Fin say fiercely.

My heart sank. Could he really be foolish enough to believe his name and title would save the day?

"Fin!" Caro whispered, and I knew she thought the same.

I felt my hands yanked behind my back and tied. The Fey who held me released my neck and looked over my shoulder, in the direction of Fin's voice. "It could be him," fe said. "He matches the stories, anyway." Fe looked me up and down, assessing. "So does this one. The princess-to-be."

"The inventor," I said. "Not the princess." I didn't know why I should care about such things at a time like this, but since I thought I might be about to die, I at least wanted to die as the person I really was.

The Fey blinked, and I thought I saw a flicker of surprise, or recognition, in fer blue eyes as fe looked me up and down. But fer face soon grew cold and impassive again.

"Inventor or princess," fe said, "you and your friends are coming with us."

I turned my head and saw several more Fey soldiers holding Fin and Caro. Others inspected Jules, who lay as still under our shelter as if he'd never moved at all. They were frowning in distaste, even disgust. Their expressions tightened further at the sight of the briefcase on Jules's back, which thankfully was closed tight again; I knew well they'd confiscate it, but I felt confident that the locks I'd adapted from Mother's designs would keep them from opening it.

One of the soldiers looked at me, and again I saw that flicker of recognition and wondered if Mr. Candery had been honest after all.

They opened the furnace hatch in Jules's belly.

"Don't hurt him!" I cried.

The Fey who had grabbed my neck frowned at me. "Send a carrier for the machine when we get to the barracks." Fe nodded toward the others. "Now turn out." Fe pivoted and began to walk back through the jungle. I felt a shove from behind and had no choice but to follow.

It was fully night now, and the only light came from the glowing orbs that dangled from the soldiers' belts. I stumbled over the uneven ground as we walked. They'd placed me in front, so I couldn't see Fin or Caro, but after a few moments I heard Caro's reassuringly gentle voice near me. "All right, both of you?"

"Yes," I said, and I heard Fin say the same from closer behind.

I still felt as if I could kill Fin for giving away his identity so easily — and I still couldn't believe he'd been so foolish. And why hadn't the rebels been expecting us?

I felt the buzzers flit one by one out of my pockets and steal away into the night, and I was glad. They were small enough to run on clockwork instead of coal, and they knew how to wind one another. Even if I never saw them again, at least they'd survive.

I don't know how long we marched. My muscles were already aching so much that every step took monumental effort and seemed to take monumental time.

At the edge of the light cast by the Fey's orbs, I watched vines slither over tree trunks like snakes, moving hopefully toward the lamps. The Fey who led us kicked away tendrils that crept around fer legs and boots. I was suddenly grateful that I didn't have a light of my own, in spite of my tendency to trip.

Far above in the trees, more lights flickered greenly among the leaves.

At last we stopped before a huge rock with a fissure down its center. I thought perhaps we'd squeeze through the crack, but instead the Fey leader walked right through the rock's apparently solid face.

I was pushed forward so harshly that I had no choice but to walk into the rockface too. I had barely enough time to remember the secret door to the underground Night Market in Esting and how I'd learned the hard way the first time I went there to hold my breath whenever I passed through it. I took in a deep breath just before the rock sucked open and closed around me.

The breath was a mistake. My torso was squeezed until every particle of air was forced past my lips. I felt my fingernails begin to crack under the pressure, and I tasted blood on my tongue.

Then I started to feel my mind being compressed too, somehow flattened and pulled apart. Every emotion inside me, every intention, was laid bare one at a time.

Some kind of entity sorted through them, rummaging past each surface thought in its search for something deeper. I was here to protect Fin, yes, and to see Mr. Candery again, yes, and also to try to help Faerie if I somehow could—I felt that last desire scoffed at and tossed aside by whatever power examined me.

But I was here for another reason as well, a secret so closely kept within my heart that I had not even known it myself, not until I felt it squeezed and excised from my brain by that strange, stony force: I was here because of my mother. By traveling to Faerie, I was doing what she had always wanted to do but had never managed in her own lifetime. In coming here, I could both love her and become her. It was why I had done so many things, so obvious now: to bring my mother back to life by building on her inventions, her engineering. Did I even want those things?

But before I had time to finish asking myself that question, to see clearly the last bit of my soul that the great pressure had laid bare, the ordeal was over. Space opened up around me, and I could breathe again.

I gasped as an infant must gasp when it is born. I knew the rock had nearly squeezed me to death, and I knew as well that if the force that had searched my mind had found something . . . distasteful to it there, I would indeed have died. My body hurt too much for me to feel real gratitude at my survival, but with each inhalation relief flooded through me.

After the complete darkness inside the rock, the light in this new place glared and fizzed angrily. My eyes burned as I waited for my vision to adjust.

"Fin? Nick?" I heard Caro say behind me. "Are you all right?"

I coughed several times before I felt able to reply; I was amazed that Caro could speak in anything more than a rasp. "Fine," I croaked eventually, although it was just barely on the edge of true. Fin kept coughing far longer than I did, but at last he was able to make a vaguely affirmative wheeze.

By then my eyes had adjusted, although they still ached. I looked down at my hands; the pressure of the rock had broken the rope that bound me. Each of my fingernails was cracked through, and each crack was edged with blood. I wiped my eyes and found blood there, too.

I saw that we were in a kind of storeroom, with stacks of muslin bags lining the wall. Our captors had kindly paused while the three of us regained our breath, and they were watching us with cautious analysis.

"I thought the rock might take you," the leader said, the one who'd seized me. Fe nodded at Fin. "Especially you."

Bruises and purplish, broken blood vessels mottled Fin's beautiful face, and I saw raw fear in his eyes. I wondered what the force in the rock had found inside his mind. He coughed again, still incapable of speech, his head bowed.

"Right," the Fey said. "You'll come with us, Heir of

Esting." Two soldiers took Fin's arms and began to lead him away.

I tried to lunge forward, but the pain in my limbs made me stumble. "Wait!" I said. "Don't take him away from us, please. You must—you must know he was telling the truth now. We all were."

The Fey snorted. "The rock may have spit you out, but that doesn't mean I trust you."

Fin raised his head with obvious effort. "That stone," he whispered in a voice like a ghost's, "it tore open my heart, it found all my—" A coughing fit seized him, and it was another minute before he could speak again. "You must know I'll die to save this place if I need to."

I remembered the feeling I'd gotten in the jungle, the sudden certainty that Faerie had nothing to do with me, that it wasn't waiting for me to come explore it, that it didn't care about me at all.

"Plenty of people have died for this place," the leader said icily, "every one of them because of Esting. One death more or less won't make any difference."

Fin, still panting and coughing, glared at the Fey.

The leader nodded at two other soldiers. "I'll deal with this one," fe said, then fe jerked fer head toward us. "Take them down."

I cried out in tandem with Caro as Fin was pulled away from us, vanishing down the stone tunnel with the soldiers who held him. The other soldiers moved behind us. Something heavy cracked against the back of my head, and then I felt nothing.

✳

The floor was cold and damp. My first thought was that I must be far underground. I remembered my mother's workshop in the cellar of Lampton Manor, and I felt sick with miserable longing. The cool, slick stone met my burned skin like a blessing, and all I wanted was to keep my face pressed against it.

But I remembered Fin and Caro, and I forced myself to sit up.

Caro was leaning against the damp, dark blue wall nearby, watching me worriedly. She took my hand, avoiding the burns as best she could, and grimaced when she saw my fingernails.

"Did the rock do that to you?" she asked.

"Yes," I said, and was relieved to find that I had my voice back. Now that I was seated and starting to really feel all the different pains again, it hurt too much even to nod.

"I knew there was more to it than the threshold spells at the Night Market," she said, "but it seems the passage was much harder on you and Fin. I wonder why."

"Maybe they weren't as suspicious of you," I said.

"No." Caro frowned. "I still felt them, it, picking me apart—tearing my heart open, as Fin said. But there were . . . what it found wasn't frightening or . . . or complicated." She shook her head. "I hadn't known it myself, the limits and dimensions of everything I want. Loving Fin, loving you, hoping we all get through this alive. Missing Bex and my family back home, and one or two secret hopes of my own." Caro touched her heart with the hand that wasn't holding mine. "That's all the desire that's in me, I guess. At least right now."

I took in as deep a breath as my injured lungs would allow. "I know what you mean. I felt it sorting through everything I wanted too. It found some things I didn't even know were there myself." I looked down at my bloody fingertips. "I think I'm lucky . . . I think I'm lucky I survived it."

Caro looked at me searchingly. "What didn't you know, Nick?"

I tried to answer, but instead I started to cry.

I felt Caro touch the corners of my eyes, trying to gather up the salt tears before they could sting my burns. I looked up at her, and her face was so open, so kind and lovely, unmarked by the stone's test in the way Fin's and my own faces were, so much the Caro I had always known.

I leaned forward, slowly, full of pain, and I touched my lips to hers.

We'd had whole conversations in one look so often, and it was the same in that one kiss. We talked about home, and love, and friendship; how good it was that here at the end of the world, captured and hidden underground while we waited to meet who knew what fate, at least we had each other. At least we had someone we loved.

The kiss ended as quietly and gently as it had begun. Caro and I leaned against each other and the cold stone wall. I closed my eyes, and we fell asleep huddled together in the cell.

Some hours later, the door opened. A Fey I hadn't seen before walked in and closed it quickly behind fer. Fe was tall and broad-shouldered, and far more blue freckles covered the left side of fer face than the right. Fe wore a blue bandanna just like the soldiers had, but the rest of fer clothes were all loosely draped white linen. I recognized them, from my reading, as healer's robes.

I didn't study fer face or clothes for long, though, because what fe carried was far more important. Fe had brought a whole basin of cool water for us, as well as threadbare but clean-looking cloths for washing and a pair of equally threadbare blue shift dresses. Fe set down the basin and took a small glass jar out of fer pocket. The unmistakable earthy, astringent smell of cap-o'-rushes filled the room.

I had been a little afraid of this new Fey's officious manner at first, but as soon as fe offered me the salve for my burns, I would have done anything fe asked.

"Did you look after Fin, too—a dark young man with curly hair?" Caro asked.

The Fey pressed fer lips together, and I remembered what

Mr. Candery had told me about Fey healers so long ago: that they didn't speak unless absolutely necessary, the better to focus their intentions and their powers on their medicine.

The healer nodded at Caro.

"Is he all right?" I asked.

Fe turned to me, and I saw boundless kindness, boundless sympathy, in fer eyes; that was perhaps more healing than the salve.

Fe nodded again, and I could have collapsed with relief.

After the healer saw to our injuries, fe gave us a spongy white fruit to eat, and I was so focused on it in my hunger that I barely noticed as we were led out of the cell and down another long tunnel, around so many turns and corners and byways that I wouldn't have been able to keep them straight in my mind even if I had been paying attention.

At last we arrived in a small, spare room equipped with a desk facing two chairs. Caro and I sank into them gladly, still chewing the rinds of our fruits. I was too tired to be anything but docile, and that was what frightened me the most.

I knew Mr. Candery as soon as he walked through the door. With a burst of strength I flung myself forward, pressed my face against his tall shoulder, and wrapped my arms around him.

I'd missed him every day since I was twelve years old.

But I quickly realized how different he was from the delicately genteel, suit-clad housekeeper I remembered.

His arms around me were wiry and hard, and he'd grown tougher and leaner about the shoulders too. I could feel the harshly raised ridge of a scar along his back where I hugged him, even through his shirt.

"Hello, Nicolette," he murmured into my hair. His voice was both the same and different; as gentle and erudite as the voice I remembered, but also lower and rougher, as if it too bore scars.

He stood there for a long time, letting me hug him and hugging me back. Eventually he pulled away to look at my face. His blue-flecked gray eyes showed such a strange, conflicting mix of emotions that I couldn't tear my own gaze from them, could only let him examine me and wait until he came to his conclusion.

"I am so glad to see you safe," he said at last in his new, scarred voice. But there was sadness in his eyes, and anger too.

The shadows of those emotions on his face, a face I hadn't seen in so long and yet remembered with such perfect clarity — more so than even my mother's — felt like the last small, unbearable burden on an already unbearable day. It was all I could do to keep my chin from trembling as I smiled at him or my voice from breaking as I said, "You too, Mr. Candery." I kept watching that sadness and anger, wondering which would win out.

I was so focused on him that I didn't notice Caro's building anger, not until it exploded.

"You're not glad to see her safe!" she cried. "Your invitation was a trap all along! That storm, the ship, all of the crew . . ." Her voice hitched. "We're lucky any of us lived." She took a calming breath. "How dare you act as if you love her when you sent her to her death?"

Mr. Candery flinched. He pulled away from me, his hands brushing reluctantly along my arms as he let me go.

"If you believe nothing else," he said softly, "you must believe—you must—that the storm was not our doing. I swear it."

Caro's anger had infected me. "Would you swear on my mother's grave?" I asked, just to hurt him. He'd loved my mother so.

He looked away, and something, some last hope, started to crumble inside of me.

"I'll swear on anything you like, Nicolette, that I have never meant you or your friends any harm," he said quietly. I didn't know what to believe. If the Fey hadn't sent that storm, who had? I knew beyond a doubt that it was no natural tempest.

A guard standing in the doorway conspicuously cleared fer throat.

Mr. Candery gave a short, curt nod. "Right," he said, the roughness, the soldier, coming back into his voice. "I know you won't like this, but I have to take you somewhere, and I can't let you see where we're going. I was about to say you needed to trust me, but . . ." He sighed. "I realize that I can't ask that of you."

"But we have to go with you, trusting or not," Caro said. "There's hardly a choice."

Mr. Candery straightened his shoulders, and he nodded slowly. The guard tied my hands behind my back again, and my old housekeeper brought a blindfold to my eyes.

We were led at a slow walk for some minutes and then helped up onto a hard, flat bench, and I felt us rolling forward, being jostled as if we were in a carriage on an uneven road. In spite of my trepidation, I was still so exhausted that I fell asleep several times.

I don't know what I expected to see when my blindfold was finally removed, but it wasn't the unassuming door in front of me. We were standing in a pleasant-looking street with wooden doors set into connected buildings built from yellowish stone. It was . . . charming. Cheerful. The sun was shining, and the pain of my burns had subsided enough that I could almost enjoy its warmth.

Some notation was written across the door, a few symbols that I thought might be numbers; I'd never learned Fey writing. All the books on the language had been burned long ago.

Mr. Candery made a quick gesture, and the silent Fey guard turned Caro and me gently but forcibly around. I saw a sunny, well-manicured courtyard. There were high walls surrounding us, to be sure, but this was hardly the dour barracks I'd imagined.

After a few long moments, I heard a loud ratcheting sound; the guard turned us back toward the now-open door, and we followed Mr. Candery into a domestic little hallway. I tried unsuccessfully to guess where we might be going, to gather clues from the framed pictures on the walls, which looked like diagrams or blueprints, but my mind was worn out and my thoughts scattered.

Only a few minutes passed before Mr. Candery stopped in front of another door. "Now," he said, bending down a little bit to speak to me, as if I were still a young girl and he my teacher and guardian, "this is where we must leave you, Miss Lampton."

The formal way he spoke my name, as if he were my housekeeper again, jarred me. Caro reacted before I did, stepping protectively in front of me.

"Absolutely not," she said. "You've taken one of my friends away already, and I won't let you take the other. I won't let you separate us." This was Palace Manager Caro with all the authority in the world in her voice; I wouldn't have dared to argue with her myself.

Mr. Candery did indeed look taken aback, and in fact it was the guard who protested. "You are a prisoner of war," fe said coldly. "You will each go, or stay, wherever we so decide."

Caro scowled, the guard frowned back, and their expressions were so similar that my exhausted brain found it funny rather than frightening.

Mr. Candery stepped between them, and I saw the soldier in him again. "These girls are no longer prisoners," he said. "It's been proven they mean no harm, and now they are under my care."

The guard saluted automatically and looked down at the floor.

"Mr. Candery," I said, "I must stay with Caro, if there's any way in the world that I can." I took a deep breath, heartened by the sympathy I saw in his face. "And we must return to Fin as soon as possible. Please, you must understand that."

Mr. Candery looked at Caro thoughtfully, at the way she still stood in front of me as if I were some treasure to be fiercely guarded. "How much do you trust this lady, my dear?" he asked, holding up one long finger when I began to give an angry retort. "Please, Nicolette. A great secret lies before you in this room, one that none but your own family should know."

I remembered suddenly another time I'd stood in a hall by a doorway with a mystery before me; I had listened to Mr. Candery and my mother talk about the future in despairing tones. I think that was when I first began to wonder about something that took me years to really acknowledge, a hope that I had never confronted in myself until the rock's pressure had nearly wrung it out of me.

I'd always believed my blue eyes came from my father; Mother had told me they did. Now I looked at Mr. Candery, standing on the threshold of some secret he swore only my family should be privy to, and I understood what the secret in his own blue-flecked eyes had been.

Mr. Candery had loved my mother so.

I started to shake, whether with hope or fear, I didn't know. I looked down at my own hands as if suddenly I would see traces of blue freckles.

Instead I saw Caro's hand clutch mine.

"She is my family," I said, looking back up at Mr. Candery. "Any secret of mine is safe in her keeping."

It took less time than I thought it would for him to nod and step back. "All right, Nicolette. Perhaps it's best, after all."

He knocked thrice on the door in quick succession. It opened with another ratcheting sound. He gave a short, brusque bow to whomever waited for us there.

I took a cautious step inside, and Caro followed me.

The room was mostly dark. The only light came from a large brick fireplace, once again surprisingly domestic — Estinger domestic — in its design.

There were a few spindly chairs around the fireplace, and in one of them a woman was sitting. She wore a slightly old-fashioned but distinctly Estinger style of dress made of pale muslin. A faint sinnum smell — ombrossus? — reached my nose.

A clockwork butterfly flitted out of a corner and alighted

on my wrist. I recognized it with a start as one of my own buzzers. My heart beat faster as I watched the rest of them flock to Caro and me, landing softly and pressing against us with little purring sounds.

"What on earth are you doing here?" I whispered. I was glad to see them, but their sudden appearance scared me. What else was waiting in this room?

I heard the door close behind us, and the woman turned in her chair. The fire illuminated one side of her face.

It was a face I'd know anywhere, the first face I had ever known. The face of my mother.

I T took me the space of several seconds, all of them ticked out in the beat of a loud clock somewhere in the room, to even register the shock I felt.

My mother. My mother, dead these eight years. My mother, the engineer and the architect of my entire life.

My mother, who'd left. She'd left me to my father, and thus to the Steps and all the misery and abuse I'd known under their so-called care. My mother, who had left a whole world of grief when she died. A world of grief I'd moved through ever since and never thought I would leave.

My mother, who was right in front of my eyes now. Who had never died at all.

I hated her more in that moment than when I'd railed against her for getting sick and dying when I was so young, when I'd thought I couldn't survive without her — when I'd nearly been right.

At the same time I was so relieved, so grateful, as if my

world had suddenly been put back on its axis again after spinning out of control through the void for all this time, for all those grief-filled years.

"Hello, darling," she said.

I took a step back. Her voice hurt more than anything.

Caro stepped back too. "Maybe I shouldn't be here," she said. "Maybe Mr. Candery was right. Nick?"

"I . . ." I wanted Caro to stay, and I wanted her to go. Both of those wants were so dwarfed by my shock that I could barely understand either of them.

Caro must have known this was my mother; the shadowed face by the fire was thinner and more sharply angled than mine, with darker eyes, but still nearly a mirror image. And Caro was so intuitive; she'd felt my reaction perhaps even before I did.

"I'll stay," she said quietly, and I knew when she said it that it was what I wanted.

But that was the last feeling I was sure of, because too many of them were filling me up at once. I was no longer in shock, and I wasn't numb; I felt all the rage and betrayal and happiness and hope and fear and longing tearing from my heart through every single vessel, throbbing into my feathery burns.

I nearly wished I could be numb instead.

I searched for something to say, a question to ask, an admonishment, a curse word strong enough. I had nothing.

"I am so proud of you, my darling girl," my mother said.

I'd heard that voice from the womb; it was stitched into my bones.

I shuddered and began to weep, and then I lunged forward into my mother's arms.

I felt the buzzers crawling over us, clicking and whirring contentedly, as if all they wanted was to see us together. My mother embraced me and rocked slowly back and forth, soothing me the same way she'd done when I was small. Her arms were hard and warm. "My darling girl. My little genius, my Nicolette. I'm here, I'm here. It's all right now."

I resented the words even as I drank them in. My rage and relief were both so strong that neither could win over the other.

But my tears eventually dried. I felt their sting in the burns on my face, a healing kind of pain. And there was a question rising on my lips that had to be asked.

"Why did you leave me?"

I felt her flinch, and my anger relished it.

"I needed to leave," she said.

I shook my head. I couldn't bear to look into her face and kept my own buried against her rigid shoulder. "I'm your daughter," I said. "I'm your daughter. You needed to stay with me."

"You were half-grown," she said quickly, and I was sure she'd been telling herself that for years. Her voice was sterner now, Nicolette's-been-naughty stern. "You could look after yourself, and you did. You've done so well, the most famous inventor in Esting, and known to be a woman! I only dreamed of such a thing. Although . . ." She shifted in her seat.

I waited out her hesitation as long as I could. When I finally opened my lips to ask her what she wanted to say, though, my voice had run away from me.

"Although?" I heard Caro speak for me. I looked back; she'd settled into one of the other chairs, but she was leaning forward, her face tense.

"Leave," my mother snapped, as imperious as any queen. "This is a matter for family."

A wheel turned inside me, love and longing submerged under righteous anger. I pulled back and would have leaped away, but her strong, hard arms held me fast.

"Caro stays," I said, hating the remnants of tears in my voice. "She's more family to me than—" I couldn't finish my sentence.

My mother straightened in her chair. Her eyes flashed cold as steel. "You have no idea what you're talking about," she said.

I fought to recoil from her then, really fought, but she was far too strong. "I didn't—didn't—how could you have . . ."

I felt a rush of blood through my head as my heart sped up. There was something else I was starting to understand.

The strength of my mother's embrace, the cold in her eyes. The overwhelming scent of ombrossus.

My mother, the great inventor, the maker of Jules, of the

buzzers, of any mechanical body she pleased. She had died, had been dying . . . her own body had begun to fail her.

She needed to leave, she said.

I understood before I drew my next breath. How she'd built herself this new body to save her own life even as she ruined mine, how she must have smuggled herself to Faerie, and Mr. Candery had covered her tracks, had stayed behind to tie up the loose threads in my upbringing before he in turn was forced to leave. How there would be a little box of Ashes set into the back of my mother's clockwork head, Ashes like the ones I'd used to animate Jules and all the buzzers. Ashes that no one had ever been willing to explain to me, or even to speak of, so taboo was their origin. So cursed.

I wanted to ask her how, why; wanted to scream at her and at all the world around me. But in my panic I had finally struggled free of her arms, and then a stronger instinct than all the others took over: the instinct to run.

I ran past Caro and out into the hallway, and the Fey guard grabbed for me but I heard my mother call, "Let her go."

Let me go, as she had done. Let me go.

But Mr. Candery followed, and in my weakened state it wasn't long before he caught up. I sobbed and struggled against him. "Where's Jules?" I said. "I know you have him. Take me to my horse."

He nodded.

Mr. Candery brought me back to that sunny courtyard,

and there was my Jules, living and moving, his furnace running hot on fresh fuel again.

Once I saw him, the world came right, and nothing else mattered. There was some mad, shaking strength in my exhausted limbs, and I shoved aside the Fey soldier who was reloading Jules's furnace and kicked its hatch closed as I jumped onto my horse's back.

"Run," I said harshly in a ragged ghost of a voice, and he was off. We leaped over the tall courtyard wall and rode hard through the jungle, over rough terrain and through slapping, tearing branches and thorns that rasped against my burns but still felt like nothing at all after the sickening plunge from the sky that we'd made only a day before.

I lay forward against Jules's neck as we ran together, as if we had only one body between us, and let myself lean fully against him.

"She's Ashes, Jules," I whispered, tears stinging my cheeks again. "My mother's Ashes."

I felt Jules wince and stumble, but just as quickly he regained his footing. He changed his course slightly, and then we were fighting our way through a jungle thicker than ever. If I had not been flat against his back, the long branches that whacked against us would have knocked me off in a moment.

I watched the dark green blur speed past me as Jules galloped, faster and faster . . . breathtakingly fast, unsettlingly fast, faster than I'd designed his legs to run. I heard steam hissing underneath me, pistons clattering as they pumped too hard, gears starting to crackle and grind as they whirred on and on, so brutally, inexorably fast.

"Jules," I said. "Jules, slow down."

But for the first time in all his life, he didn't listen.

"Jules, stop!" I cried. And then, as if I were speaking to any horse at all: "Whoa!"

He ran faster. He rampaged on through the jungle, and I didn't dare to lift myself from his neck to see where we were going. I felt the heat of his body rising the way it had done when we were fleeing the storm. I instinctively recoiled to protect my burned skin, but then I forced myself to hold on.

"Jules, please, please stop," I whispered. I clutched him with all the strength I had left and fought the temptation to squinch my eyes shut.

We rode on and on. I started to wonder how long the Fey soldiers' fuel would last.

I wondered how long their coal lasted in my mother. I wondered how she'd chosen her own design.

Heartsickness grew inside me like a cancer, and I abandoned all thought except my determination to keep hold of my runaway horse.

Eventually the green streaks around us grew paler, sparser, and I no longer felt branches whipping at me. Jules slowed and stopped. I carefully raised my head an inch or two and looked around.

We stood at the edge of a small clearing, a hollowed-out bowl of open space with jungle rising all around. The grass was pale green and looked as smooth as water, and a stream ran down one side of the meadow to collect in a pool at its center.

It should have been a lovely spot, but the air smelled acrid and wrong. There was a frightening silence around us, as if an invisible glass bell had settled over the place, sealing it away like a specimen. The sky directly overhead was wrong too, dark like the pupil of an eye. Faraway blue sky at the horizon ringed a stagnant, unmoving storm cloud. It was the too-flat shadow of the storm cloud that gave the lovely little clearing its feeling of ominous gloom.

Jules was heaving and panting like a flesh horse now, smoke and steam pouring from his mouth and nostrils and even his ears.

"You've hurt yourself, Jules," I whispered. Any anger I might have felt at his running away disappeared as soon as I started to worry that he was injured. I dismounted, ignoring the fierce trembling in my legs, and slowly examined his hooves, his hocks, his belly and head. He had strained every mechanism nearly to the breaking point, but there didn't seem to be any new damage beyond what he had sustained during our fall from the *Imperator*.

Besides, I knew now that I could repair him. If my mother kept herself in working order in Faerie, she would certainly have more than enough equipment for me to do the same for Jules.

It was strange, a kind of strange that felt like a sickness, to realize I'd accepted the idea of my mother as an automaton so quickly. Actually, I hadn't accepted it — but I understood it. I didn't rebel against the idea as I thought I should — how could I? Hadn't I been building my own living automatons for almost two years? Hadn't I joyfully accepted every automaton she'd left me?

I could understand, even, why she had done it. If I'd known I was dying and seen a way to save myself through my own invention . . .

I could imagine making the choice she had made, just barely.

But I couldn't imagine, couldn't understand, why she had let me believe she was dead. Why she had left me to endure all I had endured.

Jules had halted just before the edge of the clearing, so we still stood in the natural shadows of Fey trees and bushes rather than the distinctly unnatural, stagnant, greasy shadow of the storm cloud. He nosed my shoulders and neck, checking me for injuries as I examined him.

Then his head snapped up and he became perfectly still, a steel and copper statue.

"See," he hissed through a closed mouth, one syllable that sounded even more pained than his voice usually did.

I was crouched under his shoulder, checking a front hoof. I looked up and froze as completely as my horse had done.

There was a man walking into the clearing.

Not a Fey but an Estinger man in rough military dress,

field gear. He stalked into the center of the meadow, looking methodically from side to side, his steps practiced and utterly silent. Finally he gave a short, punctuated whistle, and several more Estinger soldiers walked into the clearing behind him. Two of them carried an unmoving man on a white cotton stretcher stained with blood.

They followed the first man toward the opposite side of the clearing from where Jules and I were hidden, just beyond the clear little pool that reflected only the greasy darkness of the storm cloud.

The soldiers who weren't holding the stretcher positioned themselves in a circle and bent to lift something that I couldn't quite see. It was flat, dark, and obviously heavy. Though they were too far away for me to be certain, I thought they looked frightened; they moved quickly, even frantically back from the dark, heavy disk they held.

A bright light shot out from where they pulled the disk away, a flame spurting into the sky like the water geysers in Nordsk that I'd read about as a child.

From the shadows of the jungle came one more soldier, this one leading a limping mare with a long gash in her flank. I looked with pity on the horse, pity that was easier to feel for the animal than for the dead man on the stretcher, whom I could hardly bear to look at. I shivered with hatred for the war and the soldiers and even for myself, that I couldn't feel what I thought I should.

I leaned closer to Jules, keeping my hand on his front foot, a contact point.

The men dragged the disk farther away, and I watched the geyser flicker and settle down from its first surge into the sky. Now it looked more like a fountain, an even, flowing fire, shooting up from the ground and fluttering in lovely patterns. It was beautiful, but within moments the acrid smell in the air increased tenfold, growing so strong that I almost gagged on it.

Wet-looking smoke rose lazily, too slowly, from the top of the plume, slithering up to join the storm cloud in the sky above us.

I covered my mouth with my arm to try to keep out the smell, but it had already soaked into the loose fabric. After a moment I took my arm away again.

The soldiers had set down that heavy disk, which seemed to be made of some kind of stone and had steel handles at its edges. The man who'd whistled the all-clear earlier now nodded, and then the soldiers with the stretcher stepped forward.

I'd thought the man they carried was dead, but as the soldiers advanced toward the flame, he began to groan, and then to weep.

"Ah, Lord," he moaned in a distinct Esting City accent. "Ah, Lord."

They brought the stretcher to the geyser, and then they

placed it in the center of the flame. The fire widened, consuming the man's body in one big, hungry bite.

He screamed, a sound that echoed around the shallow bowl of the clearing. I think I will always hear that sound echoing somewhere in the darkest and most frightened parts of my mind.

He didn't scream for long.

The smoke darkened until it looked almost slimy. The acrid air changed slightly, mixing with the smell of burning meat.

My stomach shuddered and lurched, and I brought my arm back to my mouth, resisting the urge to vomit. I knew that any sudden movement would reveal our presence to the soldiers.

Eventually the smoke lightened, both in color and weight, flickering upward like moth's wings. I couldn't see the outline of the man's twisted body in the fire anymore; it had narrowed to one slim geyser again.

I had been so consumed by staring at the fire that I hadn't noticed what the soldiers were doing. One of them had put on a bulky dark suit, leather of some kind, covered all over with chain mail. He held two long-handled iron instruments in his hands: a pan and a brush.

He gathered a small pile of ashes—Ashes!—from the center of the flame into the pan, then tipped it into a waiting box on the ground, slowly and with infinite care, so that even from a distance I could tell that he didn't spill a single tiny grain.

Just before he covered the box, a transparent, ghostly shape seemed to reach out of it, straining into the air.

He snapped the lid shut over the grasping hand.

From the side of the clearing, another soldier began to lead the horse forward.

I couldn't bear to look anymore. I rose and pulled myself onto Jules's back. The injured mare balked, but they led her closer, closer to the fire . . .

Jules stood his ground, staring into the clearing. Tears covered my face as I clutched the handles on his shoulders. I wanted more than anything to ask him to leave, run, not make us witness any more.

But I knew why he had taken me there. I knew he had more right to decide what we saw, and when we left, than I did.

I knew it had already happened to him.

Jules called to the horse in the clearing, one low, sweet neigh; the language of horses, his own tones that I knew so well. Sympathy, solidarity. Mourning and love.

The injured horse's head flung upward. She called back, a high whinny that seemed to hold both despair and gratitude. Jules had told her that she wouldn't burn alone, or unmourned.

The men in the clearing snapped their heads toward

Jules's call, but he had already turned, was already running, taking us away again.

The soldiers had been prepared for defense, not pursuit; they'd been looking for invaders. None of them rode horses, and the doomed mare was far too injured to give chase.

Still, my heart did not stop drumming with fear for a good ten minutes.

Jules did not falter once as he ran through the thick jungle. The landscape wasn't quite as dense on our return route as it had been on our rampage toward the meadow, and I was able to keep my head up. A good thing, too, because he was so overheated I could hardly bear to hold on to him.

The thought made me relax my grip; he was still running fast, but he wasn't careening with wild, dangerous speed, and I knew he wouldn't make any sudden, unpredictable jerks or jumps that might unseat me. I forced myself to breathe deeply and slow down my heart.

Jules slowed slightly too, into a smooth canter.

"Are we going back to the barracks, Jules?" I asked, truly unsure of the answer but willing to go wherever he wanted to take me. I thought I'd known heartbreak before, but the way I hurt now, understanding that Jules had endured so much pain . . . I would do anything he wanted me to do, forever. My heart broke over his pain like water over a stone, changing nothing.

But he nodded, and it's true that I was relieved. At least I would see Caro again, and maybe Fin as well. I hoped the Fey weren't treating him too badly.

Jules slowed to a trot and then a walk, and then he stopped completely. I looked around us for an entrance to the barracks, or even that terrible squeezing rock, but I could see only jungle.

"Get down," Jules rumbled.

I silently obeyed and walked around to stand in front of him. I placed my hands as gently and delicately as I could on either side of the wide, hot planes of his cheeks.

"It happened to you, too," I said.

He nodded. I saw something new in the glass eyes I'd crafted for him, some of the sad depth that shone in the dark eyes of flesh-and-blood horses. "Oh, Jules," I whispered, "I'm so sorry."

He tucked his long steel chin against my back, embracing me in his way. I felt him give one heavy shudder, and then he was still.

We stood like that for a long time; I was unwilling to let him go in spite of his heat against my burns. Gradually his overheated systems cooled, and I could see the glow in his furnace growing dimmer by slow degrees.

"We ought to get you back," I said, "or you'll run out of fuel."

I felt Jules nod. I slipped around and remounted him, and he walked us quietly back through the jungle.

Again and again as we walked, I thought I saw . . . a glimmering shadow, just geometric enough to suggest walls, a short turret . . . but I would never have seen the Fey barracks if I'd gone past them on my own. Even with Jules leading me, it was difficult to make out anything beyond the huge trees tangled into a single mass with centuries of creeping vines and hanging moss.

Jules marched me right up to an arched door that I didn't notice until two Fey soldiers opened it and walked out. Even they were hard to see—not invisible, but somehow my eyes didn't want to look at them and didn't want to focus in the few moments when I did.

They seemed to recognize me, though, or at least they did not try to accost me the way the Fey soldiers had that morning. Instead, they simply circled around behind us.

Jules walked decorously through the barely visible archway. As soon as we were inside the courtyard, I could see it clearly. I saw the guards clearly as well when they walked up to flank us again. One of them even held out a hand to help me dismount, and I thanked fer before refusing and slipping down on my own.

I opened the hatch to Jules's furnace; he was nearly empty.

"We can fetch more coal if need be," one Fey guard said, frosty, but civil enough. I supposed news had spread that my story was true. I wondered if looking like my automaton mother helped my case or hindered it.

"Please do," I said, then felt Jules nose my shoulder.

"Sleep," he rumbled.

I wanted to cry again, but I controlled myself. "Is there a place nearby where my horse can safely rest?"

The guard nodded curtly. "We've prepared one." Fe spoke grudgingly, as if they had only done so on orders.

I followed fer into a stable, where there were several other horses, all living, none of my mother's creations. No Ashes.

Again I felt the urge to be sick, and again I forced it down.

The guard brought Jules and me to a stall near the back and, after a suspicious glare, left us alone.

Jules's pace had slowed almost to a limp as we'd walked toward the stables. He settled himself down, folding his legs under his body and resting his head on the green, salty-smelling sawdust on the floor.

"Thank you for showing me, Jules," I said, kneeling by his side. "I needed to know." I wanted to say, *I'm so sorry that happened to you,* but the words didn't seem strong enough.

Jules didn't even nod, so little fuel had he left; he just looked up at me with his quiet glass eyes.

I stroked the three spirals between his shoulders that would let him sleep. He wound down to stillness.

I stayed kneeling there for a minute, and then for another, not willing to take my hand away.

Eventually I heard a tactful cough and looked up to see the guard at the stable's half door.

"Sergeant Candery requests your presence," fe said, as if fe wished it weren't true.

I got up, then gave a long look back at my sleeping horse.

"We keep someone posted at both entrances," the soldier said with a little more sympathy in fer voice. "Your horse will be quite safe."

The image of the injured mare flashed in my mind, and it took me horrid long moments to force the memory away. When I came back to the present, I nodded at the guard and followed fer out of the stable, securing Jules's door behind me.

It was strange to hear someone refer to my gentle old housekeeper as "Sergeant" with such deference, and it crystallized for me all the ways in which Mr. Candery had changed. But then I supposed that of the two of us, I had changed the more. I had been a little girl when he left, frightened and lost in a fog of mourning too overwhelming to begin to understand.

Now I was a young woman with my own business and

with people I loved around me. Mr. Candery had grown so fierce, so strong, but I had grown fiercer and stronger yet.

I wanted to believe that we would still be friends, our new versions of ourselves.

Mr. Candery leaned over a table covered with maps and letters. Beside him was a blue glass pot of tea: clary-bush. I inhaled the scent hungrily.

He looked up at me with a soft smile and poured the tea into delicate cups. "Two sugars still?" he asked.

"Just one." I stayed by the door, not quite willing to step forward. I wasn't sure why Mr. Candery remembering how I took my tea should make me angry, but it did.

He used tiny tongs to lift a single rough sugar cube from a china bowl painted with flowery vines that writhed away from his movements. He dropped the sugar into the clear tea and stirred it with a silver spoon, all with such practiced elegance that neither the spoon, nor the cup, nor the sugar made the slightest splash or clink.

I used to love watching Mr. Candery prepare tea.

He picked up the cup and held it out to me. When I didn't move, he walked around the desk. He lifted one of my hands and wrapped it around the cup, ever so gently. I didn't resist, and when he let my hand go I took a sip.

The clary-bush tasted wonderful, floral and sharp, and true to its name, it started clearing my mind immediately. I breathed in the steam, trying as I often did to give myself the gift of one moment of calm just before I plunged into a task I knew I didn't want to do. The tea cleared my head enough that I could see why I was angry now, each reason as distinct as a china vase I was ready to smash.

For each vase, I had to ask Mr. Candery a question.

I let out my breath and began.

"Why did you leave me?" *Smash.*

I saw the sudden pain in his eyes. "I had to leave, Nicolette. All the part-Fey had to leave, at least the . . . the ones like me. Look at my face." He brushed a blue-freckled hand across his even more heavily blue-freckled cheekbones. "I couldn't have stayed."

"You had ombrossus. Or you could have painted your face." I hadn't thought of either option until just before I voiced them, but they seemed so simple and obvious to me now that my anger only grew.

Crack. Smash.

"Ah." Mr. Candery began to look a little angry too. "As I imagine you've learned by now, Nicolette, if you've a sharp mind you can break the ombrossus spell once you know how to look for it. No one familiar with the oil — none of the royal brigade sent out to round up the part-Fey — would be fooled for long."

I remembered how I'd recognized that spicy scent when I confronted the automaton Fin, how once I did, the illusion of his wholeness had unraveled. How my mother had . . .

I nodded.

"And cosmetics . . ." He frowned. "Hardly reliable, and even if they were, I didn't want to hide my face. I didn't want to hide at all." He glanced from his teacup into my eyes, his gaze steady. "I saw what was coming for people like me, and I knew I had to do what I could to keep it from happening. The rebellion, it's *necessary*. You can understand that, can't you?"

I nodded, looking down at the floor. Not wanting to hide was something I understood all too well, and I was starting to feel ashamed of my questions, of my demands. I felt selfish and childish. But that shame made me angrier, too, made me want to line up more fragile things to break.

"And your mother was in Faerie, you know," he said. "It was so hard to smuggle her out, sick as she was, and harder still not to stay by her side. I wanted — oh, I know I should only have wanted to come here to fight for our freedom, but . . . I have always loved your mother, Nicolette. Surely you know that by now."

I was close to crying, or to screaming. I remembered it all, those whispered conversations late at night, the sad longing in Mr. Candery's voice when he murmured news to my mother that my Faerie-hating father refused to hear.

I hadn't understood that longing when I heard it as a child. I understood it now.

"Mr. Candery . . ." My chin trembled, and I raised my cup and took another swallow of tea to hide it. The hot drink gave me strength. "Mr. Candery, are you my father?"

Crash, crash, crash.

With a quick uncontrolled motion, he set his cup down on the table and flew to me, gathered me in his long slender arms, and buried his face in my hair.

I stood stiff as a poker in his embrace, waiting.

"I wish I were, Nicolette," he said. "You don't know how many times I've wished I were."

My arms went around him then too, and in spite of all the anger smashing its way through fragile places inside of me, I hugged him back, for the sake of every single time I had wished the same thing.

He led me to a small couch by the wall, and we sat together. He held both my hands in his as he spoke.

"The one thing I want you to understand, more than any other, is that your mother thought you were safe when she left you," he said. "I was there, and your father was too. She didn't love your father anymore, and she didn't respect his beliefs . . . but she thought that he could provide for you, and I could do enough to help you keep learning her trade. We'd both left more in that house for you than you knew, than you probably know even now." Mr. Candery squeezed my hands. "She left you safe, which is more than I can say myself. I didn't know your stepmother would treat you quite so badly as — as the stories I've heard suggested she did." Tears began to well up in his eyes. "But I knew she was not kindhearted." He shook his head. "Still, Nicolette, I thought you would be safer in your mother's house, with your mother's machines and my spells to protect and help you, than you would . . . anywhere else. I had to leave Esting, had to come to Faerie, and there was only hardship waiting here for me."

My imagination flooded with scenes from a whole other life I might have had if Mr. Candery had decided to bring me to my mother in Faerie when I was twelve years old. Announcing that he was taking an Estinger child to quarantined Faerie wouldn't have been an option, of course—he would have had to smuggle both of us out, booked us illegal passage on one of the few Nordsk trade ships that still ran to Faerie back then.

I would have grown up here, with the Fey and Mr. Candery and my mother, my automaton mother. I would have learned so much from her; I would have been a far greater inventor by now, and I would have had two people to love me and look after me all through the adolescent years that had in my reality been so cold and lonely.

True, I would not have made my own way as an inventor, would not have proved to myself that I could. I wouldn't have met Fin or Caro either; my heart couldn't comprehend that loss.

And Jules . . . Jules would have slept away in his little box in Mother's workshop forever, and all the buzzers too. I would never have known him, his help and kindness and steadfast love.

Jules, Fin, Caro, the self I had fought to become.

I didn't want to break things anymore.

I moved my hands so that they were on top of Mr.

Candery's. "I know you couldn't take me to Faerie," I said, "and I . . . I have a good life in Esting now. A life of my own, and friends that I love."

"And a kingdom to rule, Heiress," he said, a little wryness showing through his gentility. "I must admit I'm glad you don't list that first among your blessings, though."

I shook my head. "I'm not going to be Queen. Fin and I are — well, we're not getting married. We're just telling people that story, while we can use it for good. The way we used it to come here, to you. To Faerie."

He didn't even raise his eyebrows. "The way I used it to bring you both here," he said.

"You knew?" I whispered.

He nodded slowly. "Never think we didn't try to watch over you," he said. "We left you little helpmeets, too, as best we could. I know we failed in so many ways, Nicolette, but we did try. I beg —" he cut himself off.

I knew my mother had had her ways of watching me, these past eight years. I was sure Mr. Candery had helped her with them. But sitting there now, knowing that they both had seen the pain and loneliness I'd gone through . . .

I closed my eyes for a moment, forcing myself to think of other things. To think of why I was here, and what I really wanted to say right now. *Trustworthy. I beg your forgiveness.*

"You did leave a lot in Lampton that helped me," I said. "You and . . . Mother too."

It was harder to forgive her. When I remembered the

Estinger soldier's screams at the geyser, the terrified mare, I thought it might be impossible. Everything I felt about my mother threatened to rise up and drown me again . . . but I held Mr. Candery's hands and kept myself there, in that little room, in that little time, only with him. I could understand Mr. Candery right then, and that was enough.

"I can't thank you, exactly," I said, "but I think I understand. Some of it, at least."

We shared one more soft embrace, and then we finished our tea.

In place of my anger at Mr. Candery, there bloomed a curiosity more than tinged with frustration. "I wish you could have told me more in your letter," I said. "If I'd known my mother was here . . ."

"I could write nothing that might be used against any of us," Mr. Candery replied. "Your mother has been a great help to our forces in understanding and fighting back against the technology that Esting has used to dominate us. Without her . . ." He shook his head. "The war might have ended long ago, and none of us would be left even to tell stories about it."

I froze.

How long had we been in Faerie—a day? Two days? How long had we slept, that first eerie night in the jungle? The stories I'd heard about time passing differently here than it did in Esting had always seemed like xenophobic drivel, and yet . . . So many things were different here. Could Fitz have finished building his army?

"Mr. Candery," I said, "there is something terrible that I have to tell you. Something about Esting. They're—"

I stopped myself. I wished I could trust him again as completely as I had when I was a child, but we had both changed so much . . . Oh, I had said I understood, but understanding was not the same as trust.

"Fin knows the most about it," I said. "The Heir. We need to have a conference with you and with the Fey leader; we need to have the diplomatic meeting you wrote of. Then he and I both can tell you."

Mr. Candery shook his head. "I can get you back to your other friend, that Miss Caroline," he said, "but I'm afraid it's impossible to take Fin out of seclusion just now. Your arrival was so . . . complicated . . . that my superiors require time to make sure that the Heir is honest in his intentions with us."

I pulled back, sitting up straight on the couch. I tried to make my eyes flash in the righteous way a real Heiress's might. "I can promise you that Fin is honest," I said. "If you can't trust me, Mr. Candery, after all this—after what . . . well, then I don't even know why I came here." My voice stayed steady and imperious, at least.

"Of course I trust you, Nicolette, of course I do," he said. "And for your sake I trust your friends as well. But we are an army, and I am a sergeant, not such a very high rank at all. I was permitted to invite you and your fiancé here because of our previous connection, but I am certainly not permitted to try to convince my superiors of anything. Least of all could *I* convince them to trust such a potentially dangerous person as the Heir of Esting."

I stood up. "I used to think you were so wonderful," I said. "I used to think you could do anything, and Mother even more so. Now I—" I couldn't tell Mr. Candery that I knew how the Ashes were made, I realized, not then. "You can't even help me see my friend."

"Nicolette, you're a grown woman. You must see how—" Mr. Candery stood too. "Nicolette, neither your mother nor I are so wonderful as you once believed! I am not by any means all-powerful, and she . . ." He stopped. Even now he couldn't say anything against her.

I felt as if I were pounding helplessly against an unbreakable wall with Fin in danger on the other side. But as I always did, I reminded myself of all the other times I had felt helpless and how things had never been as dire as I'd thought they were. When Mother died and Mr. Candery left, when the Steps destroyed my workshop, when I thought that Fin and Caro were in love with each other and the only way I'd known to make a family was lost to me . . .

Every time, I had triumphed. I had found something in myself that let me get over that wall.

When I spoke again, my voice was as steely and strong as anything I'd ever built. "If you cannot convince your superiors to trust Fin, perhaps I can," I said. "If they wanted a conference with the Heir, they must accept one with the Heiress. Take me to them now."

I STARTED to wonder if I had done absolutely everything wrong. At least back home in Esting I had some concept of worst-case scenarios; here I had none. I couldn't even imagine the worst that could happen to me in Faerie.

I wished I'd thought of that before . . . before what? I didn't know. Before I'd boarded the airship? Told Fin about Mr. Candery's letter?

The halls Mr. Candery and I wound through seemed to have no logic at all, no sense of geometric order. I tried to picture the layout of the Fey barracks but only became more confused. I thought it must be more like a beehive than a building. I remembered the first explorers' description of the Fey capital as a honeycomb of interconnected small spaces, but even that would surely have clearer pathways, more straight lines.

Mr. Candery ushered me into another room. He was supposed to be taking me to his superiors, and I'd expected something grand, a long reception hall, perhaps, or a war room. But this office was even smaller than the last one.

Mr. Candery settled into a chair and looked at the floor, frowning. His expression was both sad and kind. I watched him for a moment, willing him to look up at me, but he wouldn't.

I forced myself to ignore the tight new knot in my stomach so that I could examine my surroundings.

The desk was small but ornate, and the chairs around it were carved from chalky, faintly translucent stone. A shade blossom floated in a shallow glass bowl on the desktop, slipping and twirling on the surface in some sourceless current.

The walls were covered in floral wallpaper like we used to have at home, before Mother died and Father'd had it painted over, with flowers that moved against their butter-yellow background, drifting in a breeze that wasn't there. They were large, blowzy pink blossoms with dense multitudes of fringed petals, and I found it hard to draw my eyes away from their delicate, shivering movements . . .

I could even smell something rich and heady, as if the flowers dripped honey. I stepped forward, barely aware of the way my feet moved, or how my hands reached out to touch the blossoms, or the slight sting as my fingertips slipped through the place where the wallpaper should have been . . .

"Nicolette!"

I nearly jumped out of my skin.

The edges of my vision seemed to tremble as I pulled

myself away from the wall. I felt something sucking at my hand, but I couldn't quite focus on what it was. I couldn't quite focus on anything.

Mr. Candery was there at my side before I'd even finished turning around. He took my hand and examined it carefully, and I was startled to see a ring of tiny marks on the tip of my index finger, like a perfectly round set of little teeth.

Mr. Candery looked in my eyes for a long moment, as if he were searching for something. There was still that trembling at the edge of my vision, but it was beginning to fade. When the last wiggling corners of my sight grew still again, he nodded and let out a long breath that he seemed to have been holding.

"You're lucky," he whispered, squeezing my finger so that a few drops of dark blood beaded out. He took a handkerchief from his pocket and wiped the blood away, then repeated the process. "You need to be careful here, Nicolette."

I swallowed, trying to clear my throat, which felt as if it were filled with syrup.

"So must we all," said someone else.

This voice was quieter and gentler than Mr. Candery's had ever been, even when I was small, and yet it held a certain authority that compelled me to look up and find the speaker.

A person a little bit shorter than I, and quite a bit wider, smiled softly at me. "I am Talis," fe said, giving a brief, fluid bow.

I knew at once that Talis was the Fey ruler. It wasn't that I'd heard the name before or seen the face that smiled at me now on any royal portraits or currency. But there was a royalty about this person that even Fin didn't have, charming prince that he was. It went deeper than likability or charisma; I felt a natural trust toward fer, the same way I trusted that each morning the sun would rise.

I reminded myself that I was supposed to be royal too: the Heiress Apparent. The syrupy feeling in my throat had finally vanished, as had the stinging in my hand, and I was able to curtsy and then hold my head high as I met Talis's level, mild gaze. My mind spun through all the tactical arguments Fin and I had talked about, all the rhetorical leaps we'd make to try to persuade this leader to trust us, despite so many reasons why fe shouldn't.

I'd had only a year to observe Fin being a prince, but I'd learned a few things. For instance: If you want to make people believe in you, you must act as if you believe in yourself.

"I am Nicolette Lampton, Heiress Apparent to Esting," I said. "I am glad to meet you at last." Each time I made myself pretend to have some authority, it came more naturally—I thought even I might believe it eventually.

"And I you," Talis said. "I was curious about your mother's daughter years before I heard you were the Esting prince's betrothed." Fe smiled. "But I'm afraid I have defined you too much by those around you," fe added thoughtfully.

I blinked. I'd worried about just that for so long: that I would always be seen in relation to Fin, that no matter what I accomplished I would always be Mechanica from the stories instead of Nick the inventor.

I looked more closely at the face of the Fey ruler. Fer skin was so covered in freckles that it was almost entirely blue; the thin skin of fer lips and eyelids was blue indeed.

Talis regarded me thoughtfully, almost shyly. I felt that sense of obvious authority again as I looked into fer blue-black eyes, even though fe was so different from the military leader I'd imagined. Talis reminded me of someone, but I couldn't place who; someone else who was quiet and shy, whose kindness spoke for itself.

Wheelock. Talis was like Wheelock. I looked down at the floor, steadying myself. For a moment I felt the pitch and roll of the *Imperator*'s deck again, and remembered the way it had felt to watch from the sky as the ship crashed into the water.

"Are you all right, *lada*?" fe asked.

I looked back up.

Talis's face showed only concern; not cunning, not even curiosity. Had fe seen what was in my mind?

And fe called me *lada*. I knew the word from the Fey history books I'd read as a child. It meant something that we didn't have a word for in Esting, something between *cousin* and *loved one* that also meant "pulse" or "heartbeat." The Fey lived in groups of friends, and they bore and raised their children that way too; they might call their children or siblings or any of their parents *lada*. It was a word for someone who wasn't just family but a part of oneself.

I looked at this person who was so gentle, so concerned, and I nodded. I remembered another moment with Wheelock: when he'd declared his allegiance to Fin after we'd saved the merman. How he had shrugged off his stiff formality like a cloak and shown us who he really was.

I understood why he'd done that now.

I reached out and took Talis's hand, ignoring Mr. Candery's soft, disapproving gasp. "Please," I said. "Please take me to Fin. I promise he means you no harm."

Talis's cool, dry, callused hand squeezed mine before letting go. Fe walked around to the chair behind the desk and sat down, gesturing with fer free hand for me to sit in the chair opposite.

Fe leaned forward. "May I tell you a story, *lada*?"

I felt my jaw tightening. I just wanted to get Fin free. What was the point of a story?

I glanced at Mr. Candery. His eyes closed and he gave the briefest, shallowest nod.

I turned back to Talis and smiled, then sat in the chair fe had indicated.

Fe settled in fer own seat, pushing back fer thick gray hair.

"Many years ago in this country," fe said, "not long

after the first arrivals from your own land, there lived a poor family who wished for a child. They kept wishing, but it took a very long time for their wish to be granted, so long that the one who gave birth, the one you would call mother, had grown old and frail, and fe died in delivery. A new illness from Esting swept through the country soon after and killed all but one of the child's other parents."

I recalled the Fey's croup that had killed Mother — that I thought had killed her. Rage and grief roiled inside me as Talis continued the story quietly.

"The surviving parent, Cal, was struck blind by the illness. Fe tried fer best to look after the child, whose name was Shim, but soon they were reduced to living in the streets, begging for scraps, and no one would help them. There was a healer in the city who Shim believed could restore fer parent's sight, but the healer's price was a hundred times more than the two of them could save in a lifetime." Talis's voice had grown louder and clearer. The idea of beggars on the streets of Faerie clearly enraged fer.

I thought of little Runner back home, the girl who had slept on a shelf to avoid the rats, when she was lucky. I thought of all the other beggars in Esting City, too many to remember, far too many to name. Fin was so concerned with righting our wrongs against Faerie, but had I ever heard him speak with such passion about the injustice at home? Was there something more glamorous about fighting for justice here? What did we really seek from our journey?

"One day, an Estinger sea merchant walked through the city, speaking with every beggar he found. The Estinger had angered a sea monster, and the monster stirred up storms whenever the merchant tried to make his voyage back home. Only the sacrifice of a child would appease the monster."

I started to feel sick.

"The merchant said that anyone willing to pay the monster's price could name their reward. Shim immediately stepped forward. 'If you will pay to bring back my parent's sight,' fe said, 'I will go to the monster for you.' Cal wept and pleaded with Shim not to make that bargain, and then fe begged the merchant not to accept.

"But the merchant laughed at them both, because to him the cost was less than a week's wages, and he could not reject such an offer. He tied the child's hands and dragged fer on board the ship, even though fe would have gone of fer own free will.

"As soon as they left the port, a storm began to rise. Huge waves slammed against the merchant's ship, and inside the masses of dark water Shim could see the shining coils of a huge sea serpent.

"Shim walked calmly to the stern of the ship and stepped overboard. The ocean grew still at once, and the merchant sailed back to Esting."

"Did he pay?" The words were out of my mouth before I could tell myself not to interrupt.

Talis's dark eyebrows rose in surprise. "Pay the monster? Of course. The storm stopped at once, as I said."

"No. The merchant. Did he pay for Cal's sight to be restored?"

Talis waved a hand. "That's not the point."

But it suddenly seemed very important to me that the Estinger in the story had stuck to his bargain. I wanted to tell Talis that it did matter—I wanted to shout it at fer—but I looked at Mr. Candery again, and I made myself remember Fin, and all the danger he was in, and how it seemed I was the only person who could get him back.

I settled into my chair and kept listening.

"As Shim plunged lower and lower into the cold darkness, fe began to see white shapes moving in the depths. They were the ghosts of Shim's other parents. 'Open your mouth,' the ghosts said, and their voices crashed and rang like waves on the shore. Shim obeyed, and even though water rushed into fer mouth, fe began to breathe.

"Shim followed fer parents' ghosts to the monster's kingdom under the sea. There were many other spirits in the serpent's kingdom, and sea-people too, thousands of them, and soon Shim found a place there among new friends. But still fe missed fer living parent and the world above the waves.

"Eventually Shim grew so sad that the serpent came to speak with fer. 'I spared your life because you gave it so selflessly,' he said, 'and I will send you back home again if you wish. But it will be different for you now.'

"Even so, Shim readily agreed. The serpent sent fer back to the land in the form of a giant shade blossom."

Talis's fingertips brushed over the water in the cut-glass bowl. The little shade blossom there twirled in the ripples.

"The flower bloomed in the river that cuts through our capital city, where Shim and fer parent had once begged together. It was so large and beautiful that every day Fey and Estingers alike came to admire it and breathe its scent.

"Every night when the moon rose, Shim emerged from the flower and walked through the streets as if fe too were a ghost, searching for fer parent. But Shim didn't recognize anyone in the city anymore. And when the moon set each morning, Shim vanished inside the shade blossom again.

"But one night, Shim saw a familiar face. It was the Estinger prince who had come to Faerie searching for a bride. Though they'd never met before, they recognized each other instantly, as if from another life." Talis smiled in a way that was both fond and lonely. I wondered whether fe had any consorts here, any family. But then, most of the citizens of Faerie were Talis's parents. When I'd learned as a child about the way Fey rulers were wished into being by the whole population, I'd envied those leaders. When my own mother and father were gone I'd imagined so many times what it would be like to have myriad parents. It had never occurred to me that it could be lonely.

"At moonset Shim brought the prince back to the shade blossom, but it had vanished. Fe was a person again.

"The prince begged Shim to return to Esting and marry him.

"'I will go with you, and gladly,' Shim said, 'but first there is something I must do.' Shim asked the prince to help fer establish a healers' hall for the beggars. 'I must bring every beggar in the city there before I leave,' fe explained.

"In the time that Shim had spent in the sea, Estinger forces had taken over all of Faerie—colonized it, you would say," Talis added drily. "It was easy for the prince to command every beggar in the city to appear at the healers' hall he and Shim established. Shim met each and every one of them, spoke to them, and made sure their ailments were treated and that each was fed and clothed. But not until fe met the very last of them did fe find Cal.

"Shim held fer parent's hand, weeping. 'It's me, *lada*,' fe said. 'I've come back.'

"'Shim is dead,' Cal said.

"'Open your eyes and look at me.'

"Shim's voice was full of so much love and conviction that Cal obeyed, and when fer eyes were opened, fe could see."

Talis leaned forward in fer chair, watching me. Watching for what? Fe said nothing. Fe barely moved.

I had tried hard to pay attention to every part of the story. I was sure the moral would be obvious at the end, like the morals in the stories that we called Faerie tales back home. I'd thought Talis might even say it directly. But now my head was full of flowers and serpents and blind parents and moon-sets—just images, and no morals at all.

"I'm sorry," I said finally. "What exactly was the point of that story?"

Talis looked behind me. "Open your eyes, Heiress," fe said.

I spun around, and there was Fin.

Haggard, thin-faced, bruised under his right eye and clutching his old bullet wound with his good arm as if it freshly pained him, but standing before me.

I sprang from my seat. With all of his injuries I couldn't embrace him; I could only lean my cheek against his. I laughed and trembled, and in spite of Talis's edict I closed my eyes as I brushed my forehead against the few days' stubble on Fin's jaw.

He leaned against me too, warm and solid.

When I opened my eyes again, I saw Mr. Candery watching us, smiling with a little bit of bemusement.

"Are you sure you're not getting married?" he asked.

Fin raised his eyebrows at me.

I glanced back at Talis, who was still seated at fer desk and watching me mildly—watching me more than Fin, which I thought was strange. But who knew how much time they'd already had to talk together.

"I never said I didn't love him," I told Mr. Candery carefully.

Fin tutted. "Well, I'm in love with her, sir, and with

Caroline Hart as well. And I don't think Nick could say anything different herself."

I grinned and found myself blushing when Mr. Candery's gaze wouldn't stop moving from one to the other of us.

Finally Talis stood. "Anyone in Faerie would call you a family," fe said. "I can see that much myself."

Fin smiled at Talis, and it wasn't just his charming-prince smile; it was warm and familiar. Had they already gotten to know each other? Had it been foolish of me to be so afraid for Fin's safety?

No. I was relieved he was near me again, and I'd stay with him now as long as I could. I'd come here vowing to keep him safe; Caro and I both had.

Mr. Candery nodded again. "I suppose I must find a way to round up this beloved Miss Hart as well," he said, as if he knew my thoughts. He cleared his throat, covering his mouth with his fist. "She might be harder to extricate than the charming prince."

My heart leaped in fear and anger.

"Where's Caro?" Fin snapped, suddenly all business.

Mr. Candery held up two open palms. "She's with your mother, Nicolette. Margot is introducing her to the healers in the nearest halls."

Fin stiffened. "Your mother?" he whispered, staring at me.

"She's here," I said. "She's . . . it's complicated."

I couldn't spare the energy to explain everything to Fin

just then. I was fixated on Caro, Caro with my mother; this felt like a greater betrayal than Mr. Candery's. Caro's own mother had nearly died of Fey's croup; she'd grown up with the motherless Fin. Did she not understand what my mother had done to me?

"Shall I take you to her?" Mr. Candery asked. "Or would you like me to bring her here, if I can persuade her?"

I recoiled at the possibility of seeing my mother again so soon.

"Not yet," I said. "There is still something I must discuss with Talis, as — as Heiress." The ruler's gentility and kindness, and the unexpected, confusing power of fer story, had lured me out of the cloak of authority I'd placed around myself. I pulled it back again. "We must tell fer now, Fin," I said. "The Estinger army —"

Talis stopped me with a raised hand. "These things will unfold in their own time," fe said. "That's the right way. Can't you see?"

Even Fin, next to me, nodded in agreement.

I wrapped the cloak up tight around me. "No, *you* don't see," I said. "You might as well be blind too, like the beggar in your story! It would be wonderful to think that — that we could give things their own time, that we could tell each other stories and weave some kind of . . . some kind of natural peace, but we can't. *You* can't. Talis, there is an automaton army coming to Faerie."

There — the words were out. Everything in the room

seemed to turn toward me, as if I were the hub of some great wheel, the rim of which I couldn't even see. Sergeant, prince, and ruler, all waiting and listening.

"I've seen the automatons. I believe they are nearly ready to sail, and I don't know how much time we have left. Whatever peace we can make together, or whatever war we can fight, we must start now."

The negotiations with Talis went on for hours, and in that time I came to respect and admire Fin in ways I'd never had the chance to before. He was so self-possessed in the face of such authority, and with breathtakingly lethal stakes at hand. He argued his case with eloquence and yet listened so humbly and open-mindedly to what Talis and fer advisors said that I began to hope we might make our peace with Faerie after all.

I came to admire Talis, too. The Fey leader was a ready match for both Fin's intellect and his rhetoric, and fer casual, forthright way of speaking made me utterly convinced of fer honesty. Talis showed me the same respect fe had for my mother, something it became more and more evident most of the Fey did not share. Now that I knew about the origins of the Ashes, I could hardly blame them. In fact, the huge scope of Talis's empathy astonished me. Even fer wish to spare the lives of Estinger soldiers was clearly sincere.

"But that's just it," Fin said. "Esting's soldiers are machines now. There are enough of them to wipe out not just your army, but all of your people, and without a single Estinger life being lost."

"How do they move? Are they only clockwork?" asked one of Talis's advisors, a slight, elderly soldier with several heavy medals pinned to fer uniform.

"Ashes," I said.

The advisors collectively hissed in their breath. "Ghost soldiers," Talis whispered.

Fin glanced at me sharply. "You didn't tell me Fitz used Ashes," he said.

I thought of the fire in the clearing, of the screaming soldier. I knew if I told him about that day it would break him.

"I . . . I wasn't sure when I saw them," I said, which was the truth.

"But you're sure now?" Talis pressed fer hands against the desk, watching me carefully.

I looked right into fer eyes. "I'm sure."

Fe sighed and looked down, then scanned the roomful of waiting advisors. "We abhor them," fe said to me. "We forbade their use long ago, and your mother . . ." Fe caught my pleading expression and Fin's confused frown, and fe paused. "I think you and I might be able to make our peace, Prince Christopher," fe said. "But if such an army is coming, we must prepare our own as well."

"More Ashes?" the small advisor asked, the one who'd spoken before. "None of us would stand for it, Talis, as you know well."

Fe shook fer head. "We will not make more." Fe was watching me again, and then every pair of eyes in the room turned to look at me too. I had the distinct feeling that Talis knew about all the Ashes I'd brought with me. Did fer vast empathy allow fer to sense them too?

Fe knew about the buzzers that had flocked to my mother's room; Mr. Candery must have told fer, or even my mother herself. And of course fe would know about Jules. I felt dizzy and weak as I started to understand, to realize just what Talis was asking of me, of us. I pictured Jules's powerful metal frame multiplied a thousandfold, and a Fey soldier riding each steel horse.

This was the price of the peace Talis would broker with Fin: my mother and I would build another mechanical army so that Faerie could fight back if the peace should fail.

FOR the next month, I barely saw Fin or Caro at all; at least not during the day. The Fey had put the three of us in one room, deep in the barracks, without question. We even shared one of the yards-wide beds designed for their large families, but we were each so busy that we didn't always share sleeping time, and when we did, we usually collapsed exhausted into bed without even speaking. Caro had fallen in love with the healers' halls, and she spent all her waking hours there, learning their trade. Fin was in meetings with Talis almost all that time, working to keep the leader's trust and broker the smaller details of the peace they both worked toward so tirelessly.

Estinger forces had already been pushed out of the capital, one of the reasons that Corsin had agreed to these negotiations in the first place. The remaining Estinger territories were isolated pockets, but they still held some crucial ground; I remembered the clearing, the fire and Ashes.

Fin insisted that we couldn't tell the Estingers we were still alive, that we were here, until negotiations were complete; it might negate the element of surprise Faerie would need if a battle proved inevitable.

"They'd call us traitors, anyway, if they knew what we were really doing here," I said to Fin one day early in the talks, in a rare moment of quiet. We were sitting by a high window in a house on the outskirts of the Fey capital; we didn't dare risk openly walking its streets, especially not Fin. But we both looked hungrily out at the winding, narrow paths and the many round turrets of gold-veined blue stone, all interconnected, vines climbing around their edges. It really was like a honeycomb, as the first explorers had described: repeating patterns of tiny structures, each one small and neat and inconspicuous by itself, building on one another into a whole that almost seemed to have a life of its own.

"But that's exactly it, Nick," Fin murmured. He placed his cup on the windowsill and ran his hands through his hair, thinking. "They say Faerie is part of Esting, that the Fey are my family's subjects . . . and then helping them, trying to keep them from dying, is treason? No. I'd be a traitor if I treated them the way my—the way so many of my family have done."

"But you don't think the Fey are your subjects," I said quietly. I understood what he was saying, and I was working toward the same goal. But ever since the first day we'd come to Faerie, my understanding of treason, of righteousness, of what was right and wrong in the first place, had grown harder and harder to parse. I didn't think I knew what was right anymore; I didn't think I knew what I felt.

"I don't think they *should* be," Fin amended. "But my family, my country—our country—subjugated them long ago. Until we can right that wrong, and I think we can, Nick, I really think Talis and I are getting somewhere . . . until then, they're as much citizens of Esting as you are, and they're equally entitled to my help. Nick, working with the Fey is the *opposite* of treason." His voice was starting to shake a little, in anger or conviction or fear.

"I know, Fin," I said, pressing my hand gently to his chest. "I know." His good intention, at least, was one thing I could be sure of. And for a while, I could think of it and feel a little surer of my own.

They hoped to have a full proposal for a cease-fire ready by the time the Estinger army appeared, an offer that King Corsin and his advisors could agree to. We would fly out to meet the attacking airships long before they reached the shore; the battle might be over before it began.

But I still spent my days with my mother preparing for that battle. I both hated and loved it, but I had to help her; we were the only ones who knew how to engineer the automatons that would give Faerie any chance of surviving the Esting attack if Fin and Talis should fail to prevent it.

Her workshop was breathtaking. She lived and worked in the house where Mr. Candery had taken Caro and me to, in twelve little honeycomb rooms of the kind that seemed so common here. Most of the rooms were underground, and walking through them was like opening those Nordsk nesting dolls, each one so intricate and meticulous that you think surely this was the end, there couldn't possibly be anything after it. And then there was.

She'd continued her studies of animal anatomy, and she seemed to have grown fixated on dragonflies and bats. My buzzers climbed inquisitively over larger, more streamlined versions of their own bodies, running their delicate legs over the improvements with what seemed to me like jealousy.

"No horses," I murmured the first time I saw her workshop, holding out my hand so the copper butterfly could perch on my finger.

Behind me my mother made a strange hissing sound, and when I turned I saw a small cloud of steam around her head.

"No more horses," she said. The furnace in her belly glowed. Her face was just a porcelain mask, and its expression was the same as ever, but her bright glass eyes looked angry.

I pushed past her and ran upstairs, back to where Jules waited for me, wound down and asleep in the courtyard. I threw my arms around him and longed for him to wake up, but I couldn't make myself draw the spiral pattern between his shoulders that would bring him to life. Jules took me back and forth between the barracks and Mother's workshop every day, and he had started to seem tired lately, in a way he never had even when we worked our hardest together back in Esting. I wondered if something about Faerie was making him sad, something he still didn't want to tell me.

The Fey had forbidden my mother to gather new Ashes even before the Estinger forces had taken over the site of their creation. We would have to make our whole army from whatever I had in my case.

When I returned, she was bent over the worktable in her first room, fiddling with a minute piece of clockwork. I could barely see the glow of her furnace now, and the steam around her head had dissipated; she seemed to have calmed down.

I set the case on the edge of the table and began to remove the thin vials of Ashes. I found myself holding my breath.

My mother glanced over at them. Her glass eyes gleamed.

"Smart girl," she whispered. "You brought those all the way here for me."

My jaw clenched. "Jules made me bring them," I muttered.

She opened the case and rifled through the glass vials with flickering, quick movements. "There isn't much, but it'll do," she said, adding bitterly: "All my other stores were destroyed long ago."

"Destroyed? How?" I was sure there was something about the Ashes that I still didn't know. What I'd already learned made me heartsick, and yet . . . I thought of Fin's talk of responsibility, of doing right by whomever was in your care, no matter how they came to be that way. If I was really sending Jules and the buzzers to war, I had to know how their Ashes could be destroyed so that I could keep them as safe as possible.

"The Fey call their destruction *releasing* the Ashes," my mother said scornfully, extending her neck just a little longer than would have been possible in her old body in order to examine a delicate gear. "They're just killing them, of course. You'd think they'd take my word for it. Yes, the burning is—painful, but . . ."

The hinges of her painted mouth closed, and her lidless eyes glanced toward me.

Then she shook herself with a jingle and kept talking, her remarkable hands working with inhuman deftness and speed as she spoke.

"But if I myself found it worthwhile, surely they could see that it isn't so terrible . . . I was going to die anyway, and so was every animal that burned! It's a blessing, the best magic Faerie has! And yet the Fey *choose* to die, of old age, of disease, in childbirth, or from injury, every one of them . . . I can't understand it."

"You don't know that," I said coldly, bending over my own work. Mr. Candery had found an old stool for me to sit on; my mother never needed one herself, and it didn't seem to occur to her that I would. I was trying my best not to envy her strength, her speed and dexterity, with mixed results.

I thought of Talis's story, of Shim stepping calmly over the side of the merchant's ship. Of the serpent who had given Shim fer life back, even if it was a new kind of life entirely.

"I do know it," she said. "Even the Fey smuggler who, ah, who helped me transform said no person in all their national memory had ever done it. It repulses them on some instinctive level. The only instinct *I* knew was the one to keep on living and working. I told fer that, and even then it took all the money I'd ever made to persuade fer to bring me to the fire . . ."

I forced myself to ignore the growing revulsion that I felt at my mother's story. "Not that," I said. "I meant that you don't know the Ashes came from creatures about to die."

Her head snapped around on her snaking neck. "No one would burn a healthy animal for no reason," she said. "Surely you don't think even I could be so cruel as that."

"The prices Ashes fetch at the Night Market — the prices *you* paid for them — would be reason enough!"

Her neck began to retract. "I didn't hear you weeping when you found Jules and my buzzers back in Esting."

I threw down the wrench I'd been holding and stood. "You didn't hear anything! You weren't there. You left me!"

She straightened up. Her new body was taller than the original had been, and our eyes were exactly level. "Didn't hear anything?" she asked, her voice oil-smooth, a perfect replica of the one that used to teach me and tell me stories. "I wouldn't be so sure of that, Nicolette." She raised one metal hand to her ceramic cheek, drummed her fingers on it lightly with a sound like four tiny hammers. "'Oh, Jules, I wonder what Fin is doing right now. Do you think he's thinking of me too?'" She pitched her voice slightly higher to mimic me, childish and silly.

I felt as if she'd struck me. Hard, in some vulnerable low-down place. I struggled to breathe, and all I could do for many long moments was glare at her, too outraged to speak. I thought I could really hit her, my own mother, for saying that, if only I knew where it would hurt her.

How many more horrible things would I learn in Faerie? Perhaps it was good that I might have to go to war. I was going to hurt someone, and soon, so it might as well be in the service of . . . something.

"I couldn't always hear you, of course," she went on in her own voice, as if it were obvious. "The spell didn't work for me as well as Mr. Candery hoped it would. After those horrid interlopers"—I realized she meant the Steps—"smashed up my workshop, it failed completely. But it was enough for me to see which way the wind was blowing, and comfort myself with the knowledge that I'd left you the tools to make a living, and a match with the Heir into the bargain." She turned away, clacking. "You used the other tools so well, I can't understand why you didn't use the best one of all when he fell right into your lap."

I snatched up my wrench again. "Neither of us understands the other, Margot," I said, enjoying her shock and hurt at my use of her given name. "I think mother and daughter should both let go of that fantasy now if we're to have any hope of working together."

Her glass eyes flicked toward me again. "Ah," she said, "it seems you have some sense after all."

They were the longest days I'd ever worked in my life. Not even when I'd been building the bigger Jules and his carriage, nor in the heady, rough first days of starting my own business after the Exposition, had I stretched myself so thin. But it would not be long before the automaton army came ashore. Mr. Candery had assured me that no more or less time had passed here than in Esting, and indeed the notion started to seem absurd to me. Based on the state of the automatons I'd seen in Fitz's storeroom, I believed we still had a month or two, but I couldn't be certain. Talis had sent twelve soldiers to assist us in our work; it would have taken a year to build our army without them, and I knew at least that that was too much time.

I was afraid my mother would ask or force me to divide Jules up into multiple bodies, but it never came to that. Unlike the loyal buzzers, Jules didn't want to see my mother; he didn't say anything to me, just gave her a wide berth on the rare occasions that she happened to be in the courtyard when we came riding in. Perhaps she sensed my protectiveness — at any rate, she never asked me about him. They never got close enough for me to see exactly what he thought of her.

So the mechanical force we built was no cavalry . . . not in the traditional sense, anyway. There were no horses. Instead we built insects, spiders, birds, and bats, all big enough to ride. Even the buzzers volunteered themselves, and like their beloved Jules they soon had much bigger and fiercer bodies.

"I'm certain I saw only foot soldiers in Fitz's warehouse," I said a few days into our work, "no horses. They were—" I'd almost mentioned the mare I'd seen at the burning site. I couldn't tell Mother; I didn't want to talk to her about the Ashes at all. "I don't think it would be reasonable to count out horses, though," I said instead. "Especially not now that Jules has become as famous in Esting as I have." For some reason, the merman Fin had freed flickered across my mind. "They could have . . . some kind of marine force too, couldn't they? Ashes of fish, or whales, or . . . sea serpents?" I pictured the serpent from Talis's story, imagined the monsters from the *Imperator*'s map made huge and metallic, and I shivered.

"Of course not, Nicolette," she said, sliding out from under the chassis of a carriage-size beetle she'd been working on. "It's completely impossible."

I bristled. "How so?"

She actually paused before responding, something that was incredibly rare for her. "You can't burn coal underwater, of course," she finally said.

Well, that was fairly obvious, and I did feel a bit foolish

for not thinking of it. Still, as my mother slid back under the beetle's chassis a little too quickly, even for her, I wondered if she was keeping the real reason to herself.

At first, I hadn't been able to tell even Fin and Caro about how Jules had taken me to the place where Ashes were made. It felt private, the most horrible kind of intimacy, to have witnessed a painful death like that. I was glad Jules had shown me for his sake, but I wouldn't share the burden of that knowledge with anyone else, especially not when even I had to admit it would be necessary to use the Ashes in the battle, if it came. Nothing could dissuade Fin from riding into the fight with the rest of us, and I couldn't have him in any further moral torture over our army and Esting's while he needed to focus on staying alive.

I had nightmares, though. One night, a little less than a week into my grueling, all-consuming work with Mother, I woke up screaming.

I was nestled between Fin and Caro when I woke. They were both sitting up by the time I came to myself, sweating and gasping.

"Nick, Nick, we're here," Caro murmured, stroking my hot forehead.

Fin's hand squeezed mine. "Are you all right?"

"Her eyes," I whispered, fighting to get my breath back. "Her eyes were rolling . . ."

"Whose eyes?" Fin asked.

"It's just us here, Nick," Caro reminded me. "No one else. You're safe here with us."

I managed a deep, shuddering breath. "I know," I sighed out on my exhale. I brought my hand up to touch Caro's, and I met Fin's reassuring glance.

"Whose eyes, Nick?" Fin asked. "Do you want to tell us about it?"

I shook my head, wishing I could spare them . . . but I knew that it would bring such relief to tell about my dream and the very real nightmare that had inspired it.

So I put my arms around both of them and pulled them down close to me, and in a shaking whisper I told them where Jules had taken me after I fled from my mother.

When I got to the part about the soldier's screams, Fin jumped out of bed and began to pace around the room, raking his hands through his curls until they stood out like a dark halo.

"Those . . . those villains," he hissed. "Those utter, utter—" He couldn't find words strong enough.

"Yes," I said quietly.

"Every one of them an Esting soldier. Every one of them burned alive." He began to breathe heavily.

My eyes stung with tears. I pulled Caro closer. "And Jules and the buzzers too. All of them burned, to make them . . ."

"And your mother," Caro whispered, shocked.

I shook my head. "At least with her, it was her own choice."

Fin was actually shaking with rage. "And to think we have to—to take advantage of—" He stopped, and I saw something settle itself into his body, something that made him stand a little taller and straighter, seem a little more assured. "If we must, then we must," he said. "Esting's rule in Faerie will be over after that army arrives if it's my own blood that brings the peace," he said. "I swear it. I swear it."

I believed him.

"All right, Fin," Caro said. "But we all have to sleep awhile first. This was Nick's nightmare, not yours. Come back to bed, because it's over now."

But all three of us knew it was not.

Still, Fin returned to the bed, and we lay on our sides and held one another, Caro behind me, Fin in front. With the familiar reassurance of their bodies around me, I began to drift back into a sleep that I felt sure, this time, would be dreamless.

When I woke in the morning, I was equally sure that Fin had stayed awake all night.

I was so bone-tiringly busy that the days flowed together into one endless stream of work and exhausted sleep. Eventually even my nightmares were welcome, because when they startled me awake I had a few moments to appreciate the sleepy intimacy I shared with Caro and Fin. On the nights I didn't wake, I hardly even noticed that we were together.

The idea that our time might be limited indeed, that the coming battle might part us with no possibility for reunion . . . it was too terrible to contemplate, so I didn't. Caro and I had fulfilled our vow to keep Fin safe so far, and if I wanted to maintain any sanity at all, I had to believe that we would continue to do so.

On the day that one of the lookouts announced a group of dark and bulky Estinger ships on the horizon, I knew we were well prepared. With the help of our many new apprentices, we had built a metal menagerie of warfare that I truly believed no foot soldiers, not even Ashes-powered automatons, could stand against. We knew from the position of the ships that they would cross the shore at the beach where Jules had crashed after his first flight. I was sure we had every advantage possible. If all Fin and Talis's negotiations couldn't win Faerie's freedom, the cavalry my mother and I had made would win it with steel and glass and smoke.

We were ready for war.

A DOZEN airships on the horizon, each of them many times larger than the *Imperator*. Lurking like black holes above the ocean.

I stood on top of the barracks wall, watching them move slowly closer. Fin, Caro, Talis, and my mother stood with me. Ombrossus oil burned in shallow bowls all around us, concealing our presence and drenching the air with its spicy scent.

Jules soared up from the ground and hovered just above the tree line. He was watching the far-off airships too.

He touched down on the wall next to me and nibbled my shoulder in greeting. I stroked his cheek.

The new wings I had built for Jules were magnificent; even then I couldn't help admiring them. Constructed from an ultra-lightweight, translucent alloy that Mother had shown me and that was found only here in Faerie, they stretched out more than thirty feet on either side of his body. They were modeled on bats' wings rather than birds', which eliminated the need for cumbersome layers of feathers and also seemed somehow more natural on Jules's mammalian body.

With these new wings, he could carry two riders hundreds of feet in the air as easily as if he bore no burden at all.

My mother didn't move when Jules touched down on the wall, but I heard her furnace rumble, and some of the gears inside her whirred as they sped up. Jules seemed to ignore her entirely. I was surprised she'd helped me with his wings at all, though she'd been building bats' wings for years before we arrived. She'd even shared her blueprints — although she couldn't bring herself to talk to me when she did so.

She didn't tell me much of anything, really. We no longer spoke unless we needed to confer on some design. It was almost as if I were working with another machine, not a woman.

Fin had wanted to go alone to meet the approaching Estinger forces, but neither Caro nor I would hear of it. Caro couldn't bear to go into the fight at all, though; if a battle ensued, she planned to spend it assisting the Fey healers who would wait at the barracks to treat any wounded who were brought to them. This was one custom the Fey had never abandoned, no matter how atrocious their treatment at Estingers' hands had become: Anyone who suffered was welcome in their healers' halls.

I wondered if that was because of Shim and the Estinger prince.

The fact that the Estingers kept alive some injured soldiers who would likely be burned for Ashes later when they returned to their own troops didn't bear thinking of.

"It's time," Fin said quietly.

The airships were close enough that I could just make out the spiny individual sails.

Talis looked at Fin a little fearfully. The peace treaty fe and Fin had brokered was a strong one, but I could tell Talis believed this would only end in violence. Secretly, I thought I might agree, but I was determined to give Fin his chance to be the diplomatic hero.

"Right," I said. I placed one foot in a stirrup and pulled myself onto Jules. Fin came after, riding in front of me this time; the Estingers needed to see him first.

Jules lifted from the wall, taking to the air as lightly as a dandelion seed.

I glanced back to see Caro, not letting myself think that it was "one last time." She was going down to join the healers as soon as we took off, but when I looked, she was still watching us. She gave me a small wave and a smile that I'm sure she meant to be encouraging.

I couldn't bear it. I looked ahead again, over Fin's shoulder at the bright sky. I tightened my arms around his waist, and he released one of Jules's handles so he could touch my wrist.

We came to the beach in no time, and as the landscape underneath us changed from green forest to blue sand, Jules rose higher still, up and up until the air grew thin and cool around us, a sweet relief after the muggy jungle heat.

We sailed over the ocean, on toward the ships. I felt a leaden weight settle in my stomach as we approached them, so heavy that it seemed hard to believe Jules could still fly.

I marveled at the airships' bulk and power, at the low predatory roar of the huge fires below the balloons. I could not quite call them beautiful, and they filled me with a sick, cold fear . . . but the inventor in me knew they were wonders.

Jules jerked and swooped. A hissing streak of a bullet only just missed us.

We dropped twenty feet in the next moment, dodging another. Jules's head strained forward, watching the lead ship, and we were close enough that I could see one dark-clad figure on the top deck holding a rifle. He reloaded and settled the butt of the gun against his shoulder.

"Hold on," Jules rumbled, gaining speed.

He reared, spreading his wings and pulling us vertical and, for a dizzying moment, upside down as he avoided the next volley of shots. I saw the rifleman suspended from the airship by his feet and an endless line of waves above my head. But Jules wheeled so quickly through the air that Fin and I were pressed against the saddle, the force of Jules's motion propelling us upward against gravity.

I understood all that, but I was grateful beyond words when he righted himself again.

We soared to the leading ship. Another crew member

had joined the rifleman on the deck, and I wondered why there weren't more of them. But the ships were so huge and bulky, and I knew what the weight of the automaton army below their decks must be. They had to keep the automatons sleeping for the voyage to avoid wasting fuel, of course . . . and only enough human crew as was needed to supervise the voyage and wake the metal soldiers when the time came.

Well, two marksmen were easier to avoid than a dozen. Only the lead airship was in range, at least for rifles.

I couldn't think about the possibility of cannons.

At the prow of the ship I saw a Brethren cleric, muttering to himself and waving incense. I shouldn't have been able to see the smoke from here, but I could: It rose thick and dark green through the clear Faerie air. In the heart of the cloud of smoke something bright flickered once, then again. The cloud grew slowly, in sudden starts and thumps, like a weak heartbeat. The brightness came back and showed itself for what it was: nascent lightning.

My own heartbeat thrummed. I knew that dark cloud, that lightning. That storm. I knew at once what the Brother on board the *Imperator* had been doing when we had approached Faerie, knew who had doomed the ship. Who had killed Wheelock and the crew and left the rest of us for dead.

The Brethren had controlled that storm, and this one, too. At Fitz's bidding, no doubt, or even the king's . . .

"Fin, the storm," I said into his ear, over the wind. "Be careful . . ."

He just nodded and urged Jules closer. He pulled a metal tube out of the leather holster on his belt and, urging Jules still farther ahead, he tossed it toward the ship's deck. My own design propelled it forward, and it landed perfectly, rolling to a stop at the second marksman's feet.

He jumped away from it as he would have from a grenade. When the tube opened with only a gentle pop, revealing a bit of paper, the two men looked at each other.

The one who had jumped away walked cautiously forward. The first kept his rifle trained on us.

The paper identified Fin in his own writing, and it guaranteed his peaceful purpose. He had signed it, as well, with some code word he'd been taught as a way to confirm the absence of Fey interference, although he couldn't tell even me or Caro what it was.

The second marksman scanned the paper and looked quickly back up at us; we drew close enough that I could see him squint.

With a start, I recognized him. The sharp eyes, the handsome creamy-pale face, the auburn hair. Fitzwilliam Covington, commanding his automaton army after all.

He spoke to the other man on deck, but the roar of the fires drowned out his words.

Both men set their guns down on the ground. Fitz beckoned us forward.

Jules approached so cautiously that it almost felt as if we were walking rather than flying. His hooves touched down lightly, and he kept his wings extended so that Fin and I could not dismount.

"Your Highness," Fitz said, bowing low. "I cannot tell you how deeply moved I am to see you alive. We attended the funerals just before our departure."

The plural of *funeral* was his only acknowledgment of me; he never even broke eye contact with Fin to look my way.

"You've read our treaty," Fin said flatly. "We know why you've come. Will you turn back now and bring the news to Esting that there will be no more killing here?"

Fitz frowned. "Such news would hardly be well received," he said. "I'm afraid your deaths stirred the whole country into bloodlust."

I stood up in Jules's stirrups. "Then our lives will bring them back to peace," I said.

Fitz looked up at me at last. "Not *your* death, Miss Nick," he said. "Although I realize it must come as a shock to you that you're not actually very important." He spoke that line with such satisfaction, I realized he'd been wanting to say it for a long time. I opened my mouth to insult him in turn, but his next words stopped me cold.

"I meant the Heir's death, and the king's."

Fin shrank back against my chest. I felt him starting to slump, and I wrapped my arms more tightly around him. "I'm here, Fin," I whispered, very low, in his ear. "I'm here."

But there was one word running through my mind: *orphan*. I'd had an intimate knowledge of that term for years; being an orphan had shaped my life as much as being an inventor had, and Fin's parentage had shaped every facet of his.

But since we'd come to Faerie, I'd found my mother again, and Fin was the orphan now.

I couldn't see his face, but I saw the smirk on Fitz's as he delivered the news. I hated him more in that moment than I'd ever hated the Steps.

"When he heard you'd died, Fin, he just . . . stopped. Like a piece of bad clockwork. The doctors said it was his heart. The country is united now, Fin—your deaths did for them what all your fiery speeches and high ideals could not." Fitz walked toward us, stopping just outside of Jules's wingspan. "The Fey are terrorists and savages. Doesn't their having killed both your parents prove that to you?"

Fin shivered, but I could feel him getting his strength back. He sat up straighter. "They didn't," he said. He looked back at me. "It's time to go."

I looked at the cleric again. His incense-storm, about the size of Jules now, had stopped growing, and he'd stopped muttering; he watched Fitz, waiting for orders.

As Jules gave a great flap of his translucent wings and hauled us back into the air, I pulled the longest wrench from my ever-present tool belt and hurled it at the cleric. Fin was right: There would be no negotiation here.

I didn't have time to see if my aim was true. As we rose

farther into the air, Fitz grabbed the rifle he'd placed on the deck and took aim at us.

Jules reacted before I could, diving down and out of range, flying right under the belly of the airship.

Those cannons that didn't bear thinking of earlier began to fire from the side of the lead ship as we came out from under it, but we were infinitely smaller and Jules infinitely faster and more agile than the airship, and he dodged out of the cannonballs' trajectories with ease.

"We tried," I called to Fin over the wind and the fiery roar, leaning forward against his shoulder to make sure he heard me.

He nodded grimly.

The other ships were approaching fast. There were shockingly few crew members on their huge decks too, and I shuddered to think of the masses of soldiers lurking below, thousands in every hull.

Jules flew us back to Faerie so fast that each beat of his wings stole the breath from my lungs.

The roar of the airships receded behind us into silence. We were high up in the cool air, but I began to sweat.

When we returned to the barracks, only Talis and a few of the highest-ranking Fey officers remained; my mother's and my menagerie was already gone, and the Fey soldiers with them. Talis had told us that they'd come together from all over the vast continent for this final defense. I looked around at the empty camp that had been so crowded mere days before, and it felt like looking at a graveyard.

Fin made his brief report to Talis, who only nodded, listening silently. But that quiet gentleness that I'd seen in fer when we first met slowly diminished as Fin spoke, like a candle dimming as the last of the wick burns up.

Fin wouldn't even dismount. I could tell he thought Jules and I might abandon him here for his own safety if he did, and it wasn't as if the thought hadn't crossed my mind.

I was afraid Jules would leave me behind if I dismounted. He protected my safety as fiercely as I protected Fin's.

So we both stayed astride, and after our few moments with Talis, we went to join the ranks.

Jules galloped along the uneven ground, his wings tucked into neat folded shields at our sides as he ran. We had to stay below the tree line to avoid the airships' lookouts spotting us. As always, Jules seemed to know exactly where to go, and we needed only to ride.

We had received helmets, breastplates, and arm guards made from some kind of plant fiber intricately woven into a scaly armor; the Fey soldiers and my mother had both assured us it was as strong as any metal, but lighter and more flexible. The same material had gone into many of our new cavalry's designs as well. The armor's gentle pressure on my head, chest, and arms didn't feel like much protection, but it didn't chafe against my nearly healed burns and distract me either.

Our forces were waiting at the very edge of the jungle, concealed with shadows and ombrossus and spells I couldn't name just behind a wide expanse of gently sloping blue beach. If we could not choose the time of this last battle, Talis had said, we could at least choose the place. When Fin suggested that the Estingers' unfamiliarity with the jungle might be a better advantage to the Fey, both Talis's advisors and my mother had shut him down. The beach was the place, they insisted.

I remembered my mother's reaction to my idea of sea automatons, and I wondered if they hoped we could simply drive the soldiers into the water and douse their furnaces . . . but I doubted it. There were far too many of them for us to have even a hope of driving them all back.

No, we had to meet them in battle.

I could feel the hushed presence of thousands of quietly breathing souls all around me. And the presence of those that weren't breathing too; all our own animals, to which Mother and I had given these new warlike bodies. They risked as much as we did, I was sure of that. And they'd already sacrificed more.

We waited, souls clothed in flesh or metal, in silence for our fate.

The airships drew steadily closer. They never gained speed. They had fired no more cannons since Fin and I left the ship.

Had they hoped to arrive unnoticed, to simply drop the

troops on top of the Fey capital with no resistance? Surely not. And Fin, Jules, and I had removed any doubt they might have had that we knew they were coming.

When they were some few hundred feet from the shore, they began to descend.

At a signal I didn't hear, the biggest dragonflies to my left took off.

They rose into the sky in an acute V formation, followed closely by giant copper bats and canaries with two Fey riders apiece. Their engines hissed and whirred in perfect synchrony.

The first Fey rider threw a grenade. It blasted into the lead airship's side, and then the cannonballs rained down.

The battle seemed to be happening in memory even as I moved through it. Part of me was there, riding Jules, clutching Fin, throwing the grenades tucked into pouches at my waist when we got above the airships again.

But the biggest part of me was detached, not even frightened or overwhelmed, just . . . watching, as if from some safe future, refusing to believe that I was experiencing these things as they happened.

The Estinger airships reached the shore. They hovered just a few yards above the ground and I watched as they dropped their cargo, seven-foot-tall toy soldiers that snapped to life under the shadows of the ships and then marched forward, gleaming in the tropical sun. Hordes of them. They were an infestation covering all the many miles of the long stretch of beach where Talis's commanders had decided that we all would live or die.

They had a cavalry. It was foolish ever to have thought they wouldn't. Hundreds of horses, so closely modeled on Jules that I was sure Fitz had somehow stolen my designs.

And yet . . . I stared down from our great height, disbelieving. The horses' heads weren't heads at all, too bulky and straight and with . . .

Not horses' heads, but human torsos, with human heads and arms above, arms that ended not in hands but in bayonets.

The clockwork centaurs clacked forward with a gait that was more insect than equine, their bayonet arms long enough to help propel them, six-legged, along the ground.

But we had a cavalry too. Our huge spiders and beetles rushed out of the jungle to meet them. The Fey soldiers astride their backs threw so many bombs that all I could see of the battle below was a muddle of smoke and fire, the occasional singing glint of steel.

Still, I could see all too well how the battle was progressing; the anguished cries of Fey soldiers soon drowned out the metallic clashing on the beach and even the great, low rumble of the airship fires. The automaton army's numbers were overwhelming, turning the blue beach black with metal and smoke.

But another battle raged in the sky. Our dozens of flying

insects zipped through the air, sending bombs down onto the shuddering airships while the ships volleyed cannon fire back.

I watched one cannonball crash into a dragonfly with a sickening crunch, a rush of flame as its furnace was exposed, and I couldn't look away as the steed and its two riders plunged down into the smoky chaos of the battle below.

Jules watched too, his spiny wings hooked into the air to glide. I tore my eyes away in time to see the rifleman on the ship below aiming his barrel, but Jules didn't.

Fin.

I'd vowed I'd be there to stop any bullet that came for him, after that first awful time at the Exposition that now seemed so long ago. Yet here in my very arms he was shot again.

I didn't scream because it would do nothing. I could do nothing.

It hit him in the belly below his breastplate, no mere shoulder wound this time, with such force that he was propelled out of Jules's saddle and nearly out of my grasp.

I clutched his right leg as he fell, his dead weight slipping away from me, dangling toward the edge of the airship's deck, toward the clashing, roaring bloodbath on the ground. We were hundreds of feet in the air.

"I can't hold him!" I called.

Jules looked back, ears flat to his head. He veered away from the airship and out toward the open water.

I heard the groan of straining ropes and sails as the ship

banked around to follow us, but I couldn't look away from the body I was barely holding on to, the bloodstain that spread below Fin's useless armor. I cursed the Fey and my mother for telling Fin it made him safe. I cursed Fin for believing them, and most of all I cursed myself.

Jules sailed away from the battle, down and down. When Fin's leg finally slipped out of my white, numb fingers, we were only twenty feet above the calm water.

His body hit with a crack like breaking bones.

But to worry about breaking bones when he might be dead . . . no. The fall at least hadn't killed him, and if I could get him back to Caro and those Fey healers . . .

I had to believe he was still living. What I had to worry about now was drowning.

I held on tight, and Jules descended until the tips of his wings and hooves splashed in the waves, throwing salt drops that clung to my skin and clothes and hair. He wasn't raising steam the way he had the day we first plunged toward Faerie three or four lifetimes ago, and he didn't struggle to stay airborne as I leaned precariously off his side to pull Fin out of the ocean.

There was blood, so much of Fin's blood, dissipating into the water. Dark, menacing red blossoming into the green like a painting of flowers.

The swirling pattern transfixed me, and even after I had dragged Fin's unconscious but still bleeding, still living body back onto Jules and he'd lifted us airborne again, I kept staring at that muddy, spreading patch of darkness, like a bruise on the skin of the sea.

I kept staring as we rose, until it vanished as suddenly as if it had been swallowed.

Fin began to shiver violently. His clothes were drenched, his fibrous armor swollen and heavy. I worried that it was constricting his breath, but I couldn't risk pulling it off; I didn't even want to risk taking one hand away from supporting him in order to try.

Jules banked as far away from the center of the battle as he could without losing too much time.

When we approached the shore, I bent forward over Fin, covering his body with my own as Jules sped past the fighting in the air and on the ground. No more bullets would reach Fin except through my own body.

I squeezed my eyes closed, sure that at any moment I would feel metal tear through my skin, shatter my bones, sure that there would be a final crack and shock of pain, and I would know no more.

But then Jules touched ground, moving smoothly from flight into his rolling gallop, and I remained whole.

I pulled my head up, keeping my arms and torso in their protective hunch over Fin, who was still shivering, still barely conscious. My whole body, my whole mind became one prayer as we sped toward the barracks and the healers' halls.

Save him. Save him.

TALIS was still standing where we'd left fer, at the top of the barracks wall. Fer skin was sallow under the blue freckles, and dark shadows lurked under fer eyes.

I saw fer with absolute clarity as we rushed past, in more detail than should have been possible. I saw fer haunted look, and I recognized it; I felt that way too. Someone I loved might be dying. I felt it now, with Fin in my arms, and I'd felt it before, when each of my parents died — or when I thought they had.

But on Talis's face, that hollow look was multiplied a thousandfold. If anyone ever doubted the multitudes of fer parentage, the look on fer face now would make it certain.

Thousands of Talis's parents were dead and dying.

My heart twisted as we sped past the ruler toward the healers' halls. For a moment even my own pain, even the pain of every soldier, flesh and metal, on the beach, was nothing to what Talis felt.

Then Fin's blood trickled across my forearm, and I forgot. I urged Jules on.

Healers were waiting to meet us at the gate, wrapped head to toe in their immaculate white, only their eyes showing through small, screened slits in their headscarfs.

Jules knelt and Fin lolled forward, still barely conscious. The healers unrolled a thin fabric stretcher, too much like the one I'd seen at the fiery geyser.

Fin couldn't even groan as the soldier in the horrible clearing had done. He was utterly still and limp and gray-skinned. He vanished down a trapdoor in the healers' hands.

Even from there, I could hear the battle raging on the shore. All I wanted was to stay away from it—not to be with Fin, because I didn't think I could bear it if I had to watch him die, but just . . . just to preserve myself.

I climbed back onto Jules before the idea could take hold. Fin was seeing out his beliefs to the bitter end, and I wouldn't let him down by giving in to my cowardice.

Jules rose from the ground, and we plunged back toward the battle.

The only word for what I saw on the beach when we returned was *carnage*. I was sure we'd been away less than an hour, but nearly all of the menagerie was demolished, wings and legs and thoraxes over which Mother and I had labored for so long strewn across the beach in pieces, while the automaton Estinger soldiers and their horribly clacking centaur cavalry seemed to dance over the wreckage. I could see human soldiers too, the colonizers who had been left in the small pockets of Faerie where Esting still ruled; it seemed as if every single one of them had joined the battle. More airships were hovering over the littered beach, releasing fresh forces in numbers unimaginable.

I looked toward the ocean—yet more airships haunted the horizon.

"Nicolette!"

My body reacted to my mother's scream before my mind did, a child that wanted its mother. I couldn't do anything but go to her, and Jules reacted just as quickly, taking me to the place where the scream came from—and wasn't she his mother too?

A centaur had stabbed her through her metal chest with a bayonet; it was trampling the pincered head of the spider steed she'd built for herself weeks before. Smoke began to pour from the hole where a human heart would have been.

Jules reared up, his wings cloaking around us for a heartbeat and then pulling us upward, and with one thrust forward he kicked the centaur's back so that it went sprawling across the bloody, oil-pocked sand. I grabbed a grenade from my pouch, removed the pin, and threw it, barely thinking as I did. When it consumed the centaur in flame I felt that same detachment, as if it were only a memory, not the result of a choice I had just made.

And then Jules turned us back toward my wounded mother, and I thought of nothing but her.

She was incredibly heavy, all iron and steel, and when I finally pulled her onto Jules's back, it took him a few heaving efforts to get airborne once more. But just as another centaur saw and lunged for us, Jules pulled up and away, and we were rising toward the darkly floating airships again.

My mother leaned forward against Jules's neck. Smoke hissed out of her chest, the fuel in her furnace burning away in the open air. Within moments her flame died and she whirred down into silence.

I started to shake as violently as Fin had when I'd pulled him out of the water. Everything I hadn't been able to feel in the rush of battle, all the rage and revulsion and pain, was swallowing me whole. I looked away from my mother's motionless second body, away from the bloody fighting. I couldn't bear it, not any of it. The only place I could look was the sea, so close to us, so calm and peaceful beyond the shallows.

But something was changing out there too. Something was shifting, a darkness far from the shore.

A bruise on the water, like the bruise Fin's blood had made.

I forced myself back into the moment, forced my mind to focus. A huge, dark, watery shape, growing closer more quickly than even the airships had done.

"Look, Jules," I said, but he was already watching it. He

reluctantly moved us nearer when I urged him, balking at first, his ears flat back against his head. He brought us higher up into the sky than we had ever been before, and we soared past the airships and far, far out to sea.

From that height, I recognized the huge, sinuous shape at once. Shim's serpent in Talis's story. The map in the *Imperator*'s library.

Here be monsters.

The creature was the shifting, unnamable color of deep water, and it was unimaginably vast. Its body twisted through the waves, thick as a ship and so long I had no scale for comparison. Even from our great height, I could look at it only in sections.

There were pale specks in the water around the serpent, as white as the beast was dark. Not sea foam, because they moved with purpose and intelligence, forward to the shore with their behemoth, only a few at first and then hundreds, thousands. We dipped down just close enough that I could see them reaching out, reaching toward the shore . . .

Then I heard them singing, and it was a song I knew.

I saw Fin cutting the merman free from the net, their blood twining together in the water. Heard the creature's keening that had turned into a song that sounded like a promise.

A promise now kept.

I shifted my grasp on my mother's body and urged Jules lower but he refused. I looked back at the shore, certain that

I was about to see a great serpent rise up and swallow the marauding forces on the beach, swallow even the airships themselves.

But as the eerie singing swelled, the throng of merfolk stopped their movement forward, and the monster stopped too. It began to circle around the singers, faster and faster, and then it reared up a narrow frilled head twice the size of any airship and dove.

Watching the slick, endless length of its body follow its head beneath the water was the most entrancing thing I'd ever seen.

Jules flapped his wings and rose yet higher, so high that I had to gasp just to get enough air into my lungs, and I began to wonder whether there would be enough oxygen to fuel the fire in his furnace.

"Careful, Jules," I croaked. But he tossed his head, staring down at the ocean.

The serpent's body was even longer than I could have imagined, and its tail rose out of the sea in front of the merfolk, whose song I could barely hear from such a height.

Then the merfolk began swimming back, away from Faerie, toward the deep open ocean again. Still singing, they swam away so quickly that I could see the water they churned up even from our great height.

Jules understood before I did. He heaved his wings through the air and headed for the mainland as quickly as he could with the weight of myself and my mother's metal body.

I looked back at the merfolk and the serpent, and I was confused because the ocean seemed to be bending, folding up toward us. A trick of perspective, an illusion caused by the path of Jules's flight somehow?

No.

A tidal wave.

A rising hump of water that dwarfed even the sea monster swelling toward Faerie, toward the invading Esting army. Ahead of us I watched the line of water recede from the shore, revealing more and more deep blue sand and then long limp stretches of kelp and the splotched, naked rainbow of an exposed coral reef. Still the water pulled away, widening the battlefield tenfold.

The automaton army continued their massacre, singleminded. I doubted even one of them turned to look.

I did, though; I looked back at the wave as Jules heaved underneath me, and I knew he was not flying fast enough. The wave that the merfolk had sent to save Fin would take us out before we even reached the shoreline. It would douse Jules's furnace and rend apart his body and my mother's as easily as it would break my own. Like the doomed armies on the shore, we would be only so much wreckage.

Jules's wings creaked and shuddered. I knew without looking that the coal in his belly was running low.

"Ballast," he growled back at me. "Margot."

I looked at my mother's body. I forced down all the many kinds of revulsion that I felt. I knew Jules was right.

I pulled my wrench from my waistcoat belt and spun the adjuster, then set to work dismantling my mother.

Her arms came off first and most easily, the jointed fingers gesturing like a ballerina's as they plummeted into the sea below us. Her legs, bolted at the hips, were heavier and harder to pull apart, but at last they tumbled away too, the abrupt absence of their weight making Jules jerk suddenly higher up into the sky. But we still weren't light enough.

I opened the back of my mother's head, under the silky brown wig that was such a close simulacrum of my own hair that I felt the ghosts of fingers at my nape too. Shivering, I withdrew the small box of Ashes that I knew would be hidden there, just as it was hidden in all the buzzers she'd made and in Jules's head too.

I tucked the box into my breast pocket, and with sudden ferocity I pushed my mother's head and limbless torso away from me as hard as I could. As I watched it fall, I felt like crying and laughing and being sick all at once.

Free of the burden of my mother, Jules flew twice as fast.

I could hear the gathering wave behind us now, a roar that made the airships' din seem as small and gentle as a purr. I could feel it, too, the sucking air behind us as the wave drew in volume and power, and the sheer unbridled force of the ocean bearing down on Faerie.

I didn't dare to look again until we were flying over jungle, Jules still plunging ahead, flying as if Hell ran behind us. I saw the wave rising like a great hand above the tree line. The huge airships in front of it were only flies to be swatted.

When it crashed down, it shook the land, shook the trees, shook the very air we flew through. The sound of impact went on and on, drowning out any screams, any sound of screeching metal. The roar blended with its own echoes, reverberating through every bone in my body, erasing any memory of silence or stillness. I watched wave after wave of aftershock push up against the beach, felling the tall jungle trees and sending ocean hundreds of feet inland.

Jules slowed at last and turned in the air, locking his wings into an updraft to save fuel. We hovered, watching the ocean shudder and gnaw at the shore. The sky was empty of airships, of flying cavalry, even of birds.

I knew the merfolk had saved us, had saved Faerie. I knew that somehow Fin's blood had called them here, and that this was something they had done for him. But how many Fey soldiers had they killed? How many automatons destroyed — and what would happen to the Ashes? Would they float bodiless on the waves now, unable to die? What happened to Ashes in seawater that my mother seemed so afraid of?

All I wanted in the world was for this to be over, but I knew it was not. I wanted to go see Fin in the healers' halls, where I made myself believe that I would find him still living.

I wanted Caro, to sleep with both of them in our wide bed for an entire week, month, for the rest of my life.

But I knew that the wave that had ended the battle so suddenly would leave many dead and dying on the beach in its wake. My battle, and Jules's, would not be over until we had brought as many of them as we could to the healers.

We flew back to the barracks only long enough to fill Jules's furnace with fresh coal, and then we headed for the beach again.

WE spent the rest of that interminable day flying back and forth between the beach and the barracks, carrying two passengers with us at a time—even three, when they could hold on to Jules themselves. The beach was strewn with tree trunks, kelp, coral . . . and bodies and metal, too, but not nearly the unconquerable numbers of soldiers that had come down from the airships. There was a slick, lacy sheen of oil on the water.

One lone black airship was marooned in the treetops a hundred yards in from the beach, its sails and the hide of its balloon draped across the branches like funeral shrouds.

Every time we looped back to the barracks I looked for Caro, but I never saw her. I told myself that it meant nothing, but every time a face that wasn't hers greeted us, my heart sank a little more. The healers we saw reminded us to bring them anyone who needed help, not just Fey. But there were few soldiers left living from either army: So many who weren't killed in the battle had drowned in the tidal wave. Every automaton had been doused in the water, and most of them were lost entirely to the sea. When I stopped to look for Ashes in the heads of those that remained, I found the boxes all empty, as clean as if they'd never been filled at all.

The little insect souls I'd loved, all gone. Dead. I knew from the look in Jules's eyes that he was mourning them too, just as I knew from the one shake of his head after I showed him the little empty boxes that they really were gone.

Any body that was still moving, we picked up and took to the healers.

I longed desperately to seek out Fin in the halls, but I knew I wouldn't be able to live with myself if I lingered there to find him while others were dying on the beach.

A few hours into my retrieval work, I saw a body I recognized drifting in the shallows, gently buffeting the shore. Fitz's skin was puffy and white, his face bloated, his eyes open and unseeing.

I had to force myself to touch him. I was almost sure he was dead, and when his lack of heartbeat confirmed it, I felt a surge of relief that was quickly overcome by guilt. The healers said everyone deserved our care; how dare I think Fitz was any different.

In a few more minutes the waves would pull him into deep water again, and he'd be lost to the sea. I dragged him onto dry sand and closed his staring eyes, remembering against my will all the times he'd winked at me and flirtatiously called me Miss Nick. He hadn't always hated me, nor I him. I could never have imagined we would end up here.

I left him there on the beach and returned to Jules, who nickered and nosed my shoulder as I walked by to remount him.

On our next stop at the healers' halls, I finally saw Caro. She nodded at me, her eyes glazed and distant, her capable hands stained with antiseptic, blood on her trainee's apron.

Fin? I mouthed, although I dreaded hearing her answer.

She blinked, startled, although I don't know what else she could possibly have expected me to ask her.

She met my eyes and nodded again. "He'll pull through," she said, and then one of the healers called for assistance and she hurried off, still with that blank, distant look.

I returned to Jules and took off toward the beach, not sure what to think. Was Fin worse off than Caro had admitted, and she just didn't want to burden me with the knowledge when I still had work to do?

No, Caro was more honest than that, and she thought better of me than that too.

Jules reached the shore again, and I scanned the littered landscape for more survivors. No one was left, only the broken machines and the broken trees and the limp, dead jellyfish that had been tossed up onto the shore along with the wave.

But, there: half buried in the sand, a lean, shuddering,

dark-haired figure trying futilely to pull himself up above the tide line.

"Look, Jules," I said, leaning forward and pointing.

We descended, keeping well clear of the lapping waves. I dismounted and rushed to the man's side.

Olive skin, black hair, tall and lean. His narrow dark eyes when he looked up at me held no trace of their secret smile, but I still knew him.

It was impossible. He'd been gone, dead, drowned, for weeks. I started to shake, and I collapsed next to him. How many resurrections would this place throw at me? How could I — could he — have been so lucky!

I checked for broken bones with my trembling hands, then heaved him into a sitting position. I put my palms on his chest to keep him from collapsing forward, and I looked into his eyes.

"Miss Lampton," he said, his voice a salty rasp. Wincing with pain, he dipped his head formally, as much of a bow as he could make.

"Nick," I said automatically, then shook myself. "How — how did you manage to live? When the ship went down . . ."

"I . . ." He coughed, and pinkish water dribbled from his mouth. "I remember so little . . ."

I could feel his heart drumming, fast and uneven. I looked up at Jules, who stamped his feet and shook out his wings.

"You don't need to tell me now," I said quickly. "Here, I'll take you to people who can help you."

I started to lift him up.

"I can walk," he insisted, pushing his hands weakly against the sand.

I hooked my arms under his and we slowly stood up. "Lean against me," I said. I half dragged Wheelock to Jules, who strained his head back to help me push him up onto the saddle, as he'd done with dozens of others already today. I pulled myself astride once more, and we took off, making a final loop over the stretch of beach to check for other survivors before we returned to the barracks.

I kept looking back at the ocean. I didn't trust it anymore. I thought I felt the pressure of a hidden wave behind me all the time, ready to drown me.

We saw no one else left alive on the beach; it was as if the ocean had been waiting to give me Wheelock until I'd saved everyone else. I tried not to think about Shim and the serpent's spirit kingdom, tried not to picture shade blossoms.

Wheelock leaned back against me, taking hollow-sounding breaths, his eyelids once in a while fluttering closed. The skin of his hands was clammy and wet, as if the water didn't want to let go of him, and I covered it with my own warm hands, finally wrapping my arms all the way around him, keeping him warm however I could as we flew.

Wheelock surrendered himself easily to the healers at

the hall, giving me another weak but formal little nod as two aproned doctors lowered him onto a narrow bed.

"Where's Caro?" I asked another healer. Fe pointed toward the far end of the hall, and I went as quickly as I could, not quite finding the strength in my exhausted limbs to run.

Caro was sitting at Fin's bedside, her back to me, holding his hand as he lay unconscious. It was much like the scene she must have come in on in Fin's palace bedroom on Exposition Day, when I stayed with him after that first wound. This was no private, sumptuous bedroom, though; it was busy and sterile and very public, and Fin was treated no differently than any of the other wounded in their beds — except that Caro was allowed to stay with him.

I walked up behind them and touched her shoulder.

She nearly jumped out of her skin.

"I'm sorry! Caro, it's just me," I said.

She stared at me as if I were a stranger. That distracted look was still in her eyes. After a moment she seemed to recognize me again, but her expression grew only more perplexed, more wondering.

"Nick . . ." she said eventually, faintly, as if she were trying out a name she'd never used before.

"Yes, Caro, I'm here," I said. I could see another reason why they'd allowed her this break to stay with Fin: She was clearly more spent than I was.

"Yes," she said slowly. "You're here." And finally she started to smile.

I took a seat on a stool that another apprentice healer brought over to me. It was only then that I noticed a faint golden glow coming from inside Fin's and Caro's hands.

In answer to my questioning gaze, the apprentice took my own hand and pressed it, then gestured toward my friends.

I rested my hand on top of Caro's. I expected to feel a spark, some sudden leap of joining or transfer of energy, but it wasn't like that. It was only the feeling I got when I woke up in the middle of the night to find Fin and Caro next to me, that I got sometimes when we were all laughing over the same joke, the feeling that I'd had when we looked at the stars on the deck of the *Imperator* the very first night of our voyage. It was the most natural feeling in the world.

I settled into the magic and closed my eyes.

They stayed closed until I heard Mr. Candery call my name.

"Nicolette," he said gently. "Nicolette."

I opened my eyes. The healers' halls were lit with glowing orbs, the same soft golden color that throbbed underneath our hands. It had grown dark outside the high windows, fully night, yet I'd felt no time pass at all.

Fin was awake now. He smiled at me and at Caro, whose eyes were fluttering open and closed, as if she didn't want to allow herself to sleep.

"Someday I'll save you instead," Fin said wryly. The effort of speaking made him grimace. "I swear."

I wanted to tell him that he did save us, in a way, that his blood had saved Faerie after all, but I thought it would be best to wait.

"No doubt you will," I said. I squeezed his and Caro's hands before releasing them.

"I'd like to speak with you, Nicolette," Mr. Candery continued, his eyes full of that familiar anxious sympathy I'd seen so often as a child as well as another emotion that it took me a little bit longer to name.

Pride. That was it, deep pride . . . because of me. I remembered that look from my childhood too, and it made my breath catch.

"All right," I said.

The ache in my muscles was like a sudden bite when I rose from my stool. I quickly took the arm Mr. Candery offered.

"You two will call if you need me, right?" I asked, although I already knew they would. They both nodded, Fin with a smile, Caro still with that absent look. I frowned a little, thinking that if she carried on that way, I'd soon be more worried about her welfare than I was about Fin's.

But Fin saw what I was thinking and gave me an extra little nod; he'd make sure she didn't slip too far into whatever place she had gone inside her head. The golden glow was still emanating from between their fingers, and I knew that would keep both of them anchored.

Leaning my head on Mr. Candery's shoulder, I walked with him out of the healers' hall and into a small private room.

There was only one chair and a desk in this windowless closet, just the same as countless other Fey rooms I'd seen. The desk was covered with stacks and stacks of medical books, the wall papered with diagrams. I knew the extent of my exhaustion when I didn't feel the least desire to examine the technical drawings.

"Nicolette, I have to tell you something," Mr. Candery said, helping me into the seat. I hissed out my breath at the relief that sitting again brought to the muscles in my legs. "But first I want to tell you how — how absolutely proud —" He lifted one elegant hand to his face and swiped away tears. I noticed that his other arm held a crutch on which he supported himself, and that his left leg was in a splint. I felt such shame that I had let him support me as we walked, that I had to force myself to keep listening to his words.

"You should rest here, Mr. Candery," I said, rising stiffly. "I'm fine, truly."

"No, Nicolette," he said. "I'd like you to be sitting down when you hear this." His lavender-blue eyelids closed, and he took one deep breath. "I know you've been busy with rescues all afternoon," he said, "and I can't tell you how much good you have done, how many people you've saved. You're a real heroine, Nicolette, and I want you to remember that, always." He took a hobbling step forward and grasped one of my hands in his. "You weren't the only person going back and forth to the beach after the battle, though, you know. We've been sending out reconnaissance people ever since the wave . . . ever since we were able. The reason you were the only one in the air is that . . ." He sighed. "It's that every other machine in the battle was doused in the water. All the Ashes were . . . were released. They died in the salt water; Ashes always do. Your dear . . ." He squared his shoulders as if to give himself courage, and he looked into my eyes. "Margot, your mother, is gone now. She was still on the beach when the wave came; I wasn't sure if you knew."

He took a deep, shaky breath. "Nicolette, I am so sorry, but your mother has passed on."

I touched my breast pocket, but he continued before I could interrupt him: "It may be for the best, after all, given her pain."

My fingers froze at the edge of my pocket. "Her pain?"

Mr. Candery clasped my hand tighter. "It's over. Whatever peace we find when we die, it's hers now."

He was so obviously stricken with grief that I forgot my question. "It's not, Mr. Candery. Jules and I saved her, just before the wave came. Her body was—it was too much of a burden for Jules, we had to, to get back to the land ahead of the wave . . ." I found I couldn't quite say it, couldn't form the words to tell Mr. Candery how I had torn apart my mother to save my own life.

Instead, I reached my trembling fingers into my pocket and withdrew the small, soldered-shut box.

Mr. Candery staggered backward, nearly losing his balance on his injured leg. "Margot?" he whispered, staring at the box. He was talking to my mother rather than to me, asking her if she was still there.

And I knew that somehow she was.

"I can make her a new body," I said. "It will take time, but . . ." I suddenly found the thought just funny enough to give one short, wry, lonely laugh. "I suppose I'm just returning the favor she once did for me. It will take less than nine months, at least."

Mr. Candery was still staring at the little box in my hand. "She's always rebuilding herself," he said. "Always . . . she has another storeroom. It will take less time than you think."

He wrenched his gaze away and began to walk toward the door. "Yes," he said, "we can start right away. We can have her back by morning. Oh, Nicolette!" He turned toward me with a wide, sweet, grateful smile, and if I had never known before how much he loved her, I would have known it just from that one look.

But I remembered what he had said a few moments before. "Mr. Candery," I said quietly, still cupping the box of my mother's Ashes in my hand, "what did you mean about her pain? Was she sick still? Did she carry the illness into her new body?"

Mr. Candery looked away. "No," he said.

With a sigh he turned away from the door. "She made me promise I'd never tell you, but I thought, if she was gone, it would be a comfort . . . Nicolette, it wasn't the croup that caused her pain. It was the burning." His gentle voice was cautious, even pleading. "I didn't know what Ashes really were until sometime after you were born, my dear, when she'd been using them for years. When I learned, I refused to buy them for her anymore. She already had so many, and I never thought . . . I never understood quite how deep her fascination with them ran until she got sick. And even then, it was only because I loved her so much, because I so selfishly didn't want her to die, that I helped her find a way to turn to Ashes herself." He sighed. "It was a long time afterward, after I left you at Lampton, that we reunited. She had been living with the pain for years by then. She couldn't ignore it, she said, but she could get used to it. She could go on working, even if the whole time . . ." He took one more breath. "Even if the whole time she felt as if she were still burning alive."

There his voice broke, and he couldn't go on.

I dropped the box of Ashes. It fell to my lap with a soft plink. The image of it blurred.

Every second. Living every second with the kind of pain that had made that Esting soldier cry out so horribly that I could still hear his scream echoing in the back of my mind . . .

"I can't bring her back, then," I said. "I can't put her into another body to feel that pain again, I can't! I wouldn't do it to anyone!"

The pity I'd felt for poor drowned Fitz on the beach evaporated away. He must have spoken with the automaton soldiers; he had to have known the pain he was forcing them into. He was an even greater monster than I had imagined.

Mr. Candery picked up the box from my lap and closed his hands gently over it in protection.

"She feels it even now," he said quietly.

I recoiled in my seat.

"At least if you bring her back, she can . . . feel other things too. See. Move. Work, she would say." He opened his hands like a shell, offering me the box. "It's what she wants, Nick. To live. To work. Please, bring her back."

I was unable to move. I felt the ghosts of imagined fire all over my body, just looking at the thing in Mr. Candery's hands.

I stood.

I forced myself to move quickly, even more quickly than I'd walked toward Caro and Fin in the healers' hall. My muscles screamed, but it was nothing to the pain the Ashes felt.

"I'll bring you to her storeroom right now," said Mr. Candery, following me out the door. "No one will blame you if you want to rest first, though, Nicolette."

I looked back at him, not trusting myself to speak.

But he must have understood.

His eyes softened, and he nodded and tucked Mother's box into his own jacket pocket, carefully, as if he could spare her some of the pain that way.

Every second. Every second, burning alive.

I took off running toward the stables.

JULES leaned his head out, looking down the stable hall, listening to one of the Fey horses nicker quietly at him. His ears were pricked forward; he looked like any happy horse.

I thought it couldn't be true. If Jules had always been in pain, I would have known. I couldn't have just sailed blithely through the past two years, seeing him every day, and not *noticed*.

I sprinted to his stall and threw my arms around him. I heard the surprised chirrup of the other horse, and the deeper, calmer noises in Jules's throat, comforting noises.

"Mechanica," he rumbled. The name had always been a badge of honor coming from him. It reminded me of what I had done, what I could do.

He was always trying to comfort me, to help me. And what had I done to help him?

I'd brought him back to life once, given him the large

quarry-horse body he had now, when he'd had only a clockwork-trinket body before that could fit in my hand.

But I knew he felt the same pain no matter what kind of body he had.

"Jules, I'm so sorry, I'm sorry," I whispered into the warm, hard expanse of his neck. I clutched at him as if I could remove the pain.

He pulled back, taking one or two steps into the stable. He gave another rumble, half voice and half engine, full of sorrow.

"Is it true?" I asked.

He looked away.

I closed the door behind me. I wanted to reach out to him, but suddenly felt as if I couldn't. I'd taken so much from him already, these two years, without knowing. To take anything else, even the solace of a touch . . .

But he came to me. He nosed my palm, pulling my hand up so that it lay on his broad cheek the way it had done so many times.

"You're always in pain."

He hesitated for a long moment, and then he nodded.

"Every second," I said.

He just watched me.

I could feel the anger coming up in my belly like bile, rage at my mother for condoning such a thing, for using her money to help make it possible. And she'd left Jules trapped in the chest in her workshop for years, for what might have been forever if her plan hadn't worked, if I had never found the secret key.

Jules and the dozens of other animals, too, trapped as Ashes in her many drawers or in sleeping clockwork bodies. Suspended in endless pain.

I felt sick, heartsick. Bone-deep sick and angry. And none of that pain was a fraction of what Jules had been feeling all along, for longer than I'd known him. Perhaps longer than I'd been alive.

Jules pressed his face against my hand. He looked down at me from the height I'd given him, his glass eyes full of compassion I didn't deserve.

"Worthwhile," he rumbled. "Worthwhile to know and . . . help you."

"You did help me, Jules," I said. "You saved me as much as I ever saved myself. You—" I wouldn't make him watch me cry. "I loved you when I had no one else to love. And you loved me. I always . . ." My voice faltered and failed me.

Jules shook his head.

I took a steadying breath that did nothing to help. I had to go shakily into the next question. I was sick with dread that I already knew his answer.

"Do you want . . ." I shut my eyes, then forced them open again. I had to show him I would be all right. "Do you want not to be in pain anymore?"

Jules stood stock-still.

Then, slowly, a quiet sigh began to sound from his body, not just from his voice but from his oiled joints, the clockwork in his head, the furnace in his belly. Every part of the machine and the horse inside breathing out together, one great exhale.

"Yes," he said.

And then again, although speaking hurt him: "Yes."

I ran my hand over his cheek.

"I'll go with you," I said.

I rode to the shoreline on Jules's back. I didn't want to ride. I hated the idea of him carrying me, of being any more of a burden than I'd already been. But he had stamped his steel hooves and huffed smoke when I'd started to walk, and I could deny him nothing now.

He ambled slowly through the jungle, across lingering rivulets of seawater from the great wave. I had thought he might fly, but I was glad he didn't. We shared the silence between us as he walked on.

I rode with my head held high. All I wanted was to fling myself down on Jules's neck and weep, but I wouldn't let myself. I would do nothing that might make him think I still needed him.

We reached the shore too soon.

It was almost dawn. The sand was dark around us, nearly the same color as the water. The sky was dusky gray-blue at the edges, still nighttime above. The jungle behind us was a dark mass.

I dismounted, and Jules stood looking at the water for a long time. I thought of all the buzzers already gone, all the Ashes of the thousands of soldiers that were released inside of yesterday's wave.

I couldn't feel sad for them, because I knew they had found peace, whatever peace comes after great suffering. I tried to feel the same for Jules. To rejoice in the death of his pain.

In the end he walked to the water alone, leaving me on the shore. I had made a small hole in the box of his Ashes back in the stable, at his request, so that it would happen quickly.

I tried to empty my head of anything but this last sight of my horse, my friend, calm and steady and wonderful as he always was, walking into the sea.

When the waterline reached the bottom of his belly, he reared up, throwing out his wings to their full span. Jules gleamed in the moonlight and the silver traces of dawn, casting spray around him like pearls.

He plunged forward, all courage and fluid grace.

I watched the reddish glow in his furnace douse under the surface.

I stood on the shore, taking one breath at a time. I saw nothing after he went under, no ghost rising from the water. Nothing.

I knelt down on the beach and watched the sun come up.

*

The air grew bright and clear, and one by one birds began to sing in the jungle at my back. I don't know how much time passed before Caro and Fin came and sat down beside me. Fin settled himself slowly, with great care, and he placed a long witchwood cane on the sand in front of him.

"Mr. Candery told us," Caro said. "Oh, Nick."

Neither of them touched me. They only sat with me, sharing my silence. The burden and the gift of it, the sadness and heartbreak and relief. There on the quiet beach, I was finding the space I needed to feel everything I'd feared would drown me if I let it in at once. It all washed over me then, all the conflict and confusion, the misery and rage and grief, and I took it in as if it were only more water. With my friends at my side, it was nothing more than that.

I turned to Caro at last, remembering the faraway look that had been in her eyes in the hall, and I was relieved to see that it had left her. There was some shadow on her still, a remnant of something she'd seen or done, but the real Caro was coming out from under it again. I knew that whatever horrors those of us in the battle had seen, Caro had fought equal horrors in the healers' halls.

Fin looked a little haunted too—which I could well understand—but there was a bigger change in him. He was staring out at the ocean, and I could see it in his profile, although I couldn't name it. He seemed older, for one thing, with a few lines at the sides of his mouth that I thought were new, and far healthier than I could have hoped he would be so soon after his grievous injury. But there was something more . . .

He broke the spell by glancing at me and smiling his Prince Charming smile, although even that had something new about it. "What is it, Nick?" he asked.

"I don't know . . ." I cocked my head a little to the side, taking him in from a different angle. "It's as if . . ." I shook my head and smiled back, my first since Jules—only a few hours, but it felt like years. "I think you look like a king now, Fin."

Fin took a deep breath. "Well, I should hope so," he said.

Caro touched his shoulder softly. Neither of us told him we were sorry for his loss. It wouldn't suffice, and it wasn't needed.

Fin turned to me. "Let's talk about Jules, Nick, if you want to talk," he said. "Politics can wait."

I felt my chin tremble. I looked out at the water. "He loved me," I said. "He loved me, and he saved me, and he was wonderful."

Fin nodded.

"That he was," Caro agreed.

They sat with me for the rest of the day. No one came to fetch us, not even Mr. Candery, and I was grateful. I knew he was longing for me to bring back my mother.

Reanimating Margot took almost no time at all. It was obvious from the moment I walked into that last storeroom that she'd been rebuilding herself constantly, working toward some newer and more perfect model of her own anatomy.

There were a dozen arms to choose from, as many legs, several torsos. I worried over which parts to choose at first, hearing her criticisms of my choices in my head even as I tried to make them, but then I remembered that she'd be able to trade them for others or even build yet more new body parts as soon as she was back.

So I did what I think no other daughter before me has ever been able to do: I remade my mother in my own image.

I chose for her the same attributes I would have chosen for myself. A right hand with tiny drill bits built into the fingernails for doing delicate clockwork; a left hand with a rubber grip and a wrist that rotated 360 degrees. Eyes with adjustable lenses, one microscopic, the other telescopic. Legs with inner springs I thought would let her walk lightly. I chose the torso with the roomiest furnace so she wouldn't have to worry about refueling herself too often; she could simply focus on her work, the reason she was willing to stay alive through so much pain in the first place. Another brown silk wig, less elaborate than her last. And a porcelain face that looked the most like the mother from my childhood, the prettiest mama in the world.

It was Mr. Candery, in the end, who wished her back. He

waited in my mother's parlor the whole time I rebuilt her body, pacing back and forth; I could hear his footsteps from the workshop below. I told him I'd thought he'd like to do it, and he was grateful, but in truth I wasn't sure if I could wish hard enough myself. I was still so angry with her, and I knew in my heart that I could never forgive her for Jules, for the buzzers, for all the many kinds of pain she'd caused.

Mr. Candery went into the storeroom and closed the door. In only a few short minutes he opened the door again and beckoned me into the room.

And there, already rummaging around in the other versions of her body, was my mother. The face she turned to me was the face I'd always loved.

"You made a good choice with the eyes," she said, tapping her porcelain temple with a drill-tipped finger. "I might have picked a stronger right arm, though." If she could have pursed the lips of her porcelain mask, I knew she would have.

I also knew that it was foolish to feel embarrassed, to let myself be vulnerable to any of her criticisms. "At least you're moving again," I said.

Her multi-lensed eyes rolled upward and she tsked at me, a sound that brought back a whole flood of squabbling, domestic memories I thought I'd lost.

Then she shuddered and sighed.

"Nicolette," she said, "thank you." She reached out the drill-bit hand.

I clenched my jaw and couldn't quite reply. The next

thing I'd have said would have been an excoriating judgment about the buzzers and Jules, and what good would it do either of us for me to dole out yet more of that pain?

I turned and left her instead.

Mr. Candery found me later, while I was eating dinner with Caro at one of the communal tables that had been set up in a long hall, the biggest room I'd ever seen in Faerie.

Both Fin and Talis were absent, although the rest of us — healers, soldiers well enough to leave their beds, officers like Mr. Candery, Caro and I — were eating together. There were quiet murmurs of conversation, but the pervading atmosphere in the room was one of stunned relief. Esting's automaton army was vanquished, and some of us, at least, had survived.

Mr. Candery touched my arm so gently that I didn't jump even though he had surprised me. "Hello, Nicolette," he said. "My dear, I just wanted to tell you . . ." He paused, sighed. "Your mother is very grateful to you. And very proud."

I tried my best to keep my face neutral; my anger wasn't at him, not truly. And was I grateful to my mother, was I proud?

Part of me was.

And part of me hated her.

"All right," I muttered to Mr. Candery. I didn't know what else to say.

"I was . . . we were talking just now. She says . . . she's too stubborn to say it herself, if you'll pardon my saying so, but she wishes she could . . . she knows you'll be heading back to Esting soon enough, you see. She wishes she could write you a letter when you're there, in the hopes that you may write back."

I blinked. I supposed I would be returning to Esting soon. The idea seemed as strange and foreign as flying to a star. It was only an ocean that separated me from my home country, but it felt like a whole other world.

I looked at Mr. Candery's worried, loving face, and I wished more for his sake than for my own that I could agree to read my mother's letters. But the knowledge of Jules's pain and of my mother's part in it still sat so heavy in my heart.

Caro regarded us both with compassion, saying nothing.

A brief burst of music, the deep harp-and-drum that announced the Fey ruler, kept me from having to answer. Like everyone else at the long table, I rose from my seat for Talis's entrance.

Fe walked into the room as calmly as ever, gesturing at once for us all to sit. Fe spoke in Fey first and then in perfect Estinger in the quiet, gentle tone fe always took.

"I'm sorry for interrupting your dinner. We have something very important, very serious, to tell you." Fe looked around the room, and I felt that shiver again when our eyes met, that moment of wondering how deep fer perceptive powers really went. Talis looked at every soul in the room that way before fe spoke again, confirming trust, offering honesty and transparency. Fe loved each and every person in the room. It wasn't a general kind of love, either; it was specific and complicated, frustrated and fierce. It was like the love all grown-up children feel for their parents.

Fin entered to stand at Talis's side. He was wearing his black dress-uniform coat, patched so well now that it looked nearly new, and over it a sash of the Fey lapis blue. The weight of sadness and that other, more welcome burden were still in his face and in the way he squared his shoulders even as he walked with the help of the witchwood cane.

I wished I could stand at his side and support him, although I realized this was something he had to do, had to let the Fey see, on his own. The sole integrity he had to show as the new ruler — the new king.

"King Corsin of Esting has died," Talis said.

All through the room a startled murmur rose. Much of the noise was joyful.

"It was no doing of ours," Talis said, holding up fer hands in reassurance, looking at us again with that perfect clarity and honesty.

"My father has been ill for years," Fin said. "The death of my mother and my brother broke Corsin's heart, depleted his health, and forced him into his extremism. Recent events proved too much for his heart to withstand." A translator standing beside Talis repeated Fin's words in Fey.

Caro squeezed my hand. We both knew the "recent

event" Fin spoke of was the news of Fin's own supposed death; more of Fitz's work.

"Any death should be mourned," Talis said, and I knew as well as everyone else in the room that fe was sincere. I thought fe locked eyes with me for another moment then, and I had the unsettling feeling that fe knew and even understood about Jules, but it was over too quickly for me to be sure that I hadn't imagined it. "But this death has brought us new life.

"King Christopher Dougray Fadhiri Anton Abdul-Rafi' Finnian," Talis said, a lilting formality coming into fer voice, "as his first official act as monarch, has cosigned a proclamation of Faerie's independence. My friends, we have our freedom."

Shocked silence in the hall—shock from everyone but Caro and me. We looked at each other with jubilation and gratitude and everything but surprise.

The room erupted into cheers, and Fin was already stepping away from the beaming Talis. His dark gaze was searching through the long room, and I couldn't bear it anymore; I took Caro's hand and rushed toward him, and we embraced, full of the same healing warmth that had glowed through our clasped hands yesterday, as radiant and natural as sunlight.

Full of love.

EPILOGUE

WE left for Esting a month later. Our ship was larger than the *Imperator* but much plainer, a supply vessel the Fey had captured in battle over a year ago. Our crew were the last remaining Estinger soldiers, all of whom would be leaving with us.

Wheelock was captaining the ship for our journey home. After he'd recovered, he told us the story of his sojourn with the merfolk, but it started to seem as if even he didn't believe it. He still moved in a daze, more the formal old man than ever, and I knew it would be a long time before I'd see that secret smile again.

But he was living, and I was more fiercely grateful for that than I could have guessed I would be.

We all needed to go home, and Fin needed to take up his crown. He had to claim his kingship in person without delay—and make the official announcement in Esting of Faerie's freedom.

"If I'd had my cabinet around me, all the advisors, they'd never have allowed me to do it so simply," Fin had told us the same night he and Talis announced the independence. "The economic ramifications, the withdrawal—but this is right. Whatever breaks because Faerie is free, I'll fix it if I can. But I couldn't be . . . king . . ."—he always pronounced the title slowly, carefully, as if the word itself contained all that heavy burden that he was working so hard to bear honorably—"a single day without giving them the freedom they should never have lost."

He was a hero now, the hero he'd always wanted to be, although he couldn't quite see it. He'd only signed his name, he insisted. Being wounded in battle to free the Fey seemed to mean nothing to him.

But I was still so proud, and I loved him so much, and I loved the king he was becoming.

I loved Fin and Caro both more than ever, and they loved me. The three of us could easily have married in a Fey ceremony before we left, but we didn't want to; Caro still had Bex waiting for her back home, after all, and none of us quite felt that marriage was the right word for what we shared. Caro and I refused the titles Fin kept offering, too, but none of that meant we weren't family.

Parting from my mother only confirmed that for me. We'd shared a cool goodbye in her parlor the day before my departure.

I agreed to read her letters, if not to write my own.

Watching Fin grapple with his father's death had made me realize that I wanted to do that much, at least for now.

But forgiving her for the pain she'd caused Jules, and the buzzers, and me, was still off the table.

My farewell with Mr. Candery was far warmer and more loving; we had a long, lingering tea together the morning of my departure, chatting over rhodopis berries and pots and pots of clary-bush.

"I will always be glad you came, Nicolette," Mr. Candery said, "and grateful to your charming prince, too, but not nearly so grateful as I am to you." He raised his hand, guessing the protest I was about to make. "I know, I know, you'll say the new king's not yours. Perhaps he isn't, in the Estinger sense. But you're in Faerie now, Nick, and everyone in this place sees you three for what you are. He is yours, as you are his, and Miss Hart's too. I am so glad to see you loved and happy."

He walked around to my side of the table. I stood, and he hugged me close, cupping the back of my head in his long, thin hand.

His embrace felt like a father's blessing, and I knew I would carry it with me all the way to Esting.

I was leaving without my beloved buzzers, without my Jules, but there were other things I would take back with me: pride, grief, gratitude. I was grateful most of all that the Ashes were destroyed. Talis had given me fer promise that fe would see the geyser stopped up, destroyed, now that the Fey controlled their own land again. When I heard that promise, the echo of the soldier's screams finally started to fade from the back of my mind.

My mother had given me something else, too. Lampton Manor was mine again, at least by law. My mother still lived, and so my father's marriage to Lady Halving had never been legally valid. The witnesses to Mother's survival included no less a personage than the king himself. And as king, Fin was head of the Brethren church now—absurd thought! I knew Lord Alming would be even more pleased with that development than with my taking back Lampton.

I thought of that large estate, of my savings, and then of Runner—of all the longing and intelligence and ambition in her, of her search for a real, caring home—and I knew exactly what I wanted to do with the place.

The Lampton Girls' School of Engineering. I was mentally drafting my letter to Lord Alming about it already.

When we stepped onto the gangplank leading up to the airship that would carry us home, I didn't get sick looking down at the receding ground. I walked confidently forward up onto the deck, and when I glanced back, the height didn't bother me at all. I'd already flown much higher through the sky on Jules.

And I was flying with people I loved again now. I stood with Caro and Fin and Wheelock at the prow of the small airship, waving down at Talis and Mr. Candery and a small throng of Fey. I thought I saw a glint of metal among them, of the hand I'd chosen for my mother waving up at me, but I wasn't sure.

It didn't matter. My family was standing right next to me.

The crew tossed down the ropes that tied us to the ground, and we sailed into the blue.